A BOUQUET OF THORNS

A BOUQUET OF THORNS

Tania Crosse

This first world edition published 2008
in Great Britain and 2009 in the USA by
SEVERN HOUSE PUBLISHERS LTD of
9–15 High Street, Sutton, Surrey, England, SM1 1DF.

British Library Cataloguing in Publication Data

Crosse, Tania Anne
  A bouquet of thorns
  1. Dartmoor (England) - Social life and customs - Fiction
  2. Love stories
  I. Title
  823.9'2[F]

ISBN-13: 978-0-7278-6696-7   (cased)
ISBN-13: 978-1-84751-087-7   (trade paper)

All Severn House titles are printed on acid-free paper.

Typeset by Palimpsest Book Production Ltd.,
Grangemouth, Stirlingshire, Scotland.
Printed and bound in Great Britain by
MPG Books Ltd., Bodmin, Cornwall.

For my three wonderful children, James, Natasha and Michael and their respective spouses and partners.

And as ever for my dear husband for his love, his strength and his understanding.

Acknowledgements

Once again, I must thank my fantastic agent and everyone at Severn House for all their hard work in publishing this novel. As with all my books, my sincere thanks go to my good friend Paul Rendell, Dartmoor guide and historian and editor of *The Dartmoor News*, for checking the manuscript for any errors regarding our beloved moor. In particular I should like to express my gratitude to Dartmoor Prison historian, Trevor James, for all his detailed information, and to our dear friend Colin Skeen, barrister and magistrate, for his research into the history of the legal system and for explaining it to me in layman's terms. I should also like to thank local historian Gerry Woodcock for his information on Tavistock, Len March for his explanation of the nature in which gunpowder would explode, The British Army Museum and last but not least, retired physician Marshall Barr. My deepest thanks to you all.

One

'Ah, Rose, my dear child, did you have a good ride?'
Henry Maddiford glanced up from his desk in the
manager's office of the Cherrybrook Gunpowder Mills high
up on Dartmoor, and beamed at his beloved daughter. Though
in his fifties, he was still a handsome man, relatively tall, and
strong and athletic from striding all over the factory site,
which, for safety reasons, was strung out across the moor on
either side of the bubbling Cherry Brook. His alert blue eyes
crinkled at the corners as he allowed himself a few moments'
break from his work to gaze lovingly on the child, a grown
woman now, and an exact replica of his wife who had died
giving birth to her.

Rose returned his smile, her full red mouth in a soft curve
and her heart running over with devotion. She was passionate
and untamed, but when it came to her father, she would sacrifice the world for him. She drew the image of him, the pride
and the warmth, into her soul, feasting on the contentment,
grasping at it, for even as the peace settled in her spirit, she
felt something wasn't quite right. His face was blurring at
the edges. Fading. Oh, please don't go. Father, come back.
Please . . .

Rose stirred as the child inside her kicked beneath her
ribs. Reality clawed at her, but she tried to ignore it, to sink
back down into the lulling cocoon of her dream where everything was calm and safe. To see her father again, to feel his
presence – ah, what bliss . . .

She groaned, and despite all her efforts to remain in the
security of sleep, her eyelids flickered open and she knew
she was awake. She closed her eyes again, trying to hold on
to the vision of her father, alive and well as he had been not
so long ago. In that magical time before the explosion, a time
she had imagined would go on for ever. A time before the

damage to his spine had paralysed his legs, before his forehead was badly burnt. Before the moment, less than a year
later, when a blood clot had lodged in his smoke-damaged
lungs and there was nothing even good Dr Power from nearby
Dartmoor Prison had been able to do to save him.

Tears welled in her eyes, and in that twilight world between
sleeping and waking, she willed the dream to be real. But
even her strong, impetuous determination could not succeed
in the impossible, and in her misery she really didn't want to
face the new day. If only she could turn back the clock, harness
that momentary joy of having her father back. But she couldn't.
He was dead. Buried in the graveyard of the prison settlement
at Princetown, two miles away across the bleak, savage moor.

The prison. Oh, dear God. The horrific event out in the
stable yard the previous day crashed into her mind like a
sledgehammer. She sat bolt upright as the hideous clarity of
it flashed into her stricken mind. Seth! All at once, her thoughts
were a mangled torment of fury, sorrow and awestruck indignation. Sweet Jesus, he didn't deserve the barbaric cruelty that
had been meted out to him by the sergeant from the Civil
Guard, who had clearly relished the power he held over the
escaped convict he had finally tracked down. Seth Collingwood
– or Warrington as Rose alone knew his real name to be –
was obviously desperately ill, weak, feverish, agonized as he
coughed up blood. And as the two soldiers had held him
securely between them, the sergeant had punched him hard
in the stomach and then kicked him as he lay writhing in
agony on the stable yard cobbles. Yet even then, Seth had
come out with a blatant lie to help protect Rose, even though
he knew he would be punished even more severely because
of it.

Punished. God Almighty. They all knew exactly how he
would be punished for his escape. Tied to the flogging frame
and tortured with up to thirty-six lashes of the cat-o'-nine-tails,
each frayed end stiffened in one of several ways to slice into
the flesh until the felon's skin hung from his back in ribbons.
Seth's beautiful back, which she had secretly admired as she
had removed the six balls of lead shot from his muscled
shoulder. Rose wanted to scream at the horrendous vision of
what would happen to him as soon as he was considered fit
enough – if he ever were. Unleashed rage flared in Rose's

breast. This was 1877. Queen Victoria had been on the throne for forty years and was considered such a fair, just monarch, and yet she permitted such sadism to continue in her gaols and, so Rose believed, in her army and navy as well.

But sitting in bed, seething with bitterness and anger wouldn't help Seth. Yesterday, Charles, her husband, had promised to listen to Seth's story of how he had come to be wrongfully convicted of robbery with violence. Of how, in a moment of madness, he had run off in to the thick fog, taking advantage of his trusted position of feeding the prison farm animals, a privilege he had earned through his previous good behaviour.

The guard had fired at him. They were supposed to aim for the legs, to wound the escapee and prevent him from getting any further. But, for one reason or another, six of the thirteen lead pellets from the cartridge had penetrated Seth's shoulder, and though in pain, he had run on, disappearing into the dense, vaporous shroud, lost and having no clue where he was going. He had discarded and hidden his prison boots that left the telltale arrow footprint, and had sped on blindly over boulders and through streams, his feet raw and bleeding as his socks disintegrated. Breathless, disorientated, he had stumbled on until his foot caught in a rock and his ankle had snapped beneath him. In agony, he had limped on until he had come to the grand, isolated house and had slipped unseen into one of the loose boxes where Rose had discovered him.

And now Charles had promised to try to help him.

Rose could scarcely believe it. Charles Chadwick had always scorned his wife's sympathy over the vicious way in which the prisoners were treated. He disapproved of her association with her dear friend Molly, because her father was a prison warder and she was of working stock. Rose and Charles had fought like cat and dog, nearly coming to blows when he had discovered that she had sneaked off to Molly's wedding to Joe Tyler, the stable lad at the gunpowder mills who as a child had been rescued by Henry Maddiford from a cruel Plymouth master, and so had been like a younger brother to Rose.

There was so much Rose and Charles disagreed over, she refusing to bend to his will. But when the vile, sickening scene had unfolded before their very eyes in their own stable yard the previous day, Charles had apparently been moved by the convict's plight. He had been incensed at the sergeant's abject barbarity in front of his heavily pregnant wife, and when she had later begged him to listen to Seth's claims of innocence, he had agreed.

Perhaps, in her headstrong stubbornness, Rose had misjudged Charles, her opinion coloured by his insatiable demands in the bedroom. Their marriage could never be perfect and Charles would always be possessive and domineering in his love for her, but perhaps there was hope yet. And when their child was born, hopefully the son that Charles craved, they would find happiness at last.

Rose hauled herself to her feet, flinging on her dressing gown, and some vain, desperate hope drew her to the window. She couldn't actually see into the stable yard from there, but somewhere deep inside her a demented disbelief willed Seth to be safely hidden in Gospel's loose box. She recognized the horrible choking void, the emptiness of total, irrevocable loss. For in her heart was a similar pain to when her father had died.

She turned away from the window and, striding purposefully across the room, her hand closed on the doorknob. And there it stayed. For though the china sphere turned, she met with unyielding resistance. She tried again to no avail. Charles was always up before her, particularly since, to Rose's relief, Dr Seaton had advised him a little while ago to desist from their marital relationship from then until six weeks after the birth. In a distracted moment, his mind preoccupied with the problem of the prisoner perhaps, Charles must have locked the door by mistake. But no matter. Rose hurried into the bathroom. There was another door directly on to the landing so that the servants could bring up hot water and later empty the tub without disturbing the master and mistress in the bedroom. Rose's hand flew to the handle, tugged it, jerked it. But it was only ever locked from the inside, and the key was nowhere to be seen. She searched round in a panic, and then the truth drove into her heart like an arrow. Charles had locked her in.

The *bastard*!

May God forgive her, but at that moment, the hatred spewed into her gullet. Damn Charles! Damn and blast him to hell! It had been a trick, a total lie, his promises to help Seth. She should have guessed that he had just been trying to pacify her, in the hope that she would forget all about the felon and return to the law-abiding, respectable reputation of which Charles was so proud. But he had seemed so genuinely shocked by what had happened that she had believed his promises, had *wanted* to believe in him, just as she had always wanted to love him. But overnight he must have reconsidered, and returned to the bigoted, implacable brute he really was. She should have known that a leopard couldn't change its spots! Not for the first time in their married life, she felt as if Charles had presented her with a bunch of beautiful roses that had quickly withered into a bouquet of thorns to scratch her and make her bleed. But if Charles thought he could treat her like that, he would have to think again. For Rose Maddiford was afraid of no man, and she wouldn't give in without a fight. Her eyes narrowed dangerously and, raising her fists, she began to pummel relentlessly on the door.

It was a full five minutes before she heard him on the other side, and the string of profanities that tumbled from her mouth shocked even herself, but she didn't care. The instant Charles opened the door, she made to dive past him, but it was impossible. He grasped her by the shoulders and forced her back into the room, using his foot to slam the door closed behind him. Mad with fury, she managed to break free from his hold and stood back, breathing heavily, her fingers ready to claw at his face.

'Shut your mouth, for God's sake, Rose!' Charles bawled at her. 'You sound like a fish wife!'

'And can you wonder at it, you treacherous sod! You—'

'Treacherous! My God, *you're* the one guilty of treachery, my girl, not me! Aiding and abetting an escaped convict, no less . . .'

'One who with half a chance can prove his innocence, and yesterday you promised to help him! You tricked me, you despicable, bloody liar!'

'Rose, how *dare* you!' The shock on Charles's face was so appalling that Rose recoiled. 'And you don't seriously think I was considering helping him, do you? A dangerous criminal who for God knows how long had been tricking my wife – *my* wife! – into concealing him—'

'Seth's no more dangerous than you are!' Rose retorted, recovering from her momentary fear. 'Less so, in fact! He risked discovery to save the life of one of the puppies when for two pins *you* would have drowned the lot of them!'

'Seth now, is it? Well, I can see, madam, that he really had you wrapped round his little finger!'

'Actions speak louder than words, Charles! And *your* actions – locking me in here – prove that your words are nothing but lies. Why did you promise to help Seth when you had no intention of doing so? You know,' she sneered sarcastically, 'I really thought for once that you were a man of principle, but how wrong I was!'

She shuddered as Charles stepped towards her, poking his nose into her face and baring his teeth as he spoke. 'I'll tell you why!' he snarled. 'Yes, I was appalled by the way that sergeant treated your convict, but I was mainly worried by the effect it was all clearly having on *you*! And God knows the effect it may have had on our son! I needed to calm you down, and that seemed to be the only way to do so! Now, I've already had a summons from the prison governor, you know. And I'll probably have to do some pretty clever talking to get you and that stupid old doctor out of trouble! I'll have to blame it all on your condition and your frail nerves, though God knows, if the governor could see you now . . . I'll have to lie through my back teeth to save your hide! And if you think for one moment I believe your story about stealing the plaster of Paris from the doctor's bag, well, I hope for the old fool's sake I can manage to convince the governor of it!'

He clamped his jaw shut, his cheeks flushed puce and his bulging eyes boring into her. She opened and closed her mouth twice, burning to make some scathing retort. But though she was poised to fly at him, she managed to restrain herself. What she really needed was to *manoeuvre* him. Besides, she recognized that she had put him in a difficult position, and she supposed she was sorry for that. And when she thought about how she had persuaded dear old Dr Seaton from Tavistock to treat Seth secretly in the stable, setting his leg and providing antiseptic for the wounds on his shoulder, Rose felt horribly guilty. She must do everything in her power to keep the elderly physician out of trouble. It had been ironic that Charles had refused to allow the prison medical officer, Dr Power, to take care of her during her pregnancy, as he would have had no option but to take the escaped convict back into custody. Rose could taste the same bitterness in her mouth as when she had argued with Charles at the time. He had considered Dr Power good enough to tend her father, but not to oversee the birth of *his son*! Well, just now she would perhaps take some vengeful satisfaction by outwitting him with a little play-acting.

She lowered her eyes and allowed the tears of anguish that were indeed blurring her vision again to meander down her cheeks. She sank down awkwardly on the edge of the bed, her head bowed over her jutting stomach, and wrung her hands.

'It really was true,' she moaned, 'even if you don't believe me. I *did* steal from Dr Seaton. He wasn't involved at all. *I* put the plaster on Seth's ankle. I don't suppose I made a very good job of it, but I didn't know what else to do. I was so confused ... But, Charles, *please*. I really do believe Seth's story. Surely if it can actually be *proved* that he's innocent ...'

Her shoulders sagged as she allowed the weary torrent to wash over her strained senses, and her hair fell forward in a widow's veil about her taut face. For a moment she looked so vulnerable, her tear-ravaged beauty so touching, that Charles's heart softened. Just as she knew it would if Charles felt he was in control of the situation.

'I'm sorry, Rose,' he said stiffly, and his hands clenched into fists at his sides. 'I'm prepared to believe that he convinced you. Some of these devils can spin a pretty good yarn, you know. Confidence tricksters. And that in your highly strung state, you were taken in by him. But I cannot forgive you for breaking the law. For your own reputation, I will support you, and even that old duffer of a physician, as I don't believe a word of your story about the plaster. But I really don't trust you, Rose. I'm sure that when the child is born, you will come to your senses and have other new priorities to govern your life. But until then, I will ensure you will keep to this room. And you had better behave yourself, for I will not be prepared to protect you from any other act of perjury.'

Keep to the bedroom! Rose's mind rose up in protest. She felt like a little child being reprimanded at school – or at least she imagined that was how it would feel, for she had never been to school, her dear father having taught her everything he himself had learnt at grammar school. Her heart cried out to retaliate, but she checked herself at once. She would play

Charles's game, but be as devious as hell. Though at present, she had no idea in what way.

'Yes, Charles,' she sighed ponderously. 'I suppose you're right. I was a fool to believe him. 'Twill be such a relief not to see him again.'

'Well, you can forget all about him, now. He'll be rightly punished for what he did. He didn't actually *hurt* you in any way, did he?'

Her eyes sparked with indignation, and she looked up sharply. 'No! Not a bit of it.'

'Just as well,' Charles snorted, 'or I'd have made sure he paid for it! But don't you think you can get round me. I'll send Patsy up with a breakfast tray, and in the meantime you can contemplate your crime alone.'

He went out, shutting the door quietly behind him and turning the key. Rose's chin quivered and she fell forward on to the bed, burying her face in the covers as she wept freely with tears of exasperation and defeat. But her self-pity didn't last for long. The image of Seth on his knees as he coughed blood on to the cobbles slashed into her mind. And there would be worse to come. Unless she did something about it.

The thoughts began to chase each other round inside her head. The baby was due in a little over six weeks, and Florrie had promised to be back in time for the birth. Dear Florrie Bennett, the loyal servant who had been employed to help when Rose herself had been born, but who had stayed on when Alice Maddiford had died in childbirth, and had been a surrogate mother to Rose. Of a like age, she had been devoted to Henry, but only as Henry lay on his deathbed had Rose realized the depth of feeling between them. After the funeral, Florrie had been so distraught that she had taken herself to stay with her widowed sister just over the Cornish border to recover from her grief. Rose had missed her dreadfully and was counting the days until her return. But she couldn't wait that long. She needed her now. Six weeks would be too late.

When Patsy came in with the tray, Rose was ready. Charles waited outside to unlock and then lock the door again, and Patsy, already too traumatized by the events of the previous day, and too young and timid to do anything beyond obeying the master in silence, simply gazed at her lovely mistress and blinked in awe as a letter was slipped surreptitiously into the pocket of her apron. The poor girl didn't have the wit to make some tiny gesture of understanding, but merely bobbed a shaky curtsy before she fled the room, and Rose was left alone once more.

Her tears were all spent now, and in their place, a squall of rage choked her rebellious heart. Rage at Charles, yes, but more so at the circumstances that had placed Seth in the position he was now. But was the sergeant right? Had Seth told her a pack of lies to gain her sympathy? No! She was convinced of his innocence, and nothing would shake her faith in him.

Her mind wandered back over the time they had spent together during the weeks she had managed to conceal him around the corner in the dog leg of Gospel's loose box. For those few moments when she had first discovered him, she had been terrified, but the instant she had seen how helpless he was, her fear had fled. He had been polite, courteous, more worried for her than for himself, and that was before they had recognized each other.

What was it, eighteen months or more ago, when she had first seen him? Back in the time when her life had been perfect, and she and her father, along with Florrie and Amber, the dog, had lived so peacefully at the manager's house at the powder mills, with Joe living over the stables. Rose's existence had consisted of running the house – with Florrie's indispensable assistance, of course – and galloping wildly all over the moor on her beloved horse, Gospel, a temperamental animal of part thoroughbred stock. Several years before, Rose had rescued him from an owner who couldn't cope with his untamed spirit, and so had employed a martingale, a harsh bit and a whip. With loving kindness, Rose had won the creature's devotion, and now they were as one with a passion Rose had never experienced in any other way. And so they spent hours together out on the moor where their hearts would run free, so that everyone for miles around knew them. And if they rightly distrusted the tall, powerful horse, they loved and respected the beautiful girl who would help anyone in distress and brighten everyone's day.

She had been out walking with her friend Molly when they had come across the work party returning from the day's gruelling labour at the prison quarry. One of the convicts had been about to attack Molly's father, who was one of the wardens on duty, and the fellow inmate who Rose knew now as Seth

Warrington had intervened and saved him from severe injury. Perhaps had even saved his life. And then two Civil Guards who hadn't witnessed the event had mistakenly thought Seth to be the guilty party and had beaten him to the ground until Rose had charged in to stop them. And when the hapless felon had looked up at her, unspoken gratitude on his anguished face, his soft hazel eyes had filled her with a strange confusion.

It wasn't the only thing that had made Rose believe in him. There was something so kind and understanding in Seth's manner, so sensitive to Rose's own distress when she had tried to keep it concealed. He was educated, said he had been a captain in the hussars – and from his obvious knowledge both of injury care and of army weaponry, that was no lie. And then there were the animals.

Gospel had retained an innate distrust of all human beings except those who emitted a deep compassion, and instead of kicking down the stable when the stranger had slipped inside, he had accepted his presence without any protest whatsoever. Even the dogs had made not a sound – not even Scraggles, who usually barked his welcome to anyone and everyone with joyful abandon. Seth had somehow calmed them all instantly, gaining their trust as he stroked them and crooned to them in a way Rose had witnessed since. And when Amber had whelped, Seth *had* risked discovery to save the poorly runt of the litter. He had a way with animals, and he shared other things with Rose besides. Nearly a month she had succeeded in keeping him hidden, and in that time she had developed a deep affinity with him, an intimacy that surpassed anything she had ever felt for Charles, even in the good days before their marriage. And now . . .

Rose thumped her fist hard into the pillow, grinding her teeth and literally tearing at her wild, raven hair as she exploded in an agony of red anger. Tearing into her heart was the thought that while Seth was locked in a punishment cell, or in the prison hospital if he was lucky, she was locked in her room in supreme comfort. Guilt and frustration crucified her, for what in God's name could she do to help him while Charles had her imprisoned? And as for Ned Cornish, well, she would kill the bastard for what he had done!

Two

It took a week before Florrie burst in upon their lives again, a week during which Rose paced the bedroom like a caged lion, raking the air with fingers stretched out like claws. She had flown at Charles with nails ready to scratch at his skin, but his superior strength was always too much for her and once he had gone, she dissolved in tears until she could weep no more. At every minute, her brain was filled with Seth and how he must be suffering. Was he any better? For all she knew, he could be dead. She hoped desperately that he was in the prison hospital with good Dr Power taking care of him. And if he improved, what then? The punishment cell where, she believed, he would have to sit on what was a section of tree trunk cemented into the floor, ankles in fixed leg-irons – although that wouldn't be possible with the plaster cast – and put to some gruelling task such as oakum picking all day long. Tough enough for a totally fit prisoner, but for Seth . . . And then he would be taken off for however many lashes the Commissioners decided was appropriate. The thought of it speared somewhere around her heart.

She couldn't eat. Although she felt hungry, the sight of food nauseated her. She could tell that Cook was sending her up the lightest, most tasty dishes, trying to tempt her appetite, but the tray was always returned virtually untouched. Besides, Rose reasoned maliciously, if Charles began to worry about the baby, the precious son he craved, he might reconsider.

Slowly, her reeling, mutinous senses started to settle and give way to rational, scheming plans. Rebellion was achieving nothing. She must attain her freedom in order to be able to do anything at all for Seth, and if the only way to do so was through submission, then so be it, though her spirit reared away from it. She didn't know if Patsy had posted the letter to Florrie, or even if the poor girl realized that Rose wanted her to, so in the meantime, she must work in other ways.

When Dr Seaton came to check on her, Charles had left the room unlocked, promising to sell Fencott Place and take her to live in his London home if she told the doctor what was going on, or even reveal to the authorities the elderly fellow's part in the felon's concealment as he still didn't believe Rose's story.

'I'm sorry your convict was recaptured,' Dr Seaton said, his voice low, as he put away his stethoscope. 'He seemed a good sort.'

Rose's throat closed. 'Yes,' she croaked. 'And I believe him. Has anyone been to see you, about the plaster, I mean? I'm still denying you had anything to do with it.'

'No.' A strange, shuttered look came over his face. 'I understand your husband had a long interview with the governor and cleared everything up. I should think Mr Chadwick could be very persuasive when he has a mind to.'

His voice had taken on a questioning tone, as if he had sensed the tension in the household, and Rose felt herself flush. Had he guessed something was wrong? He knew, after all, that Rose had kept Seth's presence secret from her husband. She trusted Dr Seaton and was tempted to blurt everything out to him. He wasn't the sort to be cowed by the authorities when it came to injustice, but the dear man had done enough and she didn't want him to be further involved.

'Yes, he can be,' she answered, forcing a smile to her lips. 'So I'm very lucky.'

Dr Seaton raised an enigmatic eyebrow. 'Well, you seem well enough, although you do look a little pale. Make sure you eat well, and I'll see you in another two weeks unless you have any problems.'

'Yes. Thank you, Doctor. And thank you for everything.'

'Hmm,' he grunted, nodding his head, not convinced, Rose suspected, as he shut the door behind him.

Rose sighed. She didn't like towing the line, but if it was the only way . . . And before the physician had turned his pony and trap out of the gates, Charles had crept upstairs and silently turned the key once more and Rose's mouth corkscrewed into a vitriolic knot.

It was the following day that Rose heard a commotion

coming from the stable yard. She had opened the window to let in the fresh May sunshine when angry shouts and Gospel's bellicose neighing reached her ears. She couldn't see into the yard, as it was at the opposite end of the house through a high wall, but she would recognize Gospel's outraged protests anywhere, and it brought a satisfied smirk to her face. Good old Gospel. She hoped he was giving Ned hell!

She had known Ned Cornish for years. Ignorant and uncouth, he had been the stable boy at the Albert Inn in Princetown. Before Molly had married Joe and gone to live at the powder mills, Rose had always given Ned sixpence to look after Gospel whenever she went to visit her friend at her parents' home in the prison barracks and then later in the warders' new accommodation block. Ned and Gospel had never mixed, the animal's teeth often finding a good grip on Ned's flesh, but Ned had always put up with it in the hope that he would be rewarded with more than a sixpenny piece.

He never was, for Rose was always one step ahead of him, until Charles had employed him to take care of their own horses – Gospel, Charles's liver chestnut, Tansy, and Merlin, the roan who went in harness. Ned had bided his time, waiting for the opportunity to waylay Rose in one of the stables. He hadn't got very far. At the time, Rose had been irritated rather than cross, seeing Ned as no more than a nuisance, but he was shrewder than he looked. She had threatened to tell Charles, but he had observed Charles's jealous attitude and had pointed out that she might come off worse! Ever since, the rancour had simmered in Ned's evil little mind, until he had found a way to get back at her refusal to grant him what he had sought for so long. He it was who had discovered the whereabouts of the escaped convict, and had surreptitiously gone off to the prison to claim his five pounds reward. Now Rose hated him, and if Gospel was kicking and biting him, well, nothing could please her more.

A smile found its way to her lips, and she sat on the edge of the bed, stroking her swollen stomach. The moment of contentment made her consider her unborn child for the first time since Seth's recapture. Would the poor thing come into a happy home? Hardly. And she wasn't sure herself that she really wanted it. Someone else's child, yes, someone she loved.

But not Charles. Someone . . . May the dear Lord forgive her, but someone more like Seth Warrington.

Once again, the anguish crippled her. Though it tore at her spirit, she would be good. Do whatever Charles wished until he released her from the room. And *then* she would see what was to be done.

Florrie arrived in Princetown on the carrier's cart and then had to allow her thick, arthritic legs to bring her all the way to the back door of Fencott Place. She was like an unstoppable whirlwind, marching through into the hallway and demanding to speak to the master. From upstairs, Rose had heard her familiar voice raised in unprecedented anger, and her heart had soared. Florrie was back!

Had Rose seen Charles's face, she would have broken into a bitter, sardonic laugh. He was so astonished both at Florrie's unexpected reappearance and at her belligerent attitude, when she had always shown him such cool deference before, that he stepped out of his study with his jaw dangling open quite stupidly. It had never crossed his mind that she looked upon Rose as her daughter, and that if the situation demanded it – which it evidently did just now – she would be willing to fight tooth and nail for her.

'They've just teld me in the kitchen that you'm keeping my Rose locked up in her room!' she exploded, remembering the exact words Rose had instructed her to say, since Charles must not know of the letter and how little Patsy had secretly posted it for her. 'I comes back here to help her prepare for the babby, and find you'm treating her like a criminal! You should be ashamed o' yoursel'!'

She stood, hands on hips and glowering at Charles from her ruddy face while Charles took the opportunity to regain his composure. 'May I remind you, Mrs Bennett,' he said coldly, 'that you are no longer a servant in this household, and that you are only here under my sufferance.'

'Don't you play Mr High and Mighty with me, young man! Your wife had already engaged me as nanny to her child, as I were to her virtually all her life!'

'And you can just as easily be dismissed by me.'

'And I could easily reveal to Mr Frean what a despicable monster you are! 'Twouldn't do your precious reputation much good, would it, especially with Mr Frean being of such influence hereabouts,' she gloated triumphantly, crossing her arms firmly over her ample bosom. 'Now I'm going up to my Rose, and from now on, that door is to remain unlocked or I shall want to know the reason why! With the way you've been treating her, and her in the last stage of her pregnancy . . . Good God, have you no soul, man? She probably don't want to go no further anyways. But she's to have the run of the house and the garden whenever she wants. Now give me the key, or I swears that by tonight the whole of Devonshire will know what sort of man you really are! '

She uncrossed her arms and thrust out her stubby palm with such force that it just missed Charles's nose. He was so dumbfounded beneath her withering stare that he reached into his pocket and carelessly dropped the key into her hand, although not without a derisive sneer.

'I was about to release her anyway as she seems to have come to her senses at last,' he drawled, 'so don't think it's anything to do with you, Mrs Bennett.'

'And I'm the Queen's hand maiden,' Florrie scoffed as she flounced past him and up the stairs.

'And do convey to my wife that if she shows the slightest sign of misbehaving, she'll be back in that room at once!' Charles called out to her back.

In the bedroom, Rose was dancing on the spot as she listened to the rumpus downstairs. Her heart was drumming hard as she heard Florrie's heavy footfall stomping across the landing, and then she stood back as the key was turned in the lock and the door opened. There was Florrie, short and plump, her face more lined than Rose remembered, warm, comforting, secure. Rose melted into her fat arms, almost knocking off her black hat. All the strain and horror of the last weeks erupted in a torrent, and she allowed it to flow over Florrie, who she knew would be an island of strength.

'Oh, my girl, my lovely girl, what have you been up to?' Florrie cried, drawing away and looking up into Rose's face, her pink cheeks wobbling. 'And look at you! Round as a ball! Whoever would have thought it!'

Rose stood back, sniffing and drawing her sleeve across her nose just like a child. Florrie was back, and even if she wouldn't approve of what Rose might be up to, she would support her in every way. Six months it was since Henry had passed on, six months of grief, but now the pair of them were back together, and Florrie would allow nothing to come between them ever again.

'Now this key stays with me,' she announced determinedly, dropping it down inside her bodice. 'And just see if his lordship tries to get it from there!'

'Oh, Florrie!' Rose had to laugh through her drying tears. 'Oh, everything will be all right now you're back, I know it will!'

'Hmm, well, we'll have to see about that! I never did want you to marry that man. He were never right for you. But I wants to know all 'bout what you've been up to before I makes any judgements one way or the other. I knows what a headstrong young maid you can be! Now I'm going to fetch some tea from the kitchen, and then you'm going to tell me all 'bout this convict fellow.'

Alone for a few minutes, the door wide open, Rose felt hopeful for the first time in a week, and when Florrie bustled back in carrying a tea tray, Rose found herself suddenly ravenous and tucked into Cook's home-made biscuits with gusto.

'Now then, cheel.' Florrie frowned and got up to close the door. 'Tell it to me from the beginning.'

Rose took a deep breath and placed her cup and saucer back on the tray. She spoke slowly, her voice quiet and subdued, as she related every detail to Florrie, of how she had found the escapee injured and hiding in the stable. Of how there was something about him that had instantly won her trust, although she was cautious at first. She explained, as Seth had to her, how he had gone to the assistance of a stranger who had been stabbed in the street, but his actions had been misinterpreted and other circumstantial evidence had led to his being wrongly convicted and sentenced to twelve years' imprisonment. The victim was a drunk who had held a grudge against Seth from an incident in an inn a little while earlier, and had sworn that Seth had attacked him so that he could keep the money involved. There had been witnesses to the truth, but as a stranger in Tavistock, Seth had no one to trace them for him and, with his money confiscated as evidence, he couldn't employ a lawyer. And so he had ended up serving his nine months' solitary in Millwall and then had been sent to Dartmoor to serve his twelve years in the country's prison for the worst criminals in the land.

'And you believed all this?' Florrie's mouth was pursed with scepticism.

Rose looked her straight in the eyes. 'Yes,' she answered firmly. 'And not just because he acted like a gentleman throughout and he were so kind and thoughtful.'

'A gentleman, eh?'

'Oh, yes, quite definitely. Of a like class to Charles, I'd say. He came from a well-to-do family in Surrey, but he were bundled off into the army at eighteen because he wanted to marry a girl who they considered far beneath them. They were out to elevate their social standing even further, and weren't going to have their younger son ruin everything for them!' Rose paused, lowering her eyes. 'A bit like me and Charles, really, though Charles has only got himself to answer to. You know, Florrie, he were absolutely furious when I went to Molly and Joe's wedding, and he does everything he can to stop me seeing all my old friends.'

'Do he, by heck?' Florrie lifted her double chin with insulted affront. 'But you was telling me 'bout this – what did you say his name were – Seth?'

Rose nodded vigorously. 'That's right. Well, his father bought him a commission because his son *had* to be an officer, but Seth hated all that sort of thing. But he managed to get transferred to the cavalry so that he could at least work with horses, which are his great love in life. And then his regiment went out to India and he were promoted to captain, and I'm sure 'twas all true because he told me so much about it. Details he wouldn't have known unless he'd actually been there. But in the end he resigned his commission without telling his family, came back to England and were just working his way about the countryside when all this happened. And there were so many other things about him. Do you remember me telling you, Florrie?' She shifted forward on the bed. 'Just before that first accident at the mills, Molly and I were out walking and we saw Mr Cartwright about to be attacked by a convict and another chap stopped it? Well, that was Seth! I recognized him at once. He was really taking a chance, and I heard from Molly that later he *were* beaten up by some other prisoners because of it. But he scarcely mentioned it, when he could have used that to gain my sympathy. Oh, I could go on, Florrie, but I really believe 'tis all genuine.'

Florrie raised her greying eyebrows. 'Well, from what you says . . .' She paused thoughtfully. 'But the truth of the pudding, you knows—'

'That's the whole problem!' Rose came back at once. 'There can't *be* any eating. Once you're convicted, that's it, even if you can prove your innocence. The only way you can be released is through a royal pardon and they're as rare as . . . as pink elephants! Only someone with contacts in high places and money can ever achieve that. And so when Charles said he'd at least listen to Seth's story, I thought . . . But the bastard only said that so as he could trick me and lock me in here!'

'Rose! You mustn't call your husband . . .'

'Well, that's what he is as far as I'm concerned! And now I don't know how on earth I can help Seth, and 'tis so unfair and unjust! And now as soon as he's fit enough, he'll be flogged for trying to escape, and he doesn't deserve it and I just can't bear it!'

Her voice had risen to a hysterical squeal as all the horror and torment of it entangled her in a vicious, strangling web. She drew in a wheezing sob as she tried to force back the constriction in her throat, pressing her hands hard over her mouth, but she was powerless against it, and with Florrie there to lean on, she broke down in floods of wrenching tears. Florrie moved from the chair and sat beside her on the bed, rocking her in her plump arms and smoothing her hair.

'There, there, my lamb, you have a good cry, and let's try to think what's to do. This lad's gotten to you, and no matter what he's done, I doesn't hold with flogging neither. But, well, Dr Power, he has to say if someone's fit for a flogging, don't he? He's a good man, is Dr Power. Look how good and kind he were with your dear father. Maybe if you was to write to him, he might be able to do summat.'

Rose snatched in her breath and her eyes flashed. 'Do you think so, Florrie?'

'Well, I doesn't know, but it must be worth a try. Now you're the one who's good with words, like.'

'Oh, Florrie, what a good idea!' Rose gripped the older woman's arm. 'What would I do without you? I'll write to

Dr Power at once,' she said purposefully, her tears subsiding as she got to her feet. 'Now you keep a look out at the door and tell me if anyone's coming. No one else must have a clue about this. If Charles found out, there'd be hell to pay.'

And the dogged determination that characterized Rose Maddiford was burning brightly inside her once more.

Three

'Well, at least I feel as if I'm *doing* something now,' Rose sighed as she folded the note and sealed it into an envelope. 'God knows if 'twill do any good, but at least I'll have tried. And maybe you could call in to see Mrs Cartwright, if you wouldn't mind,' she cajoled, 'and ask if Mr Cartwright could put in a good word for Seth. After all, Seth did save him from that attack, and Mr Cartwright always said that he were a model prisoner. He always awarded him maximum points towards his ticket of leave, and he *is* a principal warder so his opinion might count for something.'

Florrie frowned as she slid the letter down inside her full bosom to join the key. 'Like as not, your man'll lose all his points *and* have extra years added to his sentence. He were an utter fool to try and bolt.'

'But he was *desperate*, Florrie!' Rose cried, moisture glistening in her lavender-blue eyes. 'Can you imagine being imprisoned for something you didn't do? Seth's twenty-nine now, so he'll be nearly forty before he's released. The best years of his life gone. *If* he survives that long. And if 'tweren't for Ned, he'd have been away to freedom in another week from now. Away to America to make a new life for himself, just as he'd planned in the first place. Only once he got to Plymouth, he decided he wanted to visit Dartmoor before he left. Well, he's seen Dartmoor all right!'

The words had been tumbling from her mouth in an angry stream and she pulled herself up short, breathless as the bitterness stung her tongue. Her body was rigid with outrage, and Florrie patted her hand to calm her, for she was secretly concerned for the baby.

'Well, you'll have done all you can. Now, if you've been cooped up here all week, you could probably do with some fresh air and exercise. So why doesn't you go down and see that there nag o' yourn? I expect he'll have been missing you.'

'Oh, yes, what a good idea!' Rose's face brightened but then instantly contracted into a scowl. 'As long as I don't see Ned again. Oh, I'd cheerfully murder him. And I hope he's enjoying his wretched five pounds reward. Still,' she grimaced malevolently, 'the other day, I could hear Gospel playing him up something rotten. Serves him damned well right. I hope Gospel bit him where it really hurts!'

'That's my girl,' Florrie chuckled. 'I never liked that boy neither. But you watch your step, Rose. You know what they says. Discretion is the better part of valour. And you'm treading a pretty fine line just now.'

'Oh, I'll be careful, all right. I can't help Seth if I don't have my own freedom. Not that I've really a cat in hell's chance of helping him,' she muttered under her breath as she made for the door.

Her heart sang to be outside again. It was nearing the end of May, a kind, spring day when the warm sunshine lifted the scent of peat from the damp earth and into the air. Rose breathed it in deeply, pausing on the terrace for a moment to sweep her eyes over the familiar landscape of the open moor. Fencott Place was a grand house for its isolated location, built by one of the rich, so-called 'improvers' whose schemes to bring the wild moorland under cultivation had failed spectacularly at the end of the previous century. But it had been to Rose's advantage, for when she had married Charles Chadwick from London and had wanted to remain living on the moor, the house had satisfied his high demands. Huh! Everything had to be just right for him to impress his superiority upon the locals, didn't it?

She went through the gate in the high wall at the side of the house and into the stable yard, wincing at the vile memory of what had happened last time she had been there. Seth, collapsed on his knees. Oh, she must try not to think about it, but it was there, etched on her soul for ever. She shook her head, marching along the row of loose boxes. They were all empty. Doubtless the horses were out in the fields and it was far too early for Ned to bring them in for the night.

The lower half of the last stable door – the largest box with the dog leg where she had hidden Seth – was still shut, and

Rose peered over the top, her pulse suddenly racing. Surely Charles wouldn't have . . . But there was Amber, Rose's beautiful golden dog, nursing the odd assortment of her litter sired by the comical stray mongrel, Scraggles, who had limped into the yard from God knew where and become part of the household. The five pups had grown in the last week, no longer stumbling about with half-blind eyes, but finding their way confidently around the confines of the loose box. Rose slipped inside for a few minutes, Scraggles bounding joyfully around her while Amber wagged her tail contentedly as she watched her beloved mistress pick up and cuddle each little bundle of fluff in turn. When Rose held the tiny runt of the litter to her chest, two trusting, blue-hued eyes gazed up at her from the endearing little face, and Rose bit her lip. If it hadn't been for Seth, the creature would have died at birth.

'I'll call you Lucky,' Rose whispered into its fur. 'And you're the one I'm going to keep.'

She held it for a while longer, stroking its head, its round, soft body warm in her hand, before she replaced it next to its mother. It filled her with pleasure to see the happy canine family again, but the anticipation of being reunited with Gospel made her heart accelerate with joy. He was her soulmate. He shared her passion for excitement, for the freedom of the open moor, and to feel his power and strength beneath her was pure exhilaration. She couldn't wait for the child to be born so that she could ride him again.

She almost skipped out of the yard to the drove between the enclosed fields that belonged to the house. She expected at any moment to hear Gospel thundering across to her when he sensed her presence and thrust his gleaming ebony head over the high stone wall. She came to the gate into the first field and scanned it expectantly. Tansy and Merlin were cropping the fresh, spring grass, but there was no sign of Gospel. Ned must have put him in one of the other fields, perhaps to punish him for biting. Well, she wasn't having that, and she vowed soon to have them back together again. She went on. Gospel must be in the far field, she thought, and as Rose hurried to the gate, she called out jubilantly to him.

The field was green, peaceful. *Empty*. Rose's heart began to drum nervously as dread began to slither into her soul like some evil serpent. Gospel was nowhere to be seen.

She must have missed him. But . . . She ran back along the drove, calling frantically, climbing the gates, shouting, waving. Tansy lifted her head and started to amble forward. But where in God's name was Gospel?

Rose stumbled back into the yard, her pulse crashing at her temples as tentacles of ice closed around her soul, squeezing her ever more tightly. And there was Ned, sauntering across the cobbles, whistling tunelessly. *With Gospel's halter swinging from his shoulder.*

'Where's Gospel?' she demanded, but only a small, strangled sound came from her lips.

Ned shrugged disinterestedly. 'Gone,' was all he said.

'W . . . what do you mean?'

'Master sold 'en. And good riddance, I says.'

The world stood still. Horror and disbelief slashed at her, and her life shattered into tortured splinters like a breaking mirror.

She staggered, her mind grasping at emptiness. No. It couldn't be. This couldn't be for real. She was dreaming it, caught in some horrific nightmare. Oh, no. *Let me out of here!*

She blundered back into the house, groping her way as if she were blind, the floor seeming to sway beneath her feet and the familiar walls dancing a macabre, mocking waltz around her. She knew Charles would be in his study and she crashed through the door without bothering to knock. Just as she had expected, Charles was sitting at the desk, reading some company report or other, puffing nonchalantly on a cigar. Smoke floated in the room in misty ribbons, stinging Rose's eyes and catching at the back of her throat.

Charles glanced up, surprised more than anything at the intrusion. Then his brown eyes narrowed critically at the unkempt state of his wife, her thick, dark curls coming down from their pins in her headlong haste. It was all very well in the bedroom when her long, cascading tresses excited him deliciously, but it was another thing to have her running about the house like a gipsy, especially with her swollen belly. It was grotesque. He couldn't wait for the birth of his healthy, handsome son, of course. But neither could he wait to get between his wife's beautiful, slender legs again. Just the thought of it made his trousers strain, and his forehead swooped in a resentful frown as if it were Rose's fault that he was temporarily unable to satisfy his lust.

'Yes?' he barked implacably.

Rose glared at him for several seconds, hatred choking her as she tried to scrape enough air from her lungs to speak. 'What . . . have you done . . . with Gospel?' she finally managed to grate through clenched teeth.

Charles considered her for some agonizing moments, drawing languidly on his cigar and then tapping the stub into the ashtray before releasing the smoke in a slow stream. 'That wild beast was doing you no good,' he replied lazily with a shrug of his eyebrows. 'I have been most lenient with you, knowing the freedom your father always allowed you, and your understandable grief over his death. But now you must think of our son and his position in society. It's time for you to become a respectable young woman, and that does not include gallivanting across the moor and making such a spectacle of yourself on that creature's back. I will buy you a more sedate mount for our rides together, something more like Tansy. I'll feel much happier with you riding a safer animal, and it will be far more appropriate for you as my wife.'

Rose didn't move. In her breast a painful shard of glass stabbed into what might once have been her heart, and she wondered if the time when she had been truly happy had ever existed. It couldn't have done, for all that remained in her soul was a tearing, eternal agony.

She stared at the man who was her husband, unblinking, her eyes refusing to believe that what they saw could possibly be real. A demented, swirling fury was piling up inside her in a foaming tide and suddenly it exploded in a violent rage.

'How dare you!' she snarled, her cry ripping through the house. 'How bloody, sodding dare you! He wasn't yours to sell! He was *mine*! The only good thing left in my life, and you *sold* him! Well, you'd better damned well get him back!'

'Really, Rose, I won't have you using such disgusting language! It just proves that your father let you get away with far too much, though I'm sure he would turn in his grave to hear such words coming from you. And may I remind you that our son is—'

'Don't you dare come near me!' she screamed as Charles

got to his feet and stepped around to her side of the desk. 'And don't you dare talk about my father like that! He were a better man than you'll ever—'

'And one who was so deeply in debt that you had to marry me to save him from the workhouse,' Charles broke in, his voice cold and unbending. 'Don't think I hadn't guessed. But as it happens I was very fond of Henry and was quite happy to provide for him. And I had you, so we both got what we wanted. You are young and impetuous and need to be trained, but despite what you might think, I do love you, and only want what is best for you.'

'Well, you've a mighty queer way of showing it! Now you'd better get Gospel back or I'll . . . I'll . . .'

'You'll *what*, Rose? And anyway, I can't get him back. I sold him to a dealer who already had a buyer lined up. Now look, Rose.' He lifted his hands as if to place them on her shoulders, his heart softened by his wife's pale, distraught face. But she shrank away as if she couldn't bear to have him touch her and he dropped his arms limply to his sides. 'I'm sorry, but I had to teach you a lesson somehow. Aiding and abetting an escaped convict, I don't know. What next? But with a more suitable mount, a nice little mare perhaps, and ridden side-saddle, of course, now *that* would be far more respectable. Then we'll all be happy.'

'Well, *I* won't be!'

Flints of ice flashed in Rose's eyes as they speared frostily into his. Her world had disintegrated around her, and she struggled in one of the most appalling moments of her life to retain her dignity. She was so stunned that she couldn't think what to say or do next. And so she spun on her heel and flounced haughtily out of the study, head held high. But once out in the hallway, she fled back upstairs and flung herself on the bed, her fists balled so tightly that her fingernails drew blood in her palms. An untamed, unearthly howl wailed from her throat like some creature from hell, and she let it come, powerless and broken.

'Whatever be the matter, my lamb?' Florrie bustled into the bedroom, drawn from unpacking her few belongings in her old room in the attic. She came and sat on the edge of the bed, and Rose lifted herself up and turned to cling to the dear woman she loved, sobbing inconsolably.

'Charles . . . that . . . that monster . . . he's . . . he's sold Gospel.'

'He's done *what*?' Florrie's voice was high with disbelief and she was already on her feet. 'My God, I'll give him—'

''Tis no use, Florrie. 'Twill do no good.' Rose sniffed, swallowed as she clawed her way out of the drowning misery. ''Tis not the way to deal with Charles.'

'But . . . but *Gospel*?' Florrie groaned, still horrified.

Rose clamped her jaw defiantly. 'I'll find a way. Somehow. I just hope . . . I just hope whoever has Gospel just now doesn't hurt him. You know what he's like. Oh, poor Gospel! 'Tis all my fault really. 'Tis Charles's way of punishing me for helping Seth.'

'Oh, Rose.' Florrie released a huge sigh, her ample bosom rising and falling. 'I don't know why you married that man, really I don't. I always felt there were summat 'bout him.'

Rose met her gaze, her own expression tortured. She had never told Florrie the full extent of their financial straits. She had known things were tight, of course, when they had been forced to leave the manager's house at the powder mills after it had become clear that Henry would never walk again and so could not continue in his position there. Mr Frean, the proprietor, had generously given them a hundred pounds from his own pocket, but once Rose had paid all their creditors, there was little enough left and their future was uncertain.

Rose, however, had secured the lease of one of the Duke of Bedford's Westbridge cottages in Tavistock, built twenty-five years earlier for the workers of the town and the surrounding area. One of several developments, they consisted of numerous rows of sturdy stone cottages, each with two downstairs rooms, both known as kitchens, one of which would have made a bedroom for Henry, while the other had a modern range for cooking. Upstairs were three further rooms, and outside an earth closet, a pigsty, a small garden and a stand-pipe shared with one's neighbour.

It wasn't exactly what they were used to, but Rose had been determined that they would all lead a happy life together and was actually quite looking forward to it. She had even found a field with a stable to rent near the town where Gospel could be kept. The problem was how to pay for it all?

The solution, though, was quite simple. Rose would find

herself a position. It still wouldn't be easy. The rent for the cottage was to be one shilling and sixpence a week, that for Gospel's livery two and threepence, with food, fuel and other expenses on top. Rose had hoped that she could put the remainder of Mr Frean's generous gift into an interest-bearing account to supplement her wages, but she had been shocked to learn that most of the furniture in the manager's house had come with it, so to speak, so that at the very least she would have to buy beds for her father and Florrie. She herself could sleep on a straw mattress on the floor, and in all other ways they could make do, the only other essential item, as far as Rose was concerned, being a bath chair so that either she or Florrie could push Henry along the streets of Tavistock or on outings alongside the river or the canal.

She had scoured the *Tavistock Gazette* and found two adver- tisements requiring a governess. That would be right up Rose's street, and she had managed to arrange both interviews for the same day. She had dressed in an appropriate, serviceable outfit, and had taken Polly and the dog cart rather than riding Gospel since she could hardly arrive at an interview as a governess wearing her riding habit! She had stabled Polly at an inn for the day, and then had set out confidently, convinced that by the end of the day, all their problems would be solved.

She had paused with her hand on the latch of the intricate wrought-iron gate for just one fleeting moment before striding up the long, immaculately kept front garden in Plymouth Road, her heart battering against her ribcage. The tall, imposing villa was one of a terrace of opulent buildings overlooking the water meadows and the recently disused Tavistock Canal that ended, over four miles away, above the inland river port of Morwellham on the River Tamar. Only the wealthiest people of the town could afford these sought-after houses in such a pleasant situation, and though she was accustomed to rubbing shoulders with the moneyed classes, a vice of appre- hension tightened around Rose's chest: she *must* be offered the position.

Her hand pulled lightly on the bell ring. The sudden loud clang from inside made her jump, and set her shivering on the doorstep. It was March and a bitterly cold wind was making the crocuses tremble with fragility among the well-tended lawn. When the door opened and a stern grey face enshrouded in a starched white cap poked itself forward, Rose had to swallow down her nerves.

'Yes?' So blunt, the sharp eyes scrutinizing her. And she was just the maid!

'Miss Maddiford,' she answered, her voice nonetheless reproducing her usual confidence. 'I've come about the position as governess. I believe your mistress is expecting me.'

'Governess is servant, same as the rest on us,' the starched cap snapped. 'Try down there!' And it bobbed towards the steps to the semi-basement and then the door slammed in Rose's face.

The air stung in her seething nostrils. Her inborn pride lifted her head, and without a second thought, she rang the bell again. This time she was ready.

'If I am to teach the children of this house, then I deserve some respect, and I *will* enter by the front door,' she told the slack-jawed woman as she pushed past her into the hallway. 'And now, if you would tell your mistress I am here?'

She smiled with mocking sweetness and straightened her shoulders as the maid opened her mouth, but with no suitable response ready on her stunned tongue, the woman shut it again before disappearing around the corner. Rose waited patiently, approving of but not overwhelmed by the interior decoration. She heard a knock, followed by low voices, and then was shown into a lavishly furnished drawing room.

She bowed her head, for *now* was the time to show deference to the lady of the house. She waited a moment, allowing her prospective employer to study her appearance, before looking up, but remembering not to smile.

'Come forward, girl, and don't be shy.'

She obeyed, and found herself standing before a well-dressed woman of no more than thirty years old who seemed more interested in reading the letter in her hand, which Rose recognized as her application. The woman folded it with obsessive neatness, grunted, and then turned to Rose with a hostile gaze.

'So,' she began abrasively. 'You have not been a governess before, and you have no references. So why do you consider yourself qualified to teach my children?'

Rose's head tipped on her erect neck. 'Because I am educated myself, ma'am.'

'Really? At which institution?'

'My father taught me, ma'am.'

The woman's lips compressed with disdain. 'Your father? And he is, I take it, a teacher himself, or a man of the cloth, perhaps?'

'No, ma'am. A businessman, but educated at grammar school. He taught me everything – reading, writing, reckoning, history, geography . . .'

'But since you would be teaching my daughters, I assume you could pass on to them some of the more genteel skills – drawing and painting, for instance?'

'Yes, ma'am, I can paint and draw,' Rose replied, though how well was another matter, she thought grimly to herself.

'And can you teach singing and music? Play the pianoforte?'

Rose knew she stiffened. 'I'm afraid not, ma'am.'

'And do you speak French?'

Rose's heart sighed as she averted her eyes. 'I'm afraid French was not something my father had any reason to—'

'Is there *nothing* you can teach my girls, then?' The woman's gaze flashed with irritation. 'Not even needlepoint and embroidery?'

Rose jerked up her head. This so-called lady of the house seemed intent upon humiliating her, and had Rose not been so desperate, she would have given her the length of her tongue! But sewing, now that was something she knew she excelled in.

'I design and make all my own clothes.' She dared to smile. 'There's nothing I can't do with a needle.'

'Then I suggest you look for a position as a dressmaker or a seamstress! Good day to you, Miss Maddiford!'

Rose blinked at her, her wounded pride brimming with indignation. 'Oh, but, *please*, ma'am, just let me—'

'I believe you can find your own way out.'

'Oh, yes, ma'am! I believe I am quite capable of *something*!'

She spun on her heel, her jaw clamped, and swept out of the room, deliberately leaving the door, and then the front door, wide open. Good Lord! Thank goodness she hadn't been offered the position, for she could no more work for such a harridan than . . . than . . .

She stalked along Plymouth Road, the anger emptying out

of her and being replaced by tears of shame and confusion. Perhaps after all, she just wasn't suited to working. But she *had* to find a job! Her father and Florrie were depending on her! She was intelligent, diligent, polite if she was given respect in return, so there must be something she could do!

By the time she reached Bedford Square, her fury had calmed. She shouldn't expect her first interview to be a success, so she took herself off to a bench in the churchyard to consume the bread and cheese she had brought with her for lunch. She sat and trembled with cold and dejection. The wind had sharpened, snow-dust blowing in scudding circles, the sky leaden with yellow-tinged, smoky grey clouds. Winter was returning, and she felt it would break her spirit in two. But she *must* find the courage to soldier on, for the war had scarcely begun!

The second household could not have been more different. A frail young woman was sat next to a roaring fire, her two sons, aged eight and five, playing at her feet. Rose warmed to the mistress at once. They took tea like old friends, the older boy chatting away to Rose, whilst the younger child found his way on to her knee and she slipped easily into inventing a word game almost without realizing it, while their mother looked on with a contented smile.

'You are heaven sent, Miss Maddiford – or may we call you Miss Rose?' She beamed. 'My health is not what it should be, and I believe you would be of such help to me. I should like you to be as part of the family.'

A welcoming glow tingled down to Rose's feet. She had done it! And the little boys were delightful, bright, happy and interested. The world suddenly seemed a friendlier place.

'My husband and I had settled on a wage of three and sixpence a week, rising to four shillings after a year's satisfactory service. I do hope that will be acceptable to you. Payable at the end of each quarter, but we could advance you a little to begin with, if it will be of help.'

Rose felt her soul plummet like a bird shot dead in full flight. 'Three and sixpence,' she echoed tonelessly as the little boy slipped from her lap.

'Well, perhaps we could start at three and nine, if you wouldn't mind helping Nanny with her duties. She's too old to manage on her own now, but she's been with our family for so long – she was *my* nanny, you know – so we can't possibly dismiss her. You would have to share her room, I'm afraid, but it is very warm and comfortable. And our servants share our own fare. We like to look after them well, and expect their honesty and loyalty in return. Now *do* say you'll accept the offer!'

Her enthusiastic words were pricks of ice in Rose's wounded heart. There was nothing she would have loved more than to join this household, but . . . 'I'm afraid I cannot live in.' Her voice quavered as her throat closed with sadness. 'You see, my father recently had a terrible accident that has left him paralysed, and as a result he has lost his position and the accommodation that went with it. We are about to move to one of the Westbridge cottages. Our housekeeper will come with us to care for him, but there are certain things that she cannot manage alone, so I must return each evening. And . . .' She looked up and met the woman's sympathetic gaze, but would she understand? 'I have a horse. Not just any horse that I could easily sell on. He has a certain temperament . . . I fear it would mean having him put down, and I couldn't bear that. I have somewhere to keep him, but I should need to see to him every morning and night, so altogether I couldn't possibly live in.'

Her face was a mask of taut muscles, matched by the compassion of the woman who had listened to her. 'Oh, my dear, I am so sorry to learn of your plight,' she said with such feeling as she reached out and touched Rose's arm. 'If only we had space, I should willingly offer your father a home also, for I'm sure he is as amicable as yourself. As for your horse, I'm afraid we have no stables, either. Oh, dear. What a pity,' she sighed. 'But *please* think it over. I shall keep the position open for . . . a fortnight, shall we say? So, if you change your mind, just let me know. But,' she hesitated, biting her lip, 'I must warn you that *any* position as governess is bound to be live-in, you know.'

Rose lowered her eyes. 'Yes, of course. I suppose . . . I hadn't really thought about it properly. I'm so sorry to have wasted your time.'

'Not at all. The boys and I have enjoyed your visit. I just wish . . . A fortnight, remember.'

The woman's kindness had made the tears glisten in Rose's eyes and she angrily brushed them away as she walked back down the street. What a fool she had been! A governess was a servant like any other, with a servant's wage supplemented by full board. Alone in the world, the position would have been ideal, but she had responsibilities, and though she would do anything in her power, she wasn't sure she could satisfy them all. So where would they end up? In the workhouse? Good God, no! She couldn't bear the thought. They would only take her father, of course, and possibly Florrie if she could not find other employment, but male and female were strictly separated and they would never see each other again.

She shook her head. How could she even think of it! Perhaps she could set herself up as a dressmaker. But you needed time to establish a clientele, build up a business, *premises*, none of which she had. An *assistant*, then? She glanced up at the snow-laden sky. It was only mid afternoon, but growing darker by the minute. She should collect Polly and the dog cart from where she had stabled them for the day. She regretted not having ridden Gospel and having his speed to convey her quickly home. But perhaps she might just have time to make some enquiries.

She drew a blank. Apprentice to a dressmaker with lodgings but no wages; or a shop assistant on a paltry salary was the best she could find. Oh, why wasn't she a man? She groaned with such fury that she drew glances from passers-by. She could have earned eight to ten shillings a week labouring, but as a woman, you received so little reward no matter how hard you worked! Perhaps she should just find out about the workhouse . . .

The blood seemed to drain from her head and swirl about her heart as she dragged herself up Bannawell Street to the forbidding workhouse at the top, and her hand shook so violently she could scarcely knock on the intimidating wooden gates, one of which was finally opened by an even more menacing face that eyed her with hostility.

'Please,' Rose asked in a whisper as the courage flowed from her fingertips, 'how does one get into the workhouse?'

'Apply to the Board. In Bedford Square,' the voice snapped. 'They won't take a fit young woman like you. Get yersen a job. Do some work!' And the toothless mouth – whether it was man or woman, Rose could not tell – broke into a jeering cackle.

''Tis not for me, but for my father,' Rose blurted. 'He's paralysed, and—'

The face did not flinch. 'I told 'ee. Apply to the Board. Won't take anyone unless they'm destitute. Nort but the clothes on yer back, and I doesn't mean *they* sort of clothes,' the face sneered, jabbing a finger at Rose's good coat. 'I means *rags*. Then maybe they'll take 'en.'

The gate closed with a crash, but not before Rose caught sight of two stooped figures shuffling past, clad in the drab fustian of the workhouse uniform with a large 'P' for pauper on the arm. So shameful. So degrading. Rose stood for a full minute, her own shoulders slumped, battling to stop herself slithering to the frozen ground. How could she have come to this? How could fate be so cruel? A feeble, anguished moan escaped from her lips, laced with anger and frustration. It wasn't in her to give in, but at this moment, she was so lost, so defeated, so desolate that her blood seemed to have turned into water. She dropped her head back on her neck, her eyes shut as memories of her past, happy life tortured her soul, and it was only the touch of a snowflake on her frosted cheek that sparked her brain to retrieve its grip on reality. The snow was beginning to fall, the vicious wind slicing at her slender form. They were in for a snowstorm, and she had a long journey over treacherous terrain before she could reach home. She must hurry to collect Polly and set out as quickly as she could, hopefully before the snow came down too heavily.

The memory of that soul-destroying day flashed through her brain once more. When she had arrived back at Cherrybrook, frozen to the marrow, covered in snow, terrified and exhausted from battling against the blizzard, she had been too broken to relate all the details to Florrie. Too ashamed to admit that her fine plan had failed. Just as she couldn't bring herself to tell the dear woman now that on that fateful day, she had actually considered applying to the workhouse for her father. And then she had received a kind and generous letter from Charles, begging her once again to marry him. She had felt so low, so desperate, that her former hesitation was dispelled and she had joyfully accepted his proposal.

But look where it had got her!

She had been so happy until her wedding night, when she had learnt what marriage was *really* all about, and though

Charles behaved like an utter gentleman during the day, even in her ignorance Rose realized he treated her unfeelingly in their bed. And within six months, her father was dead. The only thing that had kept her sane were her mad flights of freedom on Gospel's back, and now he, too, was gone. She had lost everything she had sacrificed herself for by marrying Charles Chadwick, and her world lay in broken pieces at her feet.

'I did it for all of us,' she told Florrie now, her voice quiet and trembling. 'For you, for Father. So that I could keep Gospel. But I also did it for me.' She lifted her head and her glistening eyes fixed on Florrie's compassionate face. 'I honestly thought Charles and I would be happy together. I'd never had a sweetheart before, you know that. I'd never known what it was to love a man. And now . . .' She smiled wistfully, and even as she spoke the words, she wondered if they weren't quite true, for hadn't she felt about Seth . . .? 'And now I never will. And I can never forgive Charles for what he's done. Not ever. And if 'tweren't for this child, I'd be gone from here for ever.'

And because there was something else she had to do as well . . .

Four

Dr Power crumpled the letter into a ball in his fist and launched it into the fire, since that was the best place for it. He watched pensively as its edges scorched, then it uncurled a little before it finally fell victim to the hungry, licking flames.

Rose Maddiford. Her maiden name – for like so many of those who knew her of old, he could never think of her as Mrs Chadwick – suited her well. She truly must be mad. The letter was a full written confession of how she had willingly helped Seth Collingwood, saying that she believed unequivocally in his innocence, and that the story that he had terrified her and threatened to kill Amber's puppies was a complete and utter lie of Collingwood's fabrication told in order to protect her. She knew that he would almost certainly be flogged for his escape, but he was already so ill and could the doctor please do anything to prevent it, especially as the poor man had been wrongly convicted in the first place and didn't deserve his incarceration, let alone the terrible punishment. Dr Power had been so good to her in the past, especially with her father, and she trusted him to do what was morally right.

The good doctor slumped back in his chair and tapped his joined fingertips against his pursed lips. Ah, Rose . . . The vision of the very first time he had clapped his stunned eyes upon her crept unbidden into his brain. What was it, six years ago, when he had taken up the position of prison surgeon? It had seemed a good way to provide a roof over the heads of his growing family, and also offered him the opportunity to help the working classes of the area who could not afford the normally expensive charges of a private doctor. He was given a house of almost equal standard to that of the governor, and was paid a reasonable wage to care for both the inmates and the prison staff, so that when the local community requested his attendance, he could do so at a fee they could afford. Among them were the workers at the Cherrybrook gunpowder mills. The first time he had been summoned there, it had been at the behest of a captivating, mettlesome young girl so slender she appeared quite ephemeral, like some fanciful painting from one of his children's fairy-tale books, perched atop a massive, prancing, long-legged steed whose coat matched the shining ebony of her hair. She could have been no more than sixteen then, and at more than twenty years her senior, he was old enough to be her father, but he could not deny that, had he been younger and not already long and happily married, his heart would have been strongly drawn to her. It made him feel a little ashamed, though there was nothing more than admiration for her in his breast, not only for her undeniable beauty, but for her vivacity, her strength of character, her soul. She had such an immense capacity for compassion, whether it be for the high moorland where she lived, animals of every description, or the men and their families who had worked for her father. The father whose death, as he had witnessed for himself, had broken the poor girl's heart.

And now she had sent this plea for help.

He filled his lungs deeply, and slowly let them collapse again. Did she realize what she was asking? And yet he understood entirely. His own position at the prison was humbling and irresolute, his allegiances torn asunder. He was supposed to be a man of mercy, healer of the sick, and yet he had to uphold the cruel regime of the harshest punishment imaginable. The prison infirmary was full of convicts from other gaols across the country, sent there not because they were particularly heinous, but because they were suffering from consumption, and Dartmoor's clean air helped them to recover sufficiently to be returned to serve their sentences whence they had come. There were other inmates who feigned illness to escape the back-breaking hard labour, some who even put their own lives at risk by swallowing anything to hand – such as soap, ground glass or even pins – that would incapacitate them. Dr Power had to be equal to all their tricks. And then, ironically, perfectly fit and healthy men had their constitutions decimated by the meagre starvation diet, the vicious punishments and inhumane, gruelling tasks they were put to day in, day out, enduring conditions to which no farmer would subject his animals.

Men like Seth Collingwood.

The fellow had been in his care for a few days once before. Shortly after arriving at Her Majesty's hotel, he had apparently saved the life of Warder Cartwright as the work party returned from its racking and dangerous day's toil at the quarry. For his trouble, he had been assaulted by a group of maddened inmates – nothing too serious, but battered and bruised enough to require the medical officer's attentions. Dr Power had to admit to taking an instant liking to his patient, which was something he could rarely say of his charges. Even then, Collingwood had been protesting his innocence and Dr Power had been inclined to believe his claims, but he was hardly in a position to argue with the authorities who had committed the accused to gaol.

And then, ten days ago, the physician had been appalled to discover the poor devil chained in a punishment cell, awaiting sentence from the Director of Prisons for his attempted – and almost successful – escape. He had taken some lead shot in his shoulder from one of the guards' Snider carbines, but the wounds were healing well. How well his broken ankle inside its plaster cast was mending would only be known when it was removed. It was the doctor's considered opinion that the cast had been professionally applied and was not Rose's own remarkably successful attempt, as she claimed in the letter. However, he had determined that, were he to be questioned, he would keep that view to himself, for he would inform on neither Rose nor his respected colleague, the elderly Dr Seaton. What had horrified him, though, was that the prisoner had been set to the usual punishment task of oakum picking – teasing into shreds a statutory length of old tar-saturated ships' rope which had since dried into razor-sharp fibres that sliced into the fingertips, rendering them excruciatingly painful. This when the prisoner was most obviously running a fever and coughing up blood, sitting in a cramped position in a cold, damp cell, with nothing but bare boards for a bed and existing on the so-called jockey diet of bread and water. Dr Power didn't even wait for the result of his immediate report to the governor, but had the convict removed to the infirmary at once. Fortunately, it had been less than forty-eight hours since his recapture, but had it been much longer, it may well have been a death certificate rather than a medical report he needed to complete. The governor had, of course, been furious, and the vindictive sergeant who had lied about the escapee's state of health had been severely reprimanded, but that was it. After all, who really cared about the fate of just another convict at the isolated prison?

And now the authorization for Collingwood's sentence had arrived. The maximum of thirty-six lashes with the cat-o'-nine tails, not just for his escape, but also for his terrorizing of the heavily pregnant young woman. Dr Power ran his hand over his jaw. A few days previously, a flustered and red-faced Florrie Bennett had come to his door with the letter from her little mistress, which, once he had read it, he had secreted where no one could ever find it, and now he had committed it to ashes. What could he do? Collingwood – though of course he was referred to by his prison number only – had improved somewhat. At first, the doctor had feared consumption, but upon examination and with the history of pneumonia at Exeter gaol eighteen months previously, he had concluded that it was a recurrence of the same ailment, the patient's general health having been weakened, like so many, by the harsh prison conditions. This new episode had most likely been triggered by the inactivity of lying for days and nights on end on the stable floor, which, though dry enough for animals, was damp by human standards. The painful, scourging cough and blood-stained sputum was the first stage of pleurisy before the pleural cavity filled with cushioning fluid. After ten days propped upright in bed, with an hourly hobble up and down the infirmary to help drain the lungs, together with the superior invalid diet, the felon's constitution, which must have been generally strong, had allowed him to improve considerably. But he was nowhere near sufficiently recovered to endure the barbaric torture to which he had been sentenced.

And yet . . .

Dr Power dropped his head into his hands. It was a huge risk to take, but it was the only way to save Collingwood from the entire punishment. A total of three hundred and twenty-four strokes of each vicious tail clawing at the young, *innocent* flesh and horribly disfiguring him for life – well, it was unthinkable. Though a heavy leather hide was placed as protection over the vital organs, within a few lashes, the bruised and swelling welts would open and run with blood until the cat could cut through to the bone. The agony of it must be indescribable, the torment reaching to every fibre of the body. The physician shuddered. He had seen it many times, and now, Dear Sweet Jesus, he was to witness it again. He shook his head. What in the name of God was he doing in this job?

He stood up, his eyes screwed tightly shut at what he knew he must do.

The prisoner's face was inscrutable as his wrists and ankles were put in chains, spreadeagling him on the flogging frame. Some offered resistance as the moment of punishment came, but this fellow waited patiently while the problem of how to secure the plaster cast was solved, as the prison surgeon would not have it removed. When he offered the felon a gag for his mouth, he refused with a shake of his head, but the doctor leant forward to hiss in his ear.

'Take it, you fool. I don't want to have to stitch your tongue or your lip as well. For God's sake, do as I say. Mrs Chadwick won't want to have risked herself for nothing.'

He drew back hastily, not wanting to arouse the suspicions of the governor and the burly, unfeeling warder who had been chosen to deliver the gruesome punishment. But he caught the flash of amazed comprehension in the convict's eyes as he took up his spectator's position. And then he shuddered as he saw the governor give the nod to begin.

He had known great, swarthy bullies to holler like babies from the very first stroke, but this unfortunate lad scarcely flinched, his firm jaw set like granite and his narrowed eyes locked on to some point of focus on the far wall and merely twitching as the whipped ends of the cat raked like barbs into his exposed back. Dr Power's own sickened heart pounded inside his chest, sweat prickling beneath his shirt just as it poured from the prisoner's face and ran down his bare chest in rivulets. By the count of five, nothing had escaped his lips but a whimper, and the physician clenched his fists into tight balls. Dear God Almighty, give me something, lad! And then the pitiless warder, irritated beyond measure by his victim's silence, seemed to add extra force to the sweep of his arm as he slammed the cat through the air. The shock of the redoubled agony was so powerful, the convict could not cry out. Instead, his chest rasped with a sharp and massive intake of

breath that caused his inflamed lungs to react with a spluttering cough.

Dr Power almost rejoiced. It was what he had prayed for.
At a repeat of the warder's sadistic action, the bound man
almost choked on the prolonged coughing it drew from his
strained insides. Again and again, until it exploded into one
continuous, violent spasm. The surgeon observed carefully the
tortured criminal. With his arms spread above his head, his
already concave stomach was so taut with suffering, there
seemed little between it and his spine. The gag in his mouth
had turned scarlet, and in his already weakened state, his
head had drooped forward and his shoulders were hanging
from his stretched arms.

Dr Power held up his hand. 'That's it, sir. He's had enough,'
he pronounced, turning to the governor.

'What?' The warder's eyes bulged in his face, the veins
standing out like ropes in his thick neck. His good friend,
who had been on duty when the prisoner had made his escape,
had immediately been dismissed, he and his family being
thrown out of their home in Princetown and out on to the
street without a by-your-leave. The fact that he had been taking
a swig from his hip flask at the time and so was guilty of
gross negligence of duty didn't make any difference to his
colleague, who was gunning to take his revenge on the escapee.
'He's only had ten, the bastard!' he spat viciously.

'Eleven, actually. And if he coughs like that any more, he'll
rupture his diaphragm. Sir?' he questioned, again addressing
the governor.

'I thought you had pronounced him fit?' was the reply.

Dr Power frowned darkly. He must be careful what he said.
'Yes, I had. He seemed much recovered, but the weakness in
his lungs must be deep-rooted and so can flare up very easily.
His constitution must be considerably worse than it appears.'

The governor seemed to consider for a moment, but then
to the doctor's utter relief, he nodded his agreement.

'Take him down carefully,' Dr Power instructed at once, 'or
we'll have a corpse on our hands.'

The warder shot a disgruntled glare at the surgeon and then
gave a reluctant shrug. What would one more dead convict
matter? As far as he was concerned, he'd be pleased if the
devil died. And as the felon was released from his restraints,

he collapsed almost senseless into the doctor's arms. Raymond Power ground his teeth. He had instructed his surprised medical assistant to have a morphine injection at the ready. He would treat this poor wretch's mutilated back with the greatest care, binding down the swollen flesh and mending it where possible with the neatest stitches and the finest thread. He would be scarred, yes, but the doctor would make sure it was kept to the minimum, and nowhere near as badly as if he had taken the full thirty-six lashes. And if Dr Power's recommendations were heeded, as they most likely would be, he never would. For the doctor felt he was fully justified in writing in Collingwood's medical notes that, due to his predisposition to pneumonia, he should never be flogged again.

The physician knew he had done what he had not only for the sake of the wronged man, but for the lovely young woman who had begged for his help. And the guilt of it would go with him to the grave.

'I need to send a telegram to London,' Charles announced coolly. 'It's raining hard so I'm going to get Ned to take me in the wagonette. I trust you can behave yourself while I'm out?'

Rose was sitting in the drawing room with her feet up, supposedly reading a book. But though her eyes were travelling along each line of the page, the meaning of the words was failing to register in her brain. She was alive only to the pain in her heart, and could think only of what she could do to rectify the situation. How could she get Gospel back? The commotion she had heard out in the stable yard had been the animal kicking up a fuss, literally. But not because of his dislike of Ned, as she had thought, but because he was being taken away by a stranger. Oh, God, if only she had known what was going on! Although what she could have done, locked up in the bedroom, she didn't know.

And then there was Seth. Florrie had duly delivered the letter to Dr Power and had also been to visit Mrs Cartwright, who had promised to have a word with her husband, although she doubted there was anything Jacob could do. Rose had, of course, received no news of what had happened to Seth. In one way, it was a relief, for until she did, she could cling to the hope that he had been spared his punishment. What she could do for him in the long run, she wasn't sure either. But one thing was certain: while Charles still distrusted her, he would continue to curtail her freedom. So, although she seethed with frustration and resentment, she must play the dutiful, obedient wife until that trust was restored.

'Of course. And what do you think I'm likely to get up to, anyway, when I'm eight months pregnant? I feel like a beached whale.' She flashed him her most winsome smile, and then looked down at her hands as they lovingly stroked over her bulging belly. If there was one thing that would gratify Charles, it was the thought of his unborn son.

'Well, you just take care. I'll be as quick as I can. I don't want to be out in this any longer than I have to. You wouldn't think we're just about into summer, would you? It's bucketing down, and all we've got is that wretched wagonette. I keep promising myself to acquire some covered conveyance. I really must do so! This is bloody ridiculous. I'm going to get soaked!'

Rose smirked quietly to herself as he went out of the room tutting under his breath. She hoped he would catch a cold and die from it after what he had done. She still couldn't believe that Gospel was no longer there, and kept going out to the stables, expecting him to have escaped from wherever he was and have found his way home. But only the dogs were there to greet her, and endearing as they were, they couldn't mend her broken heart.

She hauled herself to her feet now and went over to the front window. She could scarcely see for the lashing rain that drove against the glass, but a few minutes later, the wheels of the wagonette crunched on the gravel as Ned, hunched in a sou'wester and waterproof cape, drove out from the side of the house. Charles was sitting aloft behind him, back straight as a mine rod, holding an enormous umbrella, which threatened at any moment to be turned inside out by the gusting wind. Rose gave a bitter, sardonic laugh. This was exposed Dartmoor, not a London street, and he really did look quite stupid!

But this was the moment she had been waiting for, and she lumbered over to where Florrie had been sitting in one of the more upright chairs, knitting a baby's bonnet and pretending not to observe the scene between Rose and her husband.

'Quickly, Florrie,' she hissed urgently. 'While he's gone, I'm going to look in the study. There must be a bill of sale or something in there. It might tell me who Charles sold Gospel to. The devil won't tell me. I need you to stand guard and warn me when he comes back.'

Florrie put down her knitting. 'Of course,' she whispered back. 'Quickly, then. I'll watch from the window. I'll see him first from there.'

'Thank you, Florrie.'

Rose's pulse trundled at her temples as she slipped into the study. All was neat and tidy as always. Where should she begin? Surely Charles wouldn't have been so careless as to leave such evidence on the desk, but it seemed the obvious place to start. There were two piles of papers sitting on the inlaid leather and she rifled through them at speed. Letters from his broker and solicitor, all relating to business.

She sighed, and glanced around the room. Two of the walls were lined with polished wood shelves, all nicely scrolled along the edges when they had first been installed for Sir Thomas Tyrwhitt's friend eighty years or so previously. Charles had transported some of his favourite books down from London, joining those that Rose herself had brought from Cherrybrook, but most of the shelves were empty. There certainly weren't any business papers lurking on them. She would try the drawers of the desk, then.

There were three on either side. Rose's hands shook and she realized her palms were sweating as she opened the top one on the left. Writing paper, envelopes, nothing more. The next was full of household bills, accounts. The coal merchant in Princetown. Rose remembered the horrible day she had discovered that her father's cheques were being returned by the bank, and that none of the coal they had consumed for almost a year had been paid for. It was all part of the reason why she had turned to Charles, to the man who was the answer to her prayers and who she believed she could love. And now he had betrayed her in the most cruel, unforgivable way he could.

The deep bottom drawer held company reports of the many enterprises Charles held investments in, among them the Kimberley diamond mine and the newer gold mines in South Africa. He had told her a little about them, reluctantly, as if a woman didn't have the wit to understand. But how could she possibly if he wouldn't explain it all to her? Just now, however, he was right that she wasn't interested. All she wanted was to discover who had bought Gospel so that she could try to get him back.

She went to open the top drawer on the right. It was locked, and Rose's heart sank to her boots. Of course, there could be important business papers in it, things he wouldn't want the servants to be able to see. Perhaps even documents that would show exactly how wealthy he was. There was the grand house in London, beautifully furnished, and with a fully employed staff even though Charles spent so little time there nowadays. There was never any expense spared, and he had bought Fencott Place without batting an eyelid. Rose's mouth twisted. She lived in the lap of luxury, but she paid for it dearly in Charles's bed – and now that her father was dead, he had taken Gospel, her only joy, away from her.

She went through the other drawers, scattering their contents uncaringly on the floor and then scooping them up and returning them to some sort of order before replacing them. Charles mustn't realize what she had done. She sat back, drained and defeated, in the chair, desperately eyeing the locked drawer. She had discovered no key elsewhere. Charles doubtless kept it on his person. Damn him! There was a paper knife on the fancy pen and ink set on the top of the desk. Her hand trembled as she picked it up. Could she possibly . . . without scratching . . .

'Rose, they've just turned in at the gate!' Florrie's anxious whisper came around the door.

Rose's heart tripped over itself. She replaced the knife. Everything looked as it had been. She scuttled out of the study, her mouth slackened in defeat. When would she get another chance?

Five

Raymond Power blinked his eyes and lifted his head slowly from where he had fallen asleep over the table. He hadn't been home to his own bed for two nights. How could he, when Seth Collingwood was not only in agony from his flogging, but was wheezing and coughing with frightening violence? Had the doctor done the right thing? Only time would tell. His conscience wouldn't allow him to leave the prison infirmary until he knew, and so once again he had stayed at his post all through the night. His neck was stiff from lying in such an awkward position and he wasn't quite as young as he used to be. He stretched, wincing softly, but then was racked with guilt at the low moan that came from the end bed, for surely Collingwood was suffering far worse than he was.

He had kept the poor devil floating on morphine since his punishment, stitching the lacerations to his back with the same delicacy he had once used on a young girl who had cut her cheek badly. Then he had bound the fellow's torso to compress the swelling flesh and also reduce the pain from coughing, changing the bandages each day to help prevent infection. The scars would fade to a reasonable extent as the years passed – if he survived – but he would be marked for life.

Dr Power bent over him, taking his pulse, which was near normal now and, he felt sure, a little stronger. He would normally have someone who had been flogged lying on his front, but Collingwood was in more danger from his lungs and so the physician had him propped up on several soft pillows. His face was like putty, and when his wandering eyes half opened, they stared out blankly from ink-smudged sockets.

'I didn't hurt her . . . I swear.' The words were barely breathed on a sighing whisper, his pale lips not moving so that the sounds were slurred and almost inaudible. But the agitation was clear in his feeble voice, and he whimpered as he drew in a series of tiny, snatched breaths, every one of which caused him pain. He moaned weakly again and his eyelids drooped closed, but Dr Power knew that there was consciousness behind the deathly mask.

He leaned over so that his mouth was against the convict's ear. The medical assistant was dealing with another felon who had lost some fingers at the quarry, and the doctor didn't want anyone else to hear.

'I know you didn't, lad,' he whispered back. 'But you must be careful what you say. We mustn't get Mrs Chadwick into any trouble, now, must we?'

To his amazement, Collingwood's eyes flashed wide open for just a moment with a depth of comprehension that took Dr Power by surprise. There was a strength and intelligence in this fellow that shone through his broken body, and yet again the good physician was inclined to believe that there had indeed been some grave miscarriage of justice here. And Rose Chadwick had obviously spent some time with the fellow, and he was sure she wasn't the type easily to be taken in.

'You need to start taking in some fluids,' he said, his voice at a normal level now. There was a jug of water and two feeding cups on a crude table between Collingwood's bed and the next, and the doctor filled one of them, holding the spout to his patient's lips. He always had deep misgivings about the water that came from the open leat and was doubtless the cause of the frequent bouts of diarrhoea from which all the prisoners suffered. In the infirmary, he instructed his assistants to boil all drinking water, but even so, he wasn't convinced of its safety.

Collingwood had taken several sips, but the effort appeared to have exhausted him and Dr Power allowed him to sink gingerly back against the pillows. It was too soon for another morphine injection, and he had already been on it for a couple of days. Besides, the drug was loosening his tongue and prison walls had ears. The doctor would allow him to lose himself in his rambling mind while the morphine wore off, and once Collingwood was back to normal, he would have a quiet talk with him before putting him on laudanum instead. Another derivative of the same substance, of course, but a milder, more controllable dose, it should still help suppress his cough as well as ease the pain in his back – and make him more mindful of what he was saying. And then, with inhalations, rest and the superior invalid diet, Dr Power was beginning to have more confidence that with any luck the poor sod would recover – and then be sent back to some gruelling prison work. Because of his escape attempt, he would never again be allowed on a work party outside the prison walls, and he would be extremely unlikely to be put to any of the less demanding tasks. And as for the marks he had already earned towards his ticket of leave, well, he could forget those. He was more likely to have extra years added to his sentence. And all for something he likely hadn't done in the first place.

Poor bastard!

She came to him, emerging through the vaporous shroud, gliding without movement, silent. A vivid, translucent smile lit up her face, making it glow like the sun and dissipating the mist so that she was engulfed in a shaft of golden light. The touch of a breeze kissed her cheek, lifted a tendril of her sable locks across her forehead. She drew it back with a fluid wave of her graceful hand, her eyes full of laughter and compassion, deep pools of love he felt he could happily drown in. His heart overflowed with joy and delight, and he would never want for more. He had found what he had been seeking for so long.

Pain ripped through his back, taking his breath away. Stunning him so that at first he didn't know that the agony was his own. He was almost curious. Was this what it felt like? It wasn't so bad. But by the third stroke, the shock was overpowered by the torture and every fibre of his being was alive to the sensation, tearing, burning up his arms to his fingertips. *Jesus Christ, help me to bear this.* His throat contracted, dry and choking. He heard a cry. Was it his own? He didn't recognize it, his lungs raw and stinging.

He looked up at her, pleading. The smile had slid from her beautiful face. Her brow creased with devotion, horrified, intense, distraught. Her eyes glistened a deep lavender blue. He could see the long, dark lashes as she gazed on him. She opened her slender arms, inviting him into her embrace. He fell forward, clinging to her, his head against her rounded breast, so soft, so comforting. Tears fell from beneath his closed eyelids as he felt her hold him close. Everything would be all right now. She soothed him, calmed and comforted him. The pain was easing now, melting away, and he was drifting on a rocking sea, gentle. At peace. And he was content to sink beneath the lulling waves of oblivion.

Florrie Bennett's shrewd eyes silently observed the young girl as she yet again pushed the food around her plate at dinner that evening. The older woman had been back at Fencott Place for a week, and in all that time she was convinced hardly a morsel had passed Rose's lips. Though the colossal bulge of her stomach appeared to be growing before their very eyes, the rest of her had withered to nothing more than skin-covered bone. And what made Florrie heave with anger was that, at the opposite end of the table, Charles Chadwick hardly seemed to notice as he tucked into his own meal with relish. Not that he was a fat or even well-built man, but he clearly appreciated good food. And he was quite active, walking, when the weather permitted, into Princetown to the telegraph office at least every other day, and quite often taking a ride on Tansy to some of the places Rose had shown him, and once over to Cherrybrook to check on his interests there. He was a busy, efficient businessman. Florrie only wished he were as good a husband instead of treating his wife so cruelly.

'And what have you two ladies been up to today?' he enquired as he speared his fork into the succulent slice of roast beef, doubtless from one of the many black Scottish cattle reared on the moor. He chewed for just a moment on the tender meat before swallowing it, and then washed it down with a sip of full red wine, his casual attitude demonstrating that he didn't really care as long as he would approve of their activities.

Rose slowly looked up, her sunken eyes enormous in her pale, cadaverous face. During the last few days, it had gradually sunk in that not only had Charles betrayed her over his promises regarding Seth, but that Gospel really was gone for good. She fixed her empty stare on her husband, evidently without the will to utter a word.

'Making a quilt for the babby's cradle,' Florrie answered for her, though in fact, despite Rose's exquisite skills with a needle, it had been Florrie who had been engaged on the fine embroidery while Rose had sat, gazing blindly out of the window, in the direction of the stable yard where Gospel's loose box now stood empty.

'Ah, good.' Charles nodded his constrained approbation, and Florrie burned with contempt at his desire to make everything appear normal. 'I'm glad you're making preparations for the arrival of our son. Patsy has scrubbed out the nursery and the remaining furniture is on order and should be arriving soon. By the way,' he added, 'I've told Cook to start interviewing for a second housemaid, as I believe the child will create extra work, particularly in the laundry department. And as he was leaving the other day, I instructed Dr Seaton . . .' Charles paused for an instant to clear his throat as the calming efficiency turned to a hint of disdain in his voice. 'I instructed Dr Seaton to be mindful of engaging a wet nurse.'

'*What?*'

Florrie almost rejoiced as Rose's eyes glinted with resentment, the first sign of life in them for days. 'I shall be feeding our child myself! And before you say it, I don't care if 'tis not the done thing in your mind! 'Tis not as if I've any high society engagements to attend, nor should I wish to if I had!'

She stood up so abruptly that her chair rocked on its back legs and, flinging her napkin on the table, Rose shambled out of the room with as much dignity as her swollen abdomen allowed, leaving Charles to stare after her open-mouthed.

Florrie slowly heaved herself to her feet. 'You'm destroying that girl, you know,' she announced, her chin lifted high. 'And don't you go telling me 'tis not my place. You lost any respect you deserved when you sold that there horse. She'll never forgive you, and nor will I.'

And casting a withering glance at him, she too walked quietly out of the room.

Charles leant back in his chair, his hands pushing against the edge of the table and his cheeks puffed out like ripe peaches. Women! Would he ever understand them? God damn it, he *loved* his wife. With a passion that went beyond his own reason. He *adored* her spirit, but sometimes it just went a little too far. Helping that escaped convict, well, it just wasn't on, even if he himself had been genuinely moved by the devil's plight. What could he have done, anyway? Even for someone like himself, who had money and certain connections in London, it would be impossible and he certainly didn't have the time, what with his business interests and travelling to and from the capital. If only they lived permanently in his London house, none of this would have happened. But Rose *belonged* on Dartmoor. He understood that and he wouldn't have had it any other way, but sometimes she exasperated him.

That was why he had sold the horse. It was wilder than she was. Without it, she would surely calm down just a little. To perfection. He was tempted even now to try and get the beast back. But he must stand firm. If he gave in, he would lose respect. And he *would* buy her another animal to ride – something fast, for only that would suit her, but something more reliable. And he had to admit that he really would feel more at ease and might be able to allow her a little more of the freedom she craved. Besides which, once their son was born, she might be so devoted to him that riding might become something of the past and she would forget all about the horse that had meant so much to her.

As for Florrie Bennett, well, he was quite astounded at the way the formerly meek woman had become so forthright. With Henry Maddiford's death, and with her own grief now under control, she seemed to have taken upon herself the role of Rose's protector – as if Rose needed protecting from *him*! Personally, he'd have liked to see the woman out on her ear for her insubordination, but Rose clearly loved her, and Charles really couldn't be so cruel as to dismiss her. Florrie Bennett he could put up with – and she would be useful when his son was born. But that wretched nag was an entirely different matter!

She was peering into the sepulchral darkness, her eyes dimmed with terror as she stared into the black mouth of hell. Feeling her way as she edged blindly into the deep pit of the damned. Moans, disembodied voices, wailing. Spectres with faces stretched and distorted. She saw him then, in a ghoulish flash of light, his body stretched out on the torture rack. Heard the whine of the lash as it cracked through the air. The unearthly cry from a voice she recognized, and her heart tore. There was blood. Blood everywhere. Running down a hairy, ebony hide. The great animal reared skywards, front hooves pawing frenziedly at the air, eyes rolling and ears laid back at its rider who thwacked his rump viciously with the riding crop.

Rose blinked her petrified eyes, and was overcome with relief as she realized she was sitting bolt upright in bed looking down on Charles as he lay on his back beside her, breathing heavily in an undisturbed sleep. The raging pulse in Rose's skull began to slow, and she fell back on the pillows, snuggling under the blankets, for the cold sweat that slicked her skin was making her shiver.

Relief. Just a nightmare. But it wasn't, was it? Seth either had been, or was about to be, flogged. Seth, who had resigned his army commission because he was never the fighting sort; who wanted a quiet life, a good night's sleep after an honest day's hard work. Seth, who knew and cared for God's creatures, and had saved the stunted puppy's life. Had done the same for the wretch in the dark Tavistock back street, and had ended up in hell because of it.

Rose's eyes flew open and she tossed her head from side to side in a torment of frustration. How could she go back to sleep when Seth would be suffering such agony, helplessly restrained while his back was cut to ribbons. And God alone knew what had happened to poor Gospel. Where was he now? Was he frightened and alone in a strange place? In the unfamiliar surroundings of a town, perhaps? Was someone caring for him, winning his trust, or was he being subjected to beatings to make him behave, or to a harsh martingale? Or was a cruel, pinching bit being forced into his strong, sensitive mouth? A great wave of exasperated fury threatened to drown her, so powerful that it was beyond tears, and she ground her teeth like some demented harpy.

Dawn was breaking, and she judged it must be just after four in the morning. In the faint light, she gazed on her husband's slumbering face. It was Ned's fault, not Charles's, that Seth had been recaptured. And without that, Charles would never have sold Gospel. Charles had been appalled at what she had done, she understood that. Despite the promises he had made on that terrible day, in his mind, a convicted criminal must be guilty. It was against the law to help an escapee, and the Charles Chadwicks of this world never broke the law. They adhered to every rule of society. And Rose defied them at every turn. She had pushed him too far and so it was no wonder she had incurred his wrath. She did not love him, and he could be blamed for that no more than he could for Seth's punishment. And she knew he had been genuinely shocked at the sergeant's brutality. But he had broken his promise at least to listen to Seth's story, betrayed her trust. And as for selling Gospel, she could never, *ever* forgive him.

But it didn't help. Oh, Seth. Seth . . .

She couldn't lie there a minute longer. She heaved the bulk of the unborn child upwards and, wrapping her dressing gown about her, silently let herself out of the room and padded along the richly carpeted landing. Perhaps she should go down to the kitchen, bring the banked-up range into life and make herself a soothing hot drink? But what she really needed was to talk, and there was only one person . . .

'Florrie!' she whispered urgently up in the servant's room on the top floor, wanting to wake Florrie but without too much of a start.

The older woman's eyes flickered and then stretched wide with surprise. But apart from being slightly arthritic and on the wrong side of plump, at barely fifty years old, Florrie Bennett enjoyed good health and could easily cope with being woken at the crack of dawn, though her round face immediately creased with concern.

'What is it, cheel?' she answered, her mind at once alert.

'Oh, Florrie,' Rose groaned, 'I just can't get Seth out of my mind. What they'll do to him. And 'tis so unfair . . . so unjust. And Gospel. Oh, what'll become of him? I want him back!'

Her face crumpled, her lovely eyes spangling with tears and her throat raked with pain. Her quivering lips drew back from her teeth and she managed to gasp one shuddering breath before the first howl of despair strained from her lungs. Florrie was out of bed in an instant, her arms awkwardly about the frail form of the girl who, in Florrie's heart, was her own daughter. Rose buried her head in Florrie's ample bosom, trembling against her as closely as her bulge allowed. Without a thought for the propriety of the situation, Florrie drew her into the warm bed beside her.

'If only Father were still alive,' the girl muttered desolately, and all the pent-up grief seemed to escape from her soul in an exploding stream. She shook, weeping against Florrie until the anxious woman thought the child's heart would break. 'He'd have done something about it, I know he would. Oh, I miss him so much . . .'

She was lost again in the swirl of her misery, and Florrie calmly patted her shoulder. She wasn't the only one who missed her dear Henry. If only he was still alive. Alive and fit and running the Cherrybrook gunpowder mills. Then Rose would never have married Charles, Florrie was not such a fool that she hadn't always known the truth, despite what Rose had said. The marriage must work. For the sake of Rose's sanity, it had to. But Florrie was terrified for her. The story of the wrongly convicted man was one thing. The way Rose had told it to her was another. Anger over the injustice of it was fair enough, but when Rose had spoken of the fellow himself, her eyes had shone, her face lit with something the girl herself did not recognize. But Florrie did. And Rose would hate Charles for ever for selling Gospel. The future hardly dared thinking about!

A sudden intake of breath pulled them apart.

'What? 'Tis not the babby?' Florrie demanded in a fluster.

She waited while Rose let out the breath in a slow stream. 'No.' And then she smiled at Florrie's worried face. ''Tis not due for a few weeks yet. But Dr Seaton said I'd start getting practice contractions about now. So 'tis quite normal. I've had one or two in the last few days.'

'Oh, right then,' Florrie sighed with relief. 'Now let's try to get a little more sleep, my young maid.'

Rose nodded in reply, warmed and comforted by Florrie's compassion. Her red-rimmed eyes felt tired, and it wasn't long before she drifted into a restless slumber until she at last felt Florrie stir beside her.

'I reckon as you ought to get back to your husband,' she whispered softly.

'Oh, yes, I must!'

Rose sprang to her feet, in her haste forgetting the burden of the child. A sharp pain stabbed through her as her belly hardened, taking her breath away and stopping her in her tracks. She felt something snap inside her, and then her eyes met Florrie's in horror as the warm liquid flooded down her legs and settled in a puddle on the rug.

Six

'Well?' Charles demanded tersely as Patsy showed the physician into the drawing room and then hastily retreated.

Dr Seaton glared at him darkly as he came towards him, but did not reply until he had finished rolling down his shirt-sleeves. 'Your wife, Mr Chadwick,' he began guardedly, 'has been through a most difficult labour, as I'm sure you will have realized by my sending for Dr Ratcliffe to assist. Forty-eight hours is not unusual in a first child, but the contractions were strong and close together from the start, and there is always a risk when the waters break first. Mrs Chadwick became weak and exhausted, and I had to administer chloroform. And it was a forceps delivery.'

Charles leapt to his feet, his cheeks flushed a bitter puce, and he slammed his fist so hard on the table beside him that the empty cup there rattled in its saucer. 'This is all that bastard's fault, isn't it?' he snarled, his handsome face twisted into a hideous mask. 'She's been pining for him . . . Yes, *pining*,' he repeated acidly as the doctor raised one bushy grey eyebrow, 'ever since he was rearrested. That's what brought the baby on before its time, isn't it? And you're as much to blame! Helping them like that! I had to perjure myself to get you out of trouble!' Charles barked, poking his head forward so that his nose was only inches away from Dr Seaton's.

The brittle air crackled between them, but the doctor regarded his patient's husband with a steady eye. 'I was, of course, interviewed by the authorities myself,' he said levelly, 'and perhaps I should remind you that I have a sworn duty to heal the sick no matter who they are. As for bringing on your wife's labour prematurely, well, I believe I can say quite categorically that it had nothing to do with it. She is a most passionate young woman, but emotions cannot induce labour. However, she is small of frame and not as robust as many women of her age, which may have been a contributory factor. So please, Mr Chadwick, do not make a fool of yourself by blaming things that are physically impossible.'

Charles appeared to gasp for breath, struggling to regain his composure, but one thing his pride could never allow him was to stand down from a situation. 'And what about my son, then?' he pressed menacingly.

'Your *daughter*,' Dr Seaton answered pointedly, 'is very small, as is to be expected. That in itself is not so much of a problem, but her early arrival has meant that her lungs are not quite as stable as I should have liked. And, I'm afraid, her heart is not strong.'

Charles stared at him, the colour draining from his skin, and he fumbled to sit down again in his chair. But his next words dumbfounded the doctor. 'A daughter, you say?' he mumbled. 'But . . . Rose will be able to give me a son? In the future? Next year, perhaps?'

It was Dr Seaton's turn to feel the flood of anger in his blood. 'Your wife, sir, is very ill,' he stated through tight lips. 'She is utterly exhausted, and I have given her a sleeping draught to ensure she has a proper rest. She has lost a lot of blood, and has many stitches which will be most uncomfortable for her. We have done everything in our power to save her and avoid infection, but you never can tell. Dr Ratcliffe will stay with her for the next twenty-four hours. I will return to Tavistock and arrange a wet nurse, for I doubt Mrs Chadwick will have either the strength or the milk to suckle the infant herself. She will need careful nursing, but I believe Mrs Bennett is capable of that. I can see you are . . . *disappointed* that you do not have a son,' he observed bluntly, 'but I beg you to keep that to yourself. For your wife's sake. Let us have her fully recovered before we start talking of other children.'

But he could see from the vexed expression on the man's face that it would be a tall order.

'Oh, Florrie, isn't she beautiful!'

All through her pregnancy, Rose had never really been sure that she wanted this child. She had hoped that it might heal the growing rift between herself and Charles, but she feared that his domineering attitude would extend to the nursery and that it might only lead to further rows. But now, she scarcely dared breathe as she gazed with rapt eyes on the tiny scrap of humanity that lay peacefully in the crook of her arm. She sat, propped up on a bank of pillows, her drawn face as white as their snowy covers, and her mantle of waving raven hair tangled about her in untidy confusion. She had slept for several hours, a deep, drugged unconsciousness that had nevertheless been punctuated with tormented, anguished moans that folded Florrie's brow, for she alone understood the turmoil in Rose's tortured mind.

'She certainly is!' Florrie's homely face split with an enchanted grin. 'Just like you when you was a babby.'

'Really?' Rose's sunken eyes lit with stars. She felt drained, her body so heavy it seemed welded to the soft and comfortable bed, her brain being the only part of her that seemed to have any energy. The screwed-up eyes, the rosebud mouth had instantly captivated her heart. She wanted to move the warm shawl about her daughter's head so that she could see her face a little better, but her hand felt like lead and refused to obey the order her brain was sending to it.

'Oh, yes,' Florrie smiled again. 'And you just like your mother, too.'

'Then . . . I shall call her Alice,' Rose stated fiercely.

Dr Ratcliffe's eyebrows shot up as he came across the room to them. It had been an incredibly difficult birth, the young mother struggling to bring her child into the world. It had left her in a frail and exhausted condition, and yet her voice just now had rung with defiance.

He cleared his throat. 'Now, Mrs Bennett, if you could wash Mrs Chadwick's hands and her breasts, we should get the baby to feed again. Dr Seaton should be returning with the wet nurse later this afternoon. He has someone in mind and I think she will take little persuasion. But in the meantime, we believe the mother's milk in the first few days has some particular quality . . .'

The younger physician had the same balance of confidence and understanding as his senior partner, and with his help, little Alice was persuaded to take another small feed. She was weak and reluctant, preferring just to sleep and slip quietly from life, but Dr Ratcliffe was having none of it. He showed

Rose how to place a pillow on her lap to raise the child to the right height so that she had both hands free; to express a few drops of the thick, yellowy milk on to the baby's lips, and then stroke her nipple against the child's cheek to stimulate her instinct to turn her head to suckle; to gather up her breast and be ready to thrust the entire nipple into Alice's mouth as she opened it, and hold the back of her head firmly against the breast so that she would not slip from the precious, life-giving hold. For the inexperienced mother, it seemed so much more complicated than she had imagined, especially as the infant was so lacking in strength that she was unwilling to take her part in the operation. The doctor had to resort to removing the warm and cosy shawl, and even to pinching the tiny pink feet, but eventually Alice fed for three minutes on one breast and was successfully transferred to the other. Dr Ratcliffe smiled with satisfaction as Rose experienced the drawing, gratifying sensation of giving life-sustaining nourishment to her own child.

'The waxy substance on her skin,' the doctor explained as he watched the contentment on his patient's face. 'That's because she was so early. It'll rub off on its own, and that fine down will come with it. And the tiny spots on her face, they're quite normal to any baby. But,' he continued, and a cloud passed over his brow, 'she will need the greatest care. Early babies lose their body heat even more quickly than full-term ones. And we must build up her strength, protect her from infection. But she is really lucky in that she is in the correct sort of . . . environment, shall we say, to survive.'

Rose raised her eyes to him, and he saw that the doubt had darkened them to the deepest lavender. She swallowed hard.

'Yes,' she croaked. 'Dr Seaton explained.' And noticing that Alice was slackening off from her feed, she used her newly learnt skills to rouse her enough so that she continued sucking.

'There you are! You're doing well!' Dr Ratcliffe encouraged her. 'Now, when we've finished, I want you on the commode to pass water. Mrs Bennett, I want you ready with a jug of tepid water to rinse over Mrs Chadwick's stitches afterwards. It is *essential* that you do this every time so that we minimize the chance of infection. And you must drink plenty. A glass of water or a cup of tea or whatever every hour. It will help wash out your system and make your urine less concentrated, so it will sting less when you relieve your-self.'

'Oh, Florrie, I didn't realize it would all be so complicated,' Rose sighed some ten minutes later when she was back in bed, lifeless and floppy as a rag doll and ready to sleep again. 'Amber didn't have all this terrible trouble with her puppies, did she? And . . . Oh!' She sat up with a start, her eyes wide. 'Are they all right? Who's looking after them?'

'Oh, they'm fine. And 'tis Ned who feeds the dogs, just as normal.'

But Rose's face had hardened at the mention of Ned, her heart turning to a bitter stone. 'He didn't decide to hand in his notice, then,' she snorted, 'now he's got his handsome reward in his pocket? Oh, I could murder him!' she cried with such vehemence that Florrie caught her breath. 'Just another couple of weeks, and Seth could have been away! Oh, Florrie!' She caught hold of the older woman's arm with a grip of iron, every last vestige of her strength directed into her hand. 'You must go to Dr Power for me. Find out what . . . what happened.'

Her voice faded in a choked trail, and she fell back on the pillows, her head tossing frantically in a flurry of agitation. Florrie pursed her lips, for this really would not do!

'I'm not leaving your side till you and the babby are settled,' she announced determinedly. 'But don't you fret none. I promise I'll find out for you in a few days. You did all you could, and 'tis no point in worrying your head about it no more. 'Tis the babby and yourself you've to look to now.'

Rose drew in a long breath, her face a picture of wearied consternation. 'Oh, Florrie, why has everything gone so wrong?' she groaned. 'All this, and . . . and Charles selling Gospel. And did you notice when he deigned to put in an appearance, he didn't even look at Alice? He doesn't care, because he wanted a son. And don't try telling me otherwise, Florrie, for I know 'tis true. Oh, God, what am I to do?'

She turned away, curled up in a ball on her side, biting on her knuckles as her stomach cramped with an after pain. Her beloved father was dead, she was married to a man she didn't love and who only wanted one thing in the bedroom, her tiny daughter was scarcely clinging to life, she was likely never to see Gospel again, and the one person who had brought her solace was locked away in that horrendous prison, suffering the most gruesome punishment. *If* he was still alive . . .

She wept until her very soul was emptied of its grief, and Mother Nature at last lulled her into the release of sleep.

'The child, sir, is doing as well as can be expected given the circumstances,' Dr Seaton reported a few days later. 'The wet nurse is brimming with milk, which is ideal as it means your daughter can suckle without too much effort and hopefully gain some strength that way. The woman's own infant may bawl his head off at any time of the day or night, as I believe you have complained, but his lusty feeding is stimulating his mother's milk even further, so you should be thankful.'

Charles glanced up with a scowl. He had employed Dr Seaton as the most senior and highly respected physician in Tavistock, but the elderly fellow was inclined to be blunt, and Charles, though he knew the doctor was right, resented his tone. 'And my wife?' he questioned, choosing to ignore Dr Seaton's implication.

'Ah.' The older man's face fell. 'I'm not at all happy about Mrs Chadwick's condition. Though I can assure you every precaution has been taken against it, she is a little feverish and, if you don't mind discussing such details, her stitches are showing signs of infection. I can remove them in a day or two and hopefully she will then begin to recover, but until then, I shall remain concerned. But what worries me most is her state of mind,' he went on, unhesitating, never one to beat about the bush. 'What milk she had has already dried up, which is quite a psychological blow for someone who wanted so desperately to suckle her own daughter. And I believe your own ignoring the child does not help. Your wife cannot be blamed for the gender of her baby, you know.'

Charles lifted his chin stubbornly as he met the doctor's accusing gaze. He should have been delighted at the birth of his child, be it boy or girl, he knew that. No one else knew that as a young man, he had been denied the joys of father-hood by his young mistress who, without telling him of her condition, had visited a backstreet abortionist. Not only had she taken the infant's life, but the ensuing infection had killed her as well. And all because Charles had once told her that he could not marry her as she was beneath his station. He supposed he had never forgiven himself, which was why Rose's child was so important to him, but there were reasons why he had only wanted a boy.

'I make no secret of my disappointment,' he said openly. 'I want a son who can build on the success I have worked hard for all my life. Having a wife and a male heir, or at least what I had hoped would be a male heir, has given me some purpose in life, when I was beginning to wonder quite what was the point of it all. A daughter would be no more able to cope with the business affairs I will one day leave than Rose herself would. But I love my wife dearly, for all her light-headed ways, and what you say grieves me deeply.'

'I believe you underestimate your wife's capabilities, sir, but that is none of my business. Her health *is*, however, and in my opinion a little more show of support from yourself could well be beneficial.'

Charles studied the closed expression on the doctor's face, and nodded slowly. 'So be it. I could not bear to lose my wife,' he muttered as he got to his feet and, crossing out into the hallway, made for the stairs.

'Oh, Rose, Rose, my darling,' Charles pleaded in a broken whisper, wiping her sweat-bedewed face yet again before taking her limp, fragile hand between his strong, brown ones. Her sunken eyes were closed, the long, dark lashes fanned out on her cheeks which were no longer pale, but flushed with fever. Her skin seemed transparent, and she looked more like a child than did the tiny infant up in the nursery, which Charles had not visited since his wife had sunk into the consuming delirium three days previously.

It wasn't puerperal fever, both physicians had confirmed. The bleeding from her womb was quite normal and inoffensive, and the site of the now removed stitches was only minimally infected. It went deeper than that, something Dr Seaton could not explain but had witnessed before, though usually in someone lost in grief. Rose's strength had always been in her mind rather than in her slender, waif-like form, and now that, too, had ebbed away. It was as if she could not face reality, and so had willed herself to drift into some unconscious state where it was peaceful and safe.

'Why don't you get some rest, Mr Chadwick?' Florrie suggested, for though she had never been fond of Charles and despised him as much as Rose did for getting rid of her beloved horse, he had been sitting at Rose's side for two days without a break. 'I can take over for a while.'

'No, no, Mrs Bennett,' he answered wearily. 'I can't leave her.'

He turned back to the bed, lifting Rose's hand to his lips and kissing each thin finger in turn. He wanted to pump his own strong will, his virility, into her frail body, to fill her again with that maddening resolve he had striven, he realized now, to smother.

'Rose?'

His heart soared as her eyes half opened, but he saw at once that they were unfocused, lost in some dim fever stare, some daze that she alone could see into. What was it that lurked in the dark shadows of her tortured mind? Had he done this to her, by selling Gospel? By refusing to help that black-guard out in the stable? May God forgive him! She began to whimper, as she had on several occasions in the last few days, as some hideous nightmare slithered into the deepest chasm of her soul. She threw her head against the pillows, her limbs writhing in the bed until the sweat stood out on her forehead in tiny globules and her dry lips muttered in incomprehensible anguish.

'Oh, my poor lamb,' Florrie breathed in a desperate sigh as she hurried over to the bed, the lines on her face ever deeper. 'What is it, my sweet?'

As if in reply, a tiny gasp seemed to catch in Rose's throat and a thin moan quavered from her lips. Charles met Florrie's gaze, his eyes hollow as he wrung out the cool face cloth yet again and tried to lay it over Rose's brow. But she flung her head so that the flannel slid on to the pillow.

'No!' she wailed quite distinctly now. 'Seth! Oh, Seth!'

She suddenly sat bolt upright and reached out to one side of the bed, which happened to be Florrie's, her eyes somehow wild and yet blank at the same time. Florrie wrapped Rose's wasting form in her arms, rocking her like a child until she appeared to calm, and then carefully settled her back in the bed where her sobs slowly faded and her mind was lost in sleep once more.

Florrie glanced up in despair to see Charles rise to his feet, his face rigid, and walk silently from the room.

'Right, you can sit back now.'

Dr Power put down his stethoscope. He had been listening to Collingwood's lungs having first examined the healing wounds on his back. With careful nursing, he had managed to avoid infection to the lacerations. Nature would take over now, and though permanently marked, the scars wouldn't be as horrendous as they might have been. The sounds the doctor had heard from the felon's chest, too, were encouraging, and in a few weeks' time, he should be able to leave the prison hospital and be set to some light tasks until he recovered fully.

The physician secretly breathed a sigh of relief. He had taken a huge risk, and it had paid off. He watched Collingwood pull the nightshirt back down over his torso, which was thin now from his illness, but which the doctor's experienced eye could see was normally finely muscled. The fellow's light hair had grown somewhat and he had handsome, hazel eyes. Mrs Rose Chadwick couldn't have helped but be attracted to him. It would have helped her to believe his story. But from the limited conversations Dr Power had held with him, he knew him to be refined, educated and intelligent – certainly not the kind of convict he usually had to deal with!

'Well, it's about time that plaster cast came off,' he announced gravely, drawing back the blankets from Collingwood's legs. 'It should be healed by now. Just keep still while I take it off.'

He noted that Collingwood merely looked at him without saying a word. Just as well. He didn't want any discussion over the plaster. It was obvious to him that it had been applied professionally, by his colleague, Dr Seaton, so the least said the better. Thankfully Collingwood remained silent while the doctor worked, but the moment his leg was freed, he was giving it a good scratch and his eyes opened wide.

'It looks so thin,' he observed in evident surprise.

'Wasted muscle. Tense your calf and relax it. That's it. Now push against my hand. Good. How does that feel?'

'A little strange.'

'No pain? Good. Let's try you on your feet. Take it easily.'

Collingwood swung his legs over the side of the bed and

gingerly raised himself upright. Dr Power took his arm as he put his weight on his injured leg and took a few steps, but he seemed to manage without any problem.

'All right?'

Collingwood nodded, appearing pleased. 'It feels weak and a little sore, but so much better than before. He did a good job.'

The doctor flashed him a warning glance. 'Keep your mouth shut, you fool,' he hissed at him, 'unless you want to get Dr Seaton *and* Mrs Chadwick into trouble.'

'Oh, God,' Collingwood groaned under his breath. 'What an idiot.' His eyes swept nervously about the infirmary, but it seemed that no one had heard. He dipped his head, lowering his voice to a whisper. 'I can trust you, can't I? Is she all right, do you know? No recriminations?'

'No. Not from the governor, anyway,' the doctor mouthed back, perspiration prickling at his collar.

'And has she had the baby yet? Dear God, I hope she comes through it safely.'

'I won't tell you again. I don't want to hear another word about it. Now we're going to walk up and down a few times, and then my assistant will get you an inhalation. You may have stopped coughing up blood and infected matter, but you're not entirely out of the woods yet. But you're supposed to be doing some sort of work, even in here. In my opinion, you're not up to oakum picking yet, but I reckon you can rip some old sheets into bandages for me and roll them up. That should keep the governor happy, anyway.'

And he saw Collingwood nod his gratitude and sigh deeply as he began to hobble up the ward.

Seven

R ose's heavy eyelids lifted and drooped several times before they remained open, her dulled eyes wandering uncontrolled until they finally began to focus. It was some moments before her disorientated mind placed itself back into reality, her gaze settling on the familiar room. The June sunshine entered through the large open window in a slanting shaft of silvery light, filling Rose's head with peace and tranquillity. Over by the table, a figure she recognized but somehow could not place was busy with some task, but she knew it was someone who was close to her, and inspired her with trust. She sighed softly, too weak to move, but content to float on some buoyant wave of comfort. Tugging at her memory was a horrific, half-remembered dream, but it was far, far away and mingled with a tender sweetness that had once soothed her troubled soul.

'Florrie?'

The name seemed to speak itself, and the figure turned, slow and unbelieving, before stepping on dumbfounded legs to the bed. The older woman's face was pale with shocked delight, but then the colour flooded back into her cheeks as she grinned with joy.

'Rose? Oh, my dearest! You'm back with us!'

A frown flickered over Rose's forehead. 'Florrie, I . . . I don't remember,' she croaked. 'What . . . what's happened?'

Florrie's face visibly dissolved and two fat tears trickled down her glowing cheeks. ''Tis proper poorly you've been, cheel. A fever of some sort.'

'A fever?' Rose's frown deepened, and then panic shot through her as she suddenly remembered. She tried to sit up but it was as if she was pinned to the bed and she fell back with a groan. She had no need to speak, as Florrie had guessed at once the reason for her agitation.

'You'm not to worry none. Little Alice is soldiering on upstairs in the nursery,' she said with a proud smile. 'Pretty as a picture, and putting on weight. Which is what you must do. Thin as a stick, you be.'

The corners of Rose's mouth twitched upwards as relief swamped her lifeless limbs. 'How . . . how long has it been?'

Florrie lowered her eyes. 'Nearly two weeks since you slipped away from us. Oh, little maid! You've no idea how worried we've been. But here's me wittering on, when you must be gasping for a drink. I've some nice cool water here. I bring it fresh twice a day and somehow you've managed to take a little.'

She didn't add that in Dr Seaton's opinion it was what had just about kept her alive. Florrie flustered about her charge, helping to prop her up on extra pillows so that she could sip at the refreshing liquid. Rose felt so strange, unreal, as weak as a kitten and yet relaxed and serene. Something deep and troublesome was taunting the secret depths of her mind, but for now she was happy to ignore it.

'Will you bring Alice to me, please, Florrie?' she asked eagerly.

But Florrie closed her lips firmly. 'When the doctor says 'tis safe. He'll be here after lunch, as he is every day.'

'Oh, dear, poor man. 'Tis such a long way. And . . . and what about Charles?'

The shadow flitted across Florrie's face so quickly that Rose was not aware of it. 'Been at your side constantly. Just taking a well-deserved rest right now,' she added. For how could she tell Rose that since her tortured mind had called out Seth's name, Charles had not set foot in the room?

Charles finally put in an appearance later that afternoon. Florrie had bathed Rose's skeletal body, as she had done each day since the baby was born. She had then taken the most over-whelming joy in spoon-feeding her – since Rose was too weak even to feed herself – a bowl of bland chicken broth followed at an interval by a sweet egg custard, as Florrie's instincts told her that Rose's starved stomach must be coaxed back to normality with light nourishment, little and often.

A relieved and delighted Dr Seaton had pronounced the fever gone. In his opinion, the fever itself had been mild, as had the infection in her 'down-belows' as Florrie put it, and which was now healing nicely. But the protracted labour had been exhausting, and the dread that the infant might not survive, together with the failure to feed the child herself, which was the only way she could protect it, had simply tipped her over into a state of limbo. And although he kept it to himself, Dr Seaton also believed that the traumatic event of the convict's recapture, though it could not have brought on her early labour, was bound to have upset her emotionally. Her mind and body needed time to heal, and so both had closed down while nature cured her. And now she was awake and refreshed, and though she would have to be careful not to overtire herself for some time, she should be up and about in a week or so. Her womb had contracted well, the bleeding very much lessened, and the sponginess of her stomach, the only part of her that had any flesh on it, he assured her would disappear once she was active again. He would examine her thoroughly in a month or so, but at the moment, he could see no reason why she should not bear further children in the future. In the meantime, little Alice was holding her own, though neither her heart nor her lungs were strong, and she would probably always have to be mindful of her health.

Rose was sitting up in bed now, bright and alert after a short nap, her minuscule daughter in her arms. It was a warm and sunny afternoon, and she had unwrapped the shawl to examine the tiny arms and legs, still so very fragile and covered in folds of loose, wrinkled skin. The child moved very little, and when she did, it was with the characteristic, uncontrolled jerks of a young infant. But when Rose placed her little finger across the miniature palm, Alice's hand closed about it, filling her mother's heart with unutterable joy. The grip was not strong, and there was still a faint blueness about the child's heart-shaped jaw, but when she opened her eyes – already the same violet-blue as her mother's – they bore with such intensity into Rose's face that they almost spoke to her.

'Rose, my dear,' Charles greeted her with as much emotion as if she had merely been out to the shops. But, entranced by the magical spell of her daughter, Rose did not notice.

'Oh, Charles!' Rose glanced up at him with a captivated smile. 'Isn't she lovely? Florrie says I looked like that when I were a baby.'

'You've had us worried,' Charles answered flatly.

'Yes, I know. And I'm so sorry.' There was something tugging at the back of her mind, something that she instinctively felt wasn't quite right. But she couldn't think what it was, so perhaps she was mistaken . . . She turned back to her husband, her smile broadening. 'But I feel so much better now. And isn't Alice adorable? You don't mind my naming her after my mother, do you? Why don't you sit here on the bed and have a hold of her? Only just for a few minutes, mind, because I'm so jealous that I missed the first two weeks of her life and I want to make up for it.'

She had spoken quickly, hardly drawing breath between the words that pattered from her mouth, beaming up at Charles before returning her mesmerized gaze to the precious bundle cradled in her arms, totally besotted by the tiny creature she had brought into the world. Charles's nose twitched and he took a step backwards.

'No. You hold her while you can. I'm really far too busy.'

Rose tipped her head at him questioningly. 'Can you not spare just one minute?' And then her lips pouted in that mutinous way he had come to know so well. 'I'm sorry she's a girl,' Rose went on tersely. 'I know 'twas a boy you wanted, and I promise I'll give you a son one day. But please, don't love Alice any the less because of it. 'Tis not her fault.'

'Really, Rose, I don't have time for babies no matter what their gender,' Charles snapped irritably. 'You know how time-consuming it is running my affairs from two hundred and fifty miles away. Besides, children are a woman's domain. I'm just looking forward to when I can sleep in my own bed again. And how long will that woman and her howling brat have to stay here? It may be up in the nursery, but I can hear it all night long!'

Rose flashed her eyes at him, ready to retort that the wet nurse was keeping their own child alive, but it was true that he did look tired and a little gaunt, so she bit her lip instead. 'Some time yet, I'm afraid. So, please, Charles, try to be patient. And . . . I know you don't approve, but I should love Molly to visit. I can't wait to introduce her to little Alice.'

Charles's face stiffened and he stretched his neck out of his starched collar. 'If you must. But only when Dr Seaton confirms that both you and the child are well enough.'

'Oh, thank you, Charles,' she said passionately, but when she lifted her head, it was to see his back as he left the room, and she pulled a derisory grimace at it. She had the impression he had only agreed because she had promised to produce a son. One day. But perhaps it was a promise she could not keep. And, of course . . . Her mind reared up at the thought of what had to happen in order to produce another child: the nightly ritual in their marital bed. But just now, that seemed a lifetime away as she turned her attention back to the infant who had fallen asleep in her mother's arms.

The days passed in a blissful haze, gradually establishing a routine of rest, a little exercise within the confines of the spacious room, and bonding with her daughter. She kept Alice with her for much of the day, even insisting, much to Charles's disgust, that the wet nurse come down from the nursery to feed her, chatting to the woman who was a good, homely sort and who, in turn, soon warmed to the young mistress she temporarily served. It was only at night and during Rose's daytime rest periods that Alice was taken back up to the nursery by a doting Florrie, who in her own mind, considered herself the child's grandmother. Rose grew stronger by the day, waiting impatiently for Dr Seaton to give his permission for visitors. A peaceful euphoria had taken over her spirit, her days filled with the blithe rapture of her baby, and when the occasional uneasy shadow passed over her soul, she shook her head with a scornful snort, since Alice, so far, was doing well and becoming more active as she gained a little strength.

It was Daisy who broke the spell. Daisy, the new maid, was as effervescent and garrulous as Patsy was quiet and reserved, nattering away nineteen to the dozen as she cleaned the room or saw to the fire, for though it was early July, high up on the western side of the moor, the evenings and early mornings could be chillsome even on pleasant days. That summer, the sun had only rarely appeared from behind iron-grey clouds, and today was no exception as Daisy coaxed the coal into a dancing conflagration.

'They say a prisoner fell to 'is death yesterday,' she announced cheerfully as she replaced the poker on its brass stand. 'You knows how they'm building they prison blocks up to the sky wi' convict labour. Well, he must've felled off. Still, there be plenty more to take 'is place.'

A cold, black dread slashed at Rose's heart, and somewhere deep in the sepulchre of her soul, the horror was reawakened. Her mind had somehow succeeded in shutting itself down to some hidden, lurking fear, and now the great looming monster reared its ugly head. Yes, that was it, the nameless torture that had been gnawing away inside her.

Seth.

The anguish washed over her in a drowning wave and she had to fight to draw breath, though Daisy lifted a surprised eyebrow as her mistress sighed an impassioned, 'Poor man,' almost inaudibly, and then appeared to stare blindly at the foot of the bed.

'Oh, well, there's me done,' the young maid announced with her usual merry grin, undaunted by Rose's sudden quiet. 'Be there ort else I can get 'ee, ma'am?'

'Er . . . no. No, thank you,' came the muttered reply, and Daisy waltzed contentedly out of the room.

Oh, no. Oh, no. The words wrung themselves helplessly, pathetically, from Rose's stunned mind. It mustn't be him. It mustn't. There were upwards of eight hundred men in the gaol, so why should . . .? But she didn't even know if he was still alive. He had been so ill when they had dragged him from the stables, treating him with such brutality . . . Seth, who had spoken, for want of a better word, to Gospel and instantly won over the difficult animal's trust, who had shared her enchantment of the newborn puppies, who had laughed softly with her – and who had been subjected to the most cruel injustice. How could she possibly have forgotten?

And, oh, dear God, Gospel! It wasn't a hideous dream, was it? Gospel wasn't safe out in the stable, being cared for by Ned, as her traumatized brain had allowed her to believe. Charles really had sold him. And now she didn't know where he was. She felt shot through with fury, anger at what might have happened to both Seth and Gospel, but also with a deeper, crippling guilt because her own anguish had blanked them from her mind.

She had been sitting up, cross-legged, in the bed, and now she pushed her fists into the mattress in front of her, rocking herself back and forth on her straightened arms, her teeth

gritted as she battled to stop herself from howling aloud. It
was just as when her father had died. For the Rose Maddiford
who would always fight back with the ferocity of a tigress
had finally been defeated. There was nothing she could do
now. And even in those few minutes of realization, the frustration of it, the black mist of anger, was driving her insane.

Florrie knew there was something wrong the instant she
came back into the room. There was Rose, *her* Rose, looking
almost demented, her eyes savage and haunted as she tossed
her head from side to side.

'Rose, my—'

'Oh, Florrie!' she cried distractedly, reaching out to grasp
the older woman's arms as she came towards her. 'Florrie,
you must find out for me!'

'Find out what?' Florrie frowned, but her round cheeks
flushed, as in her heart she already knew.

'I don't know how I'll ever know the truth about Gospel,
but you can find out for me about Seth,' Rose answered, her
face taut with anguish. 'Go to Dr Power. *Now!*'

Florrie's expression closed down. Not that she didn't have
the greatest sympathy with the lad's story, even though she
had been miles away at her sister's at the time and hadn't met
him. But part of her blamed him for Rose's illness, and she
had prayed that Rose's apparent loss of memory over the
events would continue. But now it seemed they had returned
to wreak havoc with her little maid's mind yet again.

'Of course, my lamb,' she soothed. 'But not now. Dr Power
will be at work in the prison, and I wouldn't be able to speak
with him. But this evening, I'll go while the master's having
his dinner.'

'Oh, Florrie . . .' Rose's face crumpled, and as Florrie held
her in her plump, comforting arms, she wept inconsolably
while Florrie's heart blackened with worry.

Where would it end?

Eight

'He were flogged,' Florrie said gently, and she watched anxiously as Rose twisted her head excruciatingly on her neck as if she would cast aside the torturing knowledge. 'A few weeks ago. But 'tweren't as bad as 'twas supposed to be. Dr Power, he said . . . he said he had to be cruel to be kind, whatever that do mean. He said . . . he only got eleven lashes, when 'twas meant to be the full thirty-six.'

The groan that came from deep in Rose's throat was like that of a wounded animal, and her hands literally tore at the tangled mass of her hair that tumbled about her in disarray. 'But they'll give him the rest some time,' she squealed, forcing the breath from her lungs. 'Oh, Florrie, I can't bear—'

'No, they won't,' she told Rose firmly. 'Or at least, 'tis highly unlikely. Dr Power has strongly recommended against it cuz of his chest.'

'He's still ill, then?'

'No. Not really. He's still in the hospital but he's nearly better. He'll be put back to work fairly soon. Summat within the prison, for he'll not be allowed on an outside work party again, not since he bolted. He weren't the one as fell to his death, so you can stop worrying and forget all about him now.'

'*Forget?*' Rose's voice was high with horror. 'How can I forget? Just being in that place is bad enough! The conditions they have to suffer, and then made to work like slaves—'

'Which is no more than most of them deserve—'

'But not Seth! Not when you're innocent!'

'Well, that's as may be, but right now, young maid, you've a tiny babby and your own health to think about!'

Rose glared at her, her mouth screwed into a rebellious pout and her eyes cobalt with frustration. But then she let herself fall back on the bed with a distraught groan. 'Oh,

Florrie, I feel so helpless! I just don't know what to do! About Seth or Gospel. But I simply *must* think of something!'

'Get yoursel' and babby Alice well, 'tis what! And then maybe, some time in the future, *then* you can see if there's ort to be done. And from what you've teld me, that fellow's a strong young man and he'll come to no harm.'

'*Was* a strong man,' Rose protested dejectedly. 'His health's been broken, and no one cares at the gaol if you live or die. All the warders want is to keep the convicts under control, and they don't care how cruel they have to be to do so! And who can blame them? You know as well as I do that any so-called neglect of duty can mean instant dismissal, and the warder's family and their possessions can be turned out on to the street the same day. 'Tis almost as hard for the warders as 'tis for the convicts, so you can understand it. There aren't many like Molly's father, who try to get to know each prisoner and treat them accordingly.'

'There you are, then!' Florrie humped up her ample bosom in triumph. 'Mr Cartwright'll look out for him.'

Rose's shoulders jolted and a strange light found its way into her eyes. 'Yes, of course! Oh, you're wonderful, Florrie! What would I do without you? When's Dr Seaton coming again?' she asked, her mind working furiously.

'Monday, as I believe.'

'Monday,' Rose repeated, unconsciously chewing on her thumbnail. 'Three days. And if he says Alice and I can have visitors, I can send for Molly. And I can write Seth a letter for her father to give him. Officially, they're only allowed a letter every three months, aren't they? And that's only supposed to be from a relative, and they'd hardly allow a letter from *me*, would they, the person who helped him when he escaped! A visit, though, 'tis what I'd really like, but they certainly wouldn't allow that. And anyway, if Charles found out . . . But a letter. Just a note to tell him I've not forgotten. Oh, I can't wait for next week. And I can't wait to show Alice to Molly! Fetch her over to me, would you?'

Florrie's expression was humourless as she took the sleeping child from her cot, but the loveliness of the enchanted, devoted smile that illuminated Rose's face as she took the tiny bundle into the protective cradle of her arms drove the doubt from the older woman's heart. For though Florrie disapproved of

Rose's association with the convict, she had accepted long ago that Rose did everything with passion. And that included being a mother.

Patsy dipped a curtsey as she finished showing the elderly gentleman into the drawing room, and Mr Frean, proprietor of the gunpowder mills and Henry Maddiford's good friend when he had been alive, stepped across the carpet, his hand held out in greeting and a broad grin on his ruddy face.

'Rose, my dear girl! No, don't get up. You need your rest and I'm sure we know each other well enough not to need to stand on ceremony. I was visiting the powder mills and they told me the happy news, so I thought I would call in to meet the new member of the family.'

'Oh, Mr Frean, how wonderful to see you! I trust both yourself and Mrs Frean are well?'

'Indeed we are, thank you, but where is this little mite?'

'She's up in the nursery while I'm supposed to be taking my afternoon nap.' Rose grinned up at him. 'But I've had enough of being in bed so I thought I'd lie here on the couch instead. I'm sure Charles wouldn't approve but he's gone into Tavistock,' she admitted in a conspiratorial whisper. 'So I'm delighted to see you. But if you pull the bell pull, I'll have Florrie bring Alice down. You're doing me a huge service as I can't bear to be apart from her for more than a moment!'

She watched, smiling at his back as he went over to tug at the tassel at the side of the fireplace, but inside her head, her thoughts were whirling. Dear, good Mr Frean. A link with the outside world. How could she make use of it without compromising him, for she'd had enough of involving innocent people in her schemes.

'Alice?' he said with approving softness. 'I believe that was your mother's name, wasn't it? I'm sure your dear father would have been touched.'

Rose lowered her eyes. Yes, Henry would have been thrilled. Her throat squeezed with sorrow. He had never known he was to become a grandfather. But she pushed her grief aside. Her father was dead. There was nothing more she could do for him now, but there were other matters she might be able to do something about.

'Ah, Patsy,' she said as the young maid popped her head

around the door, 'would you please go up to the nursery and ask Florrie to bring Alice down? Tell her Mr Frean is here.'

'Yes, of course, ma'am,' Patsy answered and disappeared again.

'Won't you sit down next to me?' Rose went on, swinging her feet from the couch and on to the floor. 'Then you can see Alice properly.'

'I should be delighted.'

'And will you take some refreshment?'

'No, thank you. I won't stay. Mrs Frean has dinner guests this evening.'

'Ah.' Rose nodded. She must think quickly if she was to take any advantage of the situation, but was it fair? She felt her heart pounding. She knew that Seth was alive, nearly recovered even. So perhaps, for now, she should wait. But what about Gospel?

'And I hear you had a pretty hard time of it, and had some sort of fever afterwards?' George Frean was asking with a concerned frown. 'Your friend Molly Tyler told me.'

'Oh, yes, but 'tis as right as rain I am now,' she assured him. 'Dr Seaton is allowing me visitors, and Molly came to see me yesterday. Ah, Florrie! You've brought my little darling down to see Mr Frean!' She held out her arms as Florrie came over to her and then, taking her tiny daughter, cradled the infant to her breast. 'Don't you think she's beautiful?' she crooned, drawing the shawl from Alice's face so that her visitor could admire her newborn child better.

Mr Frean tipped his head with a serene sigh. 'She certainly is. Just like her mother. And I wonder if she'll be as fine a horse woman?'

His innocent words speared through Rose's side, but it was the ideal opening. 'I certainly hope so,' she replied, stroking her finger against Alice's warm cheek and trying to pretend she was totally besotted with her child. Which she was. Almost. At least, she wanted – needed – Mr Frean to believe that just now nothing else mattered to her. 'But I'd never let her ride anything as headstrong as Gospel,' she went on a little quietly. 'In fact, having Alice made me realize how silly it would be of me to go on riding him. What if anything happened to me because of him, and Alice was left without a mother? So Charles and I decided to sell him. Only I do miss him so much, and I'd love to know how he is. But he went to a dealer and we don't know who owns him now, so if you ever saw him, you would let me know, wouldn't you?'

She turned her most vivid, engaging smile on him, and then looked back wistfully at Alice, not wanting Mr Frean to see just how much it meant to her. She felt guilty at the deception, but really, as far as Gospel was concerned, she would do *anything*!

'Well, my dear, I'll keep my eyes open, but I'm not sure he's the sort of animal one would see around Plymouth. He's more . . . I'm not a hunting man myself, as I believe you know—'

'No, me neither.'

'But why don't you contact local hunts? He's sure to be noticed, a fine animal like that.'

'Oh, why didn't I think of that?' It was something she had already thought of, but if she admitted so, it might make her look overeager. Mr Frean might be suspicious and, though she knew the dear man would be sympathetic if he was aware of the truth, she didn't want him to know how things stood between her and Charles. 'You clever soul! Thank you!' She beamed at him. But would she ever feel she could enlist his help over Seth? For the moment, she wasn't sure. It would perhaps be too much to ask.

'I be that sorry,' Molly said almost shamefacedly as she held out the crumpled letter. 'Father said 'twere more than his job were worth. But he said he'd have a word with him on the quiet. Tell him you'm still thinking of him.'

It was late July, and the weather in that exposed, bleak area of the moor was, for once, being kind. Rose was sitting outside under the shade of a canopy the gardener and his boy had rigged up for her between the only two trees that grew in the neatly tended garden. She was reclining on a wooden chair strewn with cushions, dressed in a simple but becoming light muslin gown that showed to perfection her regained, lithesome figure, her hair partly coiled on her head and partly tumbling down her back in a stunning balance of sophistication and rustic charm. She was propped on one elbow, gazing down quite entranced on the infant, a perfect miniature of herself, who lay on the blanket beside her, tiny legs free to kick in the warm air in jerky, uncontrolled movements, and her little starfish hands grasping at nothing. Her eyes, the exact lavender blue of her mother's, stared up at Rose as if some invisible thread were linked between them, and only Molly's arrival could distract Rose from doting over her daughter.

'Oh, I do understand,' she answered, forcing a disappointed smile to her lips though her heart dropped down inside her like a stone. ''Twas good of you to take it over to him. But could you possibly take it home with you and destroy it for me? If Charles found it—'

'Of course. You'm my best friend, Rose, and I'll do anything to help, you knows that. I just wish . . . well, that things were better between you and your husband.'

'Oh, I suppose I shouldn't have expected Charles to have done something to help a convicted criminal. But to have sold Gospel behind my back, well, I can never forgive him for that.' Rose paused with a distracted sigh. 'I feel absolutely lost without him. As if part of me is missing. And I'm so worried about him. But I have got my darling little Alice.' She brightened, and the angelic serenity that came over her face filled Molly with relief. 'Now I'm recovered, I do everything except feed her, which you know I can't.'

'Can I hold her?'

'Of course! But do be careful. You have to support her head. Look, like this. Oh, but how silly of me! Of course you know, with all your brothers and sisters!'

They sat for some minutes in relaxed companionship, worshipping the minuscule human being in their care, cherishing every detail of her curved chin, her toothless mouth, her button nose, both enthralled and seduced by her charms. They fell into a silent adoration, a deep contentment only two soulmates can know, Molly instinctively rocking Alice against her shoulder until her little head drooped and she drifted asleep. With the practised skill that came from being the eldest of a large family, Molly laid the slumbering child back on the blanket, and the two friends joined in besotted veneration of their darling treasure.

'Will . . . will you and Joe have children, do you think?' Rose asked dreamily, hesitating only minimally before broaching such a personal subject.

Molly's pretty face coloured. 'Oh, well . . . I, er . . . I hadn't said ort, cuz I thought, with Alice and everything else . . . but . . . I's already expecting. We didn't want a babby yet, and we had tried not to . . . but not too well.'

Rose felt her spirits lift. 'Oh, Molly, congratulations! 'Tis fantastic news!'

'Well, I's not too certain about that,' Molly grimaced. ''Twill really stretch what Joe earns—'

'Don't you worry none about that!' Rose fairly rounded on her. 'One thing I cannot complain about in Charles is his generosity. I have a personal allowance I really don't need, and . . . well, you're like a sister to me, and so 'twould not be charity if I were to share some of it with you. I shall be like an aunt to your baby, just as I consider you to be Alice's aunt.'

This time Molly had to lower her eyes, and if anything, her cheeks blanched. ''Twould be more than kind of—'

'Nonsense. I want you to know the same joy as I have with Alice without having to fret about money! And Joe must be thrilled, too. It must . . . it must be so good to . . . to be in bed with someone you really love.'

Her words had ended in a bitter trail, and Molly cocked one sympathetic eyebrow. 'Rather than have to suffer it with someone you doesn't,' she finished for her.

Rose's chin quivered and she bit her lip. 'I just can't love him any more. If I ever did. And since he sold Gospel, well . . . And though I suppose Charles isn't a bad man, I'm sure he thinks of me as a possession rather than a person. Not like . . .' She stopped abruptly, rearing away from the thought that had hit her like a thunderbolt and set her heart racing.

'Not like your convict, you mean?' Molly said softly.

Rose felt the blood rush from her head and her senses swooned. 'Oh, Good Lord, not like that!' she corrected awkwardly. 'But we did seem to share a lot in common.' She swivelled her eyes to glance sideways at her friend. 'Did your father say anything about him? Florrie found out he was almost better, but that were nearly two weeks ago now.'

'Father said he's doing boot-making for now, till he's fully fit. Then he'll be put to summat harder.'

'Oh, Molly.' Rose breathed in deeply and then exhaled in a long, weary stream. 'I do hope he's going to be all right. He shouldn't be in there at all. Could you ask your father, if he has the chance, to tell Seth that I said to take care? He might be put on the building works. And a prisoner fell to his death not so long ago, they're getting so high.'

Their eyes met, but not a word more was exchanged as Alice chose that moment to wake up, her little face wrinkling and her pink fists flailing as her feeble cry demanded a feed.

Nine

Rose lay in bed, her fingers entwined in the top of the sheet as they pressed against her breastbone. Her eyes moved about the pale shadows of the room, scarcely taking in the soft velvet curtains and the fine furnishings, for her mind was miles away. Where on earth was Gospel? Her lips were drawn into a seething pout, because the man who had caused her such devastating heartache was in the dressing room, changing into his nightshirt. Damn him to hell!

She heard him coming and quickly turned on her side, pretending to be already asleep. Was this to be her life from now on? Thank God she had Alice to lavish her love upon and help ease her own misery. But she didn't think she would ever recover from the loss of the spirited horse who had been a part of her life for so many years.

She listened to Charles padding around the bed in his bare feet, the puff of breath as he blew across the mantle of the oil-lamp to extinguish the low flame. She felt the blankets and the mattress move as he slid in beside her, and she screwed her eyes even more tightly shut, her heart trembling. Dr Seaton had been to examine her that afternoon, and she had heard her husband waylay him afterwards in the hallway. The recuperation period was over. She could be a wife to Charles again.

He snuggled up to her back. She could feel his breath on her neck, and a shiver of horror shot down her spine. The agony of the nightly ritual flooded into her stomach, cramping it with fear and revulsion. Please God, make him think that she was asleep and be spared for just one more night.

He moved her hair, exposing the side of her neck, and he kissed her skin, his lips leaving a drooling patch of saliva. She felt him prop himself on one elbow, the fingers of his other hand creeping across her shoulder and down, cupping her breast almost imperceptibly through the light gauze of her nightdress. He leaned over then, his tongue leaving a moist trail across her collarbone as he carefully unfastened the top button, and then the next. She hardly dared move, exhaling heavily as if she was in a deep slumber. His mouth followed his fingers, stroking her flesh, licking. Surely he must taste the sweat that oozed from every pore. And then he gave a muted grunt of pleasure, and moved away, settling down beside her.

She held her breath. Was he deliberately teasing her? Letting her think she was safe, only to be accosted fully a few minutes later? Oh, he was so vile, always forcing himself on her, taking his own pleasure without a thought for her feelings. There had been a time, up until not so long ago, when she had considered that he might be able to coax her gently to some excitement in the sexual act of which she had been totally ignorant until their wedding night. But now that he had betrayed her so deeply, all she could ever feel towards him was resentment.

She waited, immobile as a stone. Ten minutes, half an hour. Charles was breathing heavily, and she began to relax. He was asleep. But first thing in the morning, she knew what would happen. His groping had been but a prelude to tantalize his senses.

There was no way she herself could fall into the slumber her body craved. As the hours passed and she listened to the silent house, she wondered how Seth was passing the night. In an exhausted sleep, she imagined, for by now he must be back on some exacting labour, his aching body only too happy to rest on a hard, plank bed with only a thin, dirty mattress for comfort. Oh, Seth!

She sighed with a tormented tangle of wistfulness and frustration as she recalled the time when Charles had been away in London and she had despatched Ned one morning upon some fool's errand that would keep him away for some time. Using the danger to the pups as an excuse, she had told Ned to put Gospel temporarily in another stable. And knowing that Ned's main interest in life was seducing young maidens and not caring for scruffy, mongrel puppies, he would therefore have no reason to enter the loose box where Seth was concealed.

Rose had gone out to clean up after the puppies and spread clean newspaper on the floor, and then sat down on a bale of straw to watch the little bundles of fur take their first enquiring, uncontrolled steps. Seth was hobbling around the confined space of the dog leg of the loose box in an attempt to take some exercise while Rose was on guard. She had felt relaxed and happy, just wishing that Seth would always be there and hardly daring to think of the future without him.

They had chuckled together at the comical antics of the pups and Seth had asked when her own little one was due. She must be very excited about it, he had said.

'Oh, yes!' she had answered, although in her heart she hadn't been sure. The child was Charles's, after all. 'I'm hoping 'twill bring Charles and I . . .' She had broken off abruptly, realizing she had said too much. But Seth was shrewd and his eyes had seemed to bore into hers.

'Bring you closer together,' he had finished for her. 'Because you don't really love him, do you, Rose?'

She remembered it so clearly, his arresting, hazel eyes intense with compassion. She had wanted to tell him how Charles treated her like a slab of meat in their bed, but somehow, without her saying anything about it, he had understood her wretchedness, and she had cried in his arms. His strong, gentle arms that had made her feel so safe. And now he was gone, and the horror of Charles's onslaughts was upon her once more.

A frantic knocking on their bedroom door in the middle of the night roused them both with a start, and almost before Rose's heart began to crash against her ribcage, Florrie burst in without waiting for an answer. She stood in the doorway, her white nightdress voluminous in the flickering light from the candle she held in her shaking hand, and her silver-threaded hair wild and unkempt about her agitated face.

''Tis the babby, Rose!' she cried, her normal reluctant deference to Charles completely forgotten in her frenetic distress. 'She's a fever and—'

She had no time to finish before Rose fled past her, almost knocking her aside as she careered blindly along the landing and up the stairs to the nursery. She felt sick, her stomach cramped with a bottomless dread. Alice! So tiny. So helpless.

It wasn't possible. She had been doing so well. But Dr Seaton had warned them . . .

She virtually snatched Alice from the wet nurse's arms. The child was on fire, weakly fretful, and her cry no more than a feeble whimper. Rose felt strange, as if she could feel the blood coursing in aimless frustration about her limbs. Oh, Alice. Darling little Alice. With a mother's instinct, she laid the infant in her cot and tore the clothes from the bundled form, somehow knowing that her daughter's temperature must be lowered. But before she could begin to bathe the minute body with tepid water, the thin limbs went rigid, the spine arched, and the scrap of life jerked and gyrated in a violent paroxysm. Rose stood back, thorns of terror in her heart, and feeling as though she might crumple to the floor. Oh, Good God. And there was nothing she could do as Alice's tiny form shook until she suddenly turned as limp as a rag doll.

Rose stared, transfixed with horror as she gazed on her beloved daughter. *No!* . . . But there was still life! . . . The breath was crackling uncertainly in and out of Alice's lungs, and Rose grasped her in her arms again as she heard Charles enter the room behind her, bleary-eyed with sleep.

'She's had a fit,' Rose all but screamed at him. 'Go and tell Ned to ride for the doctor! Tell him . . . Oh, God . . .'

Her eyes rolled savagely. She was about to tell him to take Gospel, for surely no other horse could fly over the moor in the dark at such speed. But Gospel wasn't there, was he, and he wouldn't have allowed Ned on his back anyway. But by comparison, Tansy was so *slow* . . .

'I'll tell him to fetch Dr Ratcliffe,' Charles said efficiently. 'He'll be quicker than the old man.'

'No. Dr Power. 'Twill take half the time.'

Rose met Charles's gaze challengingly. She knew how he felt about the prison surgeon. But Charles nodded and then turned and she heard him hurry back down the stairs. She looked down again on Alice who, though her eyes were shut, seemed to be struggling for breath. Rose held her gently against her, like fragile porcelain, keeping her upright to assist her breathing, and feeling the tiny heart fluttering pathetically against her own breast. She paced up and down, hushing her though the child was unconscious, in a demented effort to staunch the flow of life from her, to pour her own strength into the failing fragment of existence.

Charles didn't reappear, but the gall barely stung Rose's throat as Alice faded in her arms. The rattle quietened to a wheeze, the wheeze to a whisper, and Rose herself hardly breathed as the room fell silent but for Florrie's muted sobs as she rocked herself in the chair.

Little Alice had gone.

And Rose slumped forward. Drained. Numbed. Empty. With no one to lean on. No one to hold her. Charles . . . Oh, how she longed for those other arms. Seth, she knew, would have known. Would have understood her pain. Seth who . . .

She jolted, her shoulders suddenly braced. The runt of the litter had apparently been dead, but Seth had breathed life into it. Literally. So could she possibly . . .? It had been like a miracle, but . . . she could never forgive herself if she didn't try.

She blew softly into the still, blue lips. And her heart soared as Alice's chest lifted. Yes! If she could just keep her alive until the doctor arrived . . . He shouldn't be long. It would take twenty minutes or so to rouse Ned, get him to saddle Tansy and ride to Dr Power's house at the prison, the same for Dr Power to answer the desperate call and arrive at Fencott Place. The intense darkness of the cruel night was already lessening, and dawn would soon be breaking over the craggy ridges and open wilderness of the moor. And Rose's very soul strained with a fearful trust.

Her ears pricked as she caught the thrumming of horse's hooves and the clink of gravel scattering on the drive. Thank God! She was exhausted, her neck aching from bending over Alice's motionless frame. But she mustn't stop. She couldn't. She must give of her own life. She didn't care what became of herself. But Alice *must* live.

She barely glanced up as Dr Power strode urgently across the room, his face in a deep study. She mustn't stop. Must not stop . . .

'Mrs Chadwick – Rose – let me see her,' the physician pleaded.

She raised her head, took a breath and bent again to transfer her own breath to her daughter. The doctor caught his bottom lip between his teeth, felt for a pulse at the tiny wrist, took the stethoscope from his bag and listened intently to the infant's chest.

'A light, please, Mrs Bennett,' he called over his shoulder.

Florrie obeyed at once, her face taut with distress. Dr Power took the nursery lamp from her, held open each of Alice's eyes in turn, and waved the source of brightness in front of them. There was no reaction.

The doctor sighed regretfully as he folded the long tube of his stethoscope and replaced it in his bag, then his eyebrows swooped as he contemplated the new mother as she breathed tirelessly into her baby's mouth. He shook his head, putting out his hand to touch her arm.

'Mrs Chadwick, I'm so sorry, but your daughter is dead.'

Rose blinked at him, the blank look in her haunted eyes slicing into his soul. 'No, no, look!' she stammered, her voice vibrant. 'She's breathing—'

'No,' he repeated with firm compassion. '*You* are breathing for her. There's no pulse, no heartbeat. No eye movement. She's turning cold. I would say she's been gone a little while.'

Rose stared at him, her head tilted and her brow corrugated with incomprehension. Slowly, very slowly, she lowered her gaze to Alice's motionless face as the horrible, vile, crucifying truth slithered into her rebellious, unaccepting mind, and her lips rested on the tiny marble forehead.

'From what your husband said, I think it must have been some sort of chest infection,' the doctor whispered reverently. 'I understand she was born quite early, and Dr Seaton was concerned that her heart and lungs were not strong. So this sudden illness, it was just too much for her. Nobody's fault. No medicine we have could have saved her.'

Whether young Mrs Chadwick heard or not was debatable. She began to rock back and forth, crooning to the child in her arms as if she were soothing her to sleep, humming softly, her face translucent like some serene Madonna. She scarcely flinched when her husband came and sat beside her on the bed, not until he put his hands about the diminutive corpse.

'She's dead, Rose,' he said without expression. 'Let the doctor take her now.'

She flicked up her head like a lioness, her raging eyes flashing dementedly as she hugged Alice tightly against her. 'No!' she wailed, lashing out at Charles, and when he tried to take the child by force, she bit into his hand and began to scream, a deep, howling, unearthly lament that made his blood run cold.

'For God's sake, man, isn't there something you can give her?' he demanded.

Dr Power considered the broken, grief-stricken figure before him. What she needed was time. Time to say goodbye to her child. Time her husband was unlikely to grant her. And so Dr Power reached sadly into his bag.

The warder strode across the prison yard. He had just returned from three days' leave, two because he had worked two six-day shifts back to back and one in lieu of the August bank holiday. What good the break had done him, though, he didn't know. With eight offspring all under twelve years old, they couldn't even afford to take the carrier into Tavistock for the day. So he had spent the days at home with the children under his feet, walks on to the moor being the only respite from their cramped flat. He had returned to duty in a dark mood, to be told he was to be in charge of boot-making. It was considered a fortunate post so he should have been pleased, but he wasn't. Convicts should all be put to hard labour, in his opinion, even if they had to earn the privilege of being in one of the workshops. Scum, they were, the lot of them.

He nodded at the other warders as he entered the building, enjoying his recently elevated status to senior officer. He walked menacingly up and down the rows of work benches, burly arms crossed over his intimidating uniform. The inmates had their heads down as they worked in silence, since any exchange of words was punishable, each man shuddering as the principal warder passed. He picked up a half-made boot, inspected it and replaced it with a grunt, irritated as there was nothing he could criticize.

And then he spied him. The yellow particoloured uniform of the escapee made him easily distinguishable from the others who wore the garb of more trusted men. The felon glanced up as more pieces of leather were added to the pile before him, and the warder glimpsed his face. He recognized him at once. The bastard who had run off in the fog and forced a young woman to hide him when he broke his ankle. The warder had been delighted to be chosen as the one to administer the flogging, as his colleague who had been guarding the scoundrel when he had made his escape had met with instant dismissal. He and his family had been evicted from their home the very same day. They had been next-door neighbours, friends. Though he had put his full and considerable force into each stroke, the warder had been devastated when the bugger had only been given a few lashes. Well, now it was time to make up for it.

'Get up, you,' he ordered. He saw the blackguard catch his breath, freeze. 'I said get up!'

This time the convict sprang to his feet and stood erect in a military stance, staring straight ahead at the opposite wall. The warder looked up at his impassive face, cursing himself. He had forgotten the fellow was so tall, touching six foot, while he was barely five feet eight, though as swarthy and strong as a bull. His face twisted in a sadistic leer to compensate.

'You were talking just then,' he accused him with a sneer.

The prisoner didn't move, didn't fall into the trap of denying his alleged crime so that the warder could reply that he had certainly spoken now and would be punished. The warder fumed with frustration.

'You shouldn't be in here,' he spat. 'Come with me.'

The assistant warder at the other side of the room dared to object. 'He's here temporarily, sir, because of his health.'

'Malingering, more like. Looks fit enough to me. Let's find some proper work for you.'

The junior officer shrugged and turned away as his superior marched the felon to the door. The fellow hadn't been an ounce of trouble, but it wasn't worth standing up for him. He was just another number – not worth risking the prospect of promotion for!

The principal warder led his captive through the work yards into the relative pleasantness of what had been the market square during the old prisoner-of-war days, and thence through the gate into the most secure part of the gaol. Up the side of the kitchens, then, and around the back of the chapel to an area the prisoner had never been to before. It was quiet, a hidden corner. Dear Lord, he wasn't in for an unlawful beating, was he? But now he recognized the smell as they passed the recently completed piggery, could hear the snorts of the sows and the squeals of their young. Well, he wouldn't mind working with any animal, and he rather liked pigs.

But no. The fetid odour became worse as they approached a shed about ten-foot wide and twenty in length. This wasn't just the fresh whiff of animal manure that he was well used to and didn't dislike. It was mixed with the reek of decaying human sewage that grew more pungent as they advanced towards the building, stinging the eyes and burning at the back of the throat. Jesus, the cesspits. The warder took out his hand-kerchief and held it over his mouth and nose. The convict at once broke out in a coughing fit that he struggled to suppress.

He was pushed down a set of steps and the warder knocked on the door to the sunken shed. It was opened by another warder wearing a mask.

'Another one for you. Make sure he works hard.'

If the stench outside was rank and putrid, inside the shed it was like running full pelt into a wall of stinking, choking gas. Seth Collingwood could taste the foulness of the air, feel it on his tongue, seeping into his ears, his skin. He could scarcely see for the thick, clogging dust that at once seared into his lungs and he instantly started to wheeze. But it was the vile fumes of putrefying bones, of rotting, noxious excre-ment that clenched at his stomach. He felt the bile, the nausea rising to his throat. He tried to force it down, struggling, retching, but the rancid, suffocating atmosphere was over-whelming, swirling down inside him. He found himself on his knees, vomiting up his breakfast of watery gruel, on and on, uncontrollably, until there was nothing left to bring up and yet his insides still heaved in violent spasms. He felt a hand under his arm, dragging him upwards. Through his streaming eyes, he made out a haggard, grimacing face against the pall of dust that surrounded them.

'Welcome to hell, pal,' the voice hissed in his ear.

Ten

Charles watched through slitted eyes as Rose bent to lay a delicate posy of flowers on the tiny coffin as it was lowered into the ground. So graceful, so dignified, so *glorious* in her sorrow. The lashing rain that had driven into their faces as they had arrived at the church had eased, but a gust of wind lifted the jet-encrusted mourning cape about her shoulders, revealing the slenderness of her narrow waist and the swathes of edged silk that cascaded from the small bustle into a billowing train at her ankles. She straightened up, her neck as long and elegant as a swan's, and beneath the veil of her black hat, her lovely face was as white and as set as alabaster.

Oh, how he yearned to have her in his bed again. Of course, he had been back *sleeping* in their marital bed for weeks. And what a torture that had been, not being able to touch her. Penetrate her. At long last, Dr Seaton had examined her and pronounced her fit to resume her duties as a wife, provided Charles was gentle with her. He had planned to take her the very next morning, when he would expose every part of her to the daylight, but the child had died that very night, and even he could not be cruel enough to impose himself upon her.

Did he care so much about his daughter? His own flesh and blood? It was difficult to say, when he had hardly got to know her. He had never even held her. But what he *did* care about was the gnawing misery that had enshrouded his wife ever since. Her spirit had withered. Even the two dogs sensed it, laying their heads on her knee and looking up at her with doleful eyes while their offspring romped and rolled beside them. She didn't even notice.

Charles bit his lip as he contemplated her wilted form. Perhaps if he hadn't got rid of that ferocious beast she loved so much, the creature would have brought her comfort, breathed life back into her. But it was too late now. The dealer would have sold the animal on to heaven knew who, and when it became clear that its temper was untameable, it would probably have changed hands again. Charles *almost* regretted it, especially each time his wife wandered off into the pouring rain, a desolate, inconsolable figure lost in some macabre, gruesome world of her own. He would run out after her with a coat to shield her from the unseasonable weather, as, despite the odd day of brilliant sunshine, it was turning into one of the wettest summers in years, and farmers were worried about their crops. She would let him lead her home, malleable as a child, not uttering a word, nor swallowing a morsel of the tempting food Florrie and Cook between them produced on her plate at meal times, and only drinking when Florrie forced her to.

Charles came and put his arm about her now, for without it, he feared she might fall. It was time to leave the graveside, to allow the little soul to rest, to lie in eternal peace beside the grandfather she had never known in this earthly life, but who she would come to know in the next. Rose moved with faltering steps, turning just once to glance back with a feeble whimper, not seeing the tear-filled eyes of Florrie Bennett, George Frean, Molly and Joe, and all those who had come to share in her grief.

They made their silent and hesitant way through the graveyard to the iron gates, the hem of Rose's gown dragging along the sodden path and soaking up the rainwater from the puddles. But she seemed oblivious to everything around her until they came out to the road, and Charles hailed to the hired carriage that had been waiting at a respectful distance to drive them back to the house, seeing as he had considered their own wagonette inappropriate for such a sombre occasion. Just at that moment a group of six or seven people, dressed more suitably for the fashionable streets of London and shielding themselves with huge umbrellas even though the rain had virtually stopped, hurried gaily along on the opposite side of the street in the direction of the prison.

'Oh, what a frightfully grim place!' one of the ladies tittered gleefully, with a plum the size of a melon in her mouth.

'What do you expect, my dear?' a gentleman replied with equal delight. 'This *is* the worst prison in the country. You have to be a pretty dastardly criminal to be sent here, you know!'

'Of course!' another fellow declared with enthusiasm. 'I wonder who they'll show us? Thieves and murderers, I expect!'

'Not murderers! They hang *them*!'

And with a chorus of laughter, they marched on up the road.

Rose halted, a spark of hatred igniting in her breast. It was despicable, this custom of showing people over the gaol as if it were some sort of holiday attraction, pointing out to them the worst criminals, the gruelling labour they were put to for their punishment and the horrendous conditions in which they existed; whose sufferings were to be found amusing and entertaining, when many of them had only been caught up in a life of crime in the first place through poverty and starvation, and not every inmate was guilty of heinous acts that warranted such callous retribution. And, to add insult to injury, these tours were relatively frequent, but a prisoner was only permitted three twenty-minute visits every six months. Not that many ever experienced such a happy interlude, as most relatives were too impoverished to afford the journey to such a remote place. But that was part of it, wasn't it, to scorn and humiliate the convicts so that upon their final release they made the effort not to return – or at least not to get caught again.

Rose's mouth thinned into a fine line. On the opposite side of the road stood the tall, quite attractive building of the warders' new flats where Mr and Mrs Cartwright now lived in relative comfort with their remaining children. Beside it, much of the former soldiers' barracks where Molly and her family had previously lived in cramped accommodation beset by damp and crumbling decay, were being demolished, and beyond them, Rose could just glimpse the forbidding walls of the prison blocks and the building site that would eventually stand five storeys high to match the first rebuilt edifice that had been completed a few years earlier. Away in the distance stretched the extensive lands of the prison farm that had been, and continued to be, cleared and drained in the most impossible conditions by the human sweat and toil of convict labour.

Rose frowned. Teasing her brain was an emotion triggered by the sight of the gaol, a tenderness, a faint memory of something that had once soothed her aching soul. And then her heart tripped and began to beat faster as a vision of that lean, strong face with its expressive hazel eyes formed itself in her mind.

A long, sighing breath fluttered from her lungs, and her husband caught her as she slithered to the ground.

Charles padded across the thick bedroom carpet and came up behind her as she sat at the dressing table, mechanically brushing at her hair that swung in a living waterfall of thick raven waves against the foaming white of her nightgown. In the mirror, he met her dulled eyes that stared sightlessly at him from dark sockets in her sculptured face, her skin taut and pale as ivory. Dear God, she was so beautiful, and he already felt the uncomfortable rising in his loins.

He smiled benevolently, and felt his heart expand as her eyes widened a little and her lips curved upwards in a strained response. His hands came to rest on her shoulders. She tilted her head, but the hope expired inside him, since she did not turn to brush her cheek on the back of his hand, nor lean against him to take the comfort he was attempting to offer her.

He cleared his throat. 'I'm so sorry, Rose. I know the child meant more to you than to me. I suppose a man doesn't become close to his children until they're older. But a mother . . . Well, I *am* sorry.'

She remained motionless, as if his words could not penetrate her grief, and he was about to turn away when she mumbled something under her breath.

'Pardon, my dear?' he prompted her at once, seeing as it was the first word she had spoken that day.

'I said, her name was Alice. Our daughter's name was Alice.' Her voice was empty, devoid of expression, as if coming from some other, ethereal being, and Charles felt not the least reprimanded.

'Of course it was,' he replied tentatively, anxious to seize any shred of communication. 'And we will always remember her. But there will be others. This time next year, there will be another little Chadwick, I promise you. And over the years, we will fill the nursery with our children. So the sooner we start, the better.'

He just caught the thin sound that gurgled at the back of her throat, but chose to ignore it. Instead, he bent to kiss the bare milky skin at her neck, and his hand found its way beneath the yoke of her nightdress to the warm, soft mound of her breast.

She flinched. Her shoulders instantly stiffened and she jerked up her head so that she narrowly missed butting him in the mouth. 'Charles, I really don't think . . .' she croaked hoarsely.

'And why not, my dear?' he purred, his voice oily. 'Dr Seaton pronounced you fit and well a week ago. And the sooner we conceive another child, the better.'

'But not when we've only just laid Alice in her grave.' Her tone was stronger now, a blend of sadness and resentment that was beginning to try Charles's patience. But anger was not the way to get what he wanted, and he was determined that he would.

He withdrew his hand and instead began to stroke her hair. 'I understand how you feel, my darling,' he said persuasively. 'But surely you must see it would be for the best? Another child would give you something else to think about. Help you to get over Alice more quickly.'

He saw in the mirror that she lowered her eyes, and a glow of satisfaction warmed his blood. He was winning her over and, turning her about on the stool, he knelt down before her and with one hand on the back of her head, placed his lips forcefully on hers and used his tongue to probe into her mouth.

She pulled away. 'Charles . . . please . . .' she moaned. 'Not now . . .'

'Oh, but you know I'm right,' he murmured into her ear now as his hands began to fumble between her thighs. 'Another child . . .'

The sensation of disgust shot up to her stomach, and her muscles cramped. She instinctively pushed him away, and the words were out of her mouth before she had time to think what she was saying.

'But I'm not certain I *want* another . . .'

They both froze, two statues glaring at each other from eyes stretched wide with horror. Rose wanted to swallow, but it seemed a stone had lodged in her gullet. The buried truth had wormed its own way to the surface without her having consciously considered it. Charles's slack-jawed mouth gradually closed into a hateful knot, and his eyes narrowed

as he raised his hand which shook with the effort it was taking
not to slam it across her face.

'Don't want any more children!' he spat venomously. 'You
little bitch! It's your duty as my wife to give me as many children as you can! *Sons*, to carry on my work! I know you
dislike the act of love-making—'

'*Love-making!*' Rose reared up her head. 'There's nothing
loving in it, the way *you* do it. You're like an animal!'

Charles jerked as if he'd been shot by a bullet, and then
his eyes bulged with unleashed rage. 'And how would you
know any different, madam? It was that bloody convict, wasn't
it? You made love to him, but you refuse to make love to your
own husband! Well, I'll show you, you bloody little—'

'No! How dare you! There was nothing like that—'

But the rest of her incensed words were lost as he grasped
a hank of her flowing locks and dragged her across the room
by it. She couldn't even scream for the pain as her hair was
almost torn from her scalp, and as he hurled her on to the
bed, the breath was entirely knocked out of her so that she
struggled for some moments to remain conscious. She almost
wished she hadn't, for a few seconds later, he plunged himself
into her. She cried out, transfixed with the sudden pain of it,
and at that precise instant, she truly wished herself dead. She
turned her head away, gasping for breath, and praying that
Charles would hurry up with the business. He was right, of
course. She was his wife, and it was her duty. And, in time,
she probably *would* want more children. Thousands of mothers
lost their infants each year, and went on to find solace in
further offspring. But it didn't help her just now, and her spirit
heaved with a powerless contempt.

When Charles had finished, he was full of remorse, kissing
her, telling how much he loved her. She remained silent, tight-
lipped, finally turning her back on him in the bed until his
heavy, even breathing told her he was asleep. She let her tears
come then, quiet tears of despair that soaked into the pillow
and washed away the grief-numbed sterility of her mind. There
was nothing she could do for herself. The laws of both God
and man said so. She was Charles's wife, as her bruised and
stinging flesh reminded her. And she would be so until one
or the other of them died – which could be twenty, thirty years
– and she would have to live in that knowledge for the rest

of her days. She could bring back neither her father nor her daughter. Perhaps other children, the son that Charles craved, would bring her contentment in the future. But that time seemed a long way off, in some distant haze that her present pain could not begin to envisage.

Her own soul was eternally lost. But there was something she could perhaps do to save someone else's. At least she could try . . .

It was still dark when she rose, sleep having eluded her all night. She slipped quietly into the dressing room, managed to light the lamp and dug out her riding habit from the back of her wardrobe. It fitted her regained figure perfectly. She crept silently down the stairs, carrying her cleaned and polished boots, and let herself out of the back door with the stealth of a cat.

A dank drizzle somewhat akin to a heavy mist fell steadily from the sky. Dawn would rise late that foggy August morning. The house still slept, but not so the horses in the field. Though moist, the atmosphere was warm, and Tansy was delighted to see the gentle mistress who was always so kind to her. Rose fetched just a handful of oats and while the mare munched happily, she stole into the tack room. She must be careful as Ned – Ned whom she now hated – slept above it with only the floorboards between them. She could hear him snoring soundly, and though Tansy's bridle jangled on her shoulder as she heaved the saddle from its bracket, the rhythmical droning above her was not interrupted.

It felt so good when she finally mounted Tansy's back. She hadn't ridden for months and it was wonderful to be astride an animal again. If only it had been Gospel! She would have felt him quivering with excitement, his muscles bunched beneath her, but she must put such morose thoughts aside. She had another mission, and though the loss of her beloved horse would tear at her for ever, surely the life of a human being must be more important.

Within minutes they were off at a trot, keeping to the grass beside the gravelled driveway to deaden the sound of Tansy's hooves, and evaporating into the swirling mist like some mythical spectre. They were gone. Free. As if Charles and her life at Fencott Place no longer existed.

Even so, Rose was cautious. She wasn't nervous, but rather

fired with humiliation and deranged bitterness, and the desire to lash out in revenge. But she knew that the shadowy gloom of the gauzy mist as morning broke could confuse and disorientate, and so she kept Tansy at a steady trot so that they didn't lose the track in the half light. When they came into Princetown, the village was still deserted. What time was it? Half past five? Six o'clock? Back home, Cook and Patsy and Daisy would be up, building up the heat in the kitchen range, kneading the day's bread. Florrie would not be far behind, wondering what she would do now her darling little Alice was dead and buried. Ned would doubtless still be snoring his head off, and though it would not be long before he awoke, Charles would remain in blissful ignorance of his wife's disappearance.

Nobody saw them slide through the vapour-enshrouded prison village. She could scarcely distinguish the massive buildings of the gaol, but could just about make out the flickering lights at what she knew were row upon row of small, high-up, barred windows. After a long night locked away in their lonely cells, and sleeping on hard wooden beds, with a thin straw mattress if they had behaved themselves, the inmates would already be up, slopping out, eating their dry bread and watery porridge, going to morning prayers to ask God's blessing on the gruelling day of punishment ahead. And tomorrow. And the next day.

Rose paused for an instant near the gates. Somewhere inside those soulless walls, in an unforgiving, damp cell, Seth would be preparing for another long day of back-breaking labour when not even a word of companionship was permitted to ease one's misery. The Silent Rule. Just another cross to bear.

Rose gritted her teeth as she urged Tansy onwards. The injustice of it erupted inside her yet again. She wanted to rebel, to hit out. At Charles, for his possessiveness, his lack of understanding, his jealousy. His betrayal. Most of all, at Fate, or whatever force it was had taken her darling, innocent Alice. And somehow doing whatever she could to help Seth was a way of cleansing her soul of its black anger. Of allowing herself to find some peace.

They trotted on to the small settlement at Rundlestone, then turned left along the old toll road across the moor. Rose knew it like the back of her hand. Though there had been no visible

sunrise at her back, daylight was penetrating the mantle of
fog. They passed on their left the track that led off to the
massive quarries of Foggintor, King's Tor and Swell Tor,
reminding Rose of happier times when she had accompanied
her father on many a visit to the busy, hard-working community there. She wondered vaguely if they still used gunpowder
rather than the new dynamite that was available now. She was
sure they would. The men at the quarries were experts with
explosives and didn't welcome change, and with the powder
mills being so close . . . Ah, but those halcyon days at
Cherrybrook seemed an eternity away.

The bank of mist suddenly rolled away as they descended
the hill to Merrivale and the new Tor Quarry just beyond the
inn. The world seemed to explode into life as men were
arriving for work, astounded to see the beautiful young woman
of obvious class out so early on the lonely moor – and *alone*.
But perhaps the heavenly vision was no more real than the
devilish pixies and other sprites that some believed roamed
the moor.

Now that they could see clearly, Rose urged Tansy into a
sedate canter. Had she been riding Gospel, he would have
catapulted forward, neck arched, fine legs stretched as they
ate up the ground. Oh, she must stop grieving for him and
concentrate instead on breathing in the freedom of the moor
that she had not experienced for so long. The joy of the rugged
landscape began to lift her heart, allowing her to leave her
sorrow behind, if only for a short while. As they reached the
top of Pork Hill, the familiar, magnificent view down over
the Tamar River to Plymouth was stunning, and Rose slowed
Tansy's pace to negotiate the steep downhill incline. And then,
at long last, they turned right down the lane that would eventually lead to Peter Tavy.

Eleven

The village was just as Rose remembered it from her visit with her father several years before. People were up and about their business, mainly farmers, one or two of whose farms were actually within the village centre, which once again struck her as unusual. She noticed a straggling group of men heading down towards a lane beside the inn. They looked like miners, and she recalled driving down the lane with Henry in the dog cart. It led down to the River Tavy and they had crossed by the ford rather than the sturdy wooden bridge, since the water in the river had been low. On the far side lay Wheal Friendship, once the most extensive copper mine on the moor, but now, like many that hadn't been forced to close altogether, turned over to arsenic production. Whether or not the mine still used gunpowder, she didn't know. And with Henry and her life at Cherrybrook gone for good, it was no longer her concern.

What *was* her concern was to try to find the man Seth had told her he had befriended during his brief spell in the police cells in Tavistock nearly three years previously. Since Charles had broken his promise to listen to Seth's story and see if he could do anything to help, Rose would have to seek out this Richard Pencarrow instead. His farm was not *in* but *near* Peter Tavy, so she would have to ask. But while she had stopped to remember her trip to the mine with Henry, the people she had seen earlier had disappeared, so for a few minutes, she ambled around the village wondering what to do next. She discovered there was a grassy square in front of the church, wide enough for a funeral carriage to turn, she considered grimly. And coming across it was a likely looking couple, middle-aged and, by their attire, quite respectable.

'Excuse me, sir, ma'am,' she said politely, bringing Tansy

to a standstill. 'I'm looking for a Mr Richard Pencarrow. I believe he has a farm somewhere near.'

The man raised his eyebrows at being addressed so respectfully. 'Up at the Hall, miss. He be the maister. Though what a pretty cheel like thee wants with 'en, I cas'n imagine.'

A shadow of doubt clouded Rose's heart at the man's words. In her headlong haste, she hadn't considered that she knew nothing about the stranger she was seeking. Seth himself had known precious little. The friendship that had developed between them was limited, even though Seth seemed to trust the other fellow entirely. From what the man before her had just said, this Richard Pencarrow must indeed have been released, but what if he really was a violent criminal – a murderer as it had involved the Coroner's Court – and she would be putting herself in danger? But to be quite honest, at that particular moment, she didn't really care.

'But p'raps 'tis 'is wife you wants,' the woman put in with a reassuring smile. 'Our village wise-woman?'

'Ah,' Rose answered with some relief, for she indeed welcomed the information. Richard Pencarrow was considered 'the maister', the charges against him had evidently been dropped, and the husband of a caring and respected member of the community was unlikely to be a vicious brute. Altogether, Rose felt encouraged. 'Well,' she prompted, 'perhaps you'd be so kind as to direct me to the Hall?'

'Yes. Rosebank Hall. Follow this road,' the man indicated, waving his arm. 'And arter aboot a mile, thee turns up a track on to the moor. Just keep following. 'Tis a long way, mind, but thee cas'n miss it.'

'And mind you goes in the back door. 'Tis always open.'

'Oh, er, right,' Rose replied with surprise. 'Thank you kindly.'

She flashed her lovely, natural smile, making the man's day, and turned Tansy along the way he had pointed out. As he had said, the track was easy to find, and as they gradually climbed out of the valley, Rose relaxed in the saddle and admired the view as a watery sun began to break over the higher ground. It was as if she was in a different world, one in which the pain in her heart ceased to exist. And when Rosebank Hall – a square building of some size although nowhere near as imposing as Fencott Place – came into view, Rose began to focus her thoughts and wonder about the said

Mr and Mrs Pencarrow. A wise-woman would surely be of a certain age, and she prayed they would both be sympathetic to her cause.

Mrs Pencarrow was nothing like she had imagined. Crossing what was clearly a farmyard, Rose found somewhere to tether Tansy and then knocked tentatively on what appeared to be the back door. There was no answer, and when she tried the handle, it turned and she found herself in an inner hallway with a second door immediately opposite. This time, she rapped loudly, and started when a voice at once called out to her to enter.

She was in a farmhouse kitchen, but rather than the aroma of cooking, an overwhelming fragrance she recognized but could not immediately name permeated the air. And then she noticed the bunches of different herbs hung in rows from drying racks, and the mystery was solved. Jars lined the walls, filled with powders from green to brown, or liquids of all manner of colours. Not just a wise-woman then, but a herbalist. Rose was amazed.

'Good morning, miss. Can I help you?'

Mrs Pencarrow's voice was quiet and gentle, and Rose's eyes widened even further, as its owner was not many years older than herself. A petite young woman, dressed in a simple blouse and skirt and with a riot of golden hair secured only with a ribbon, was coming towards her with an outstretched hand which Rose instinctively took in hers. The pretty face was smiling in welcome, the eyes the most striking, translucent amber Rose had ever seen.

'Mrs Pencarrow?' she mumbled.

'Why, yes. But do call me Beth. Now, what can I do for you? You're not from round here, are you?'

But before Rose could reply, a further door opened, and an attractive girl of about twelve years old bounded into the kitchen, an infant struggling in her arms. Rose might have been punched in the chest, and she felt the room spin around her.

'*Elle s'est réveillée,*' the girl said casually as she handed the child into the waiting arms of Elizabeth Pencarrow. '*Tu veux que je fasse la vaisselle?*'

'*Oui, s'il te plaît.* Oh, I'm sorry. This is my daughter, Chantal.'

'Pleased to meet you, madame.' And bobbing a curtsy, the girl went over to the deep stone sink.

Rose had to swallow hard and make a conscious effort to take a grip on herself. A baby. Much older than Alice. But a baby. And its presence slashed at her heart, throwing her bereaved soul into turmoil. Elizabeth Pencarrow and the older girl might have been speaking in a foreign language, she thought, and then, as her mind cleared, Rose realized that they *had* been.

She shook her head, blinking hard as she battled to put her thoughts straight. 'I'm sorry,' she muttered in bewilderment. ''Tis Mr Pencarrow I need to see. I have a message for him from . . . from someone he met in the Tavistock police cells.'

Elizabeth Pencarrow's smiling face became still, and the colour drained from her cheeks. She fumbled for one of the kitchen chairs and lowered herself into it, dandling the infant subconsciously on her knee. 'Oh, dear,' she finally breathed. ''Tis an episode we thought were behind us.'

In her own anguish, Rose recognized the friendly woman's distress. 'Oh, no, 'tis nothing for you to worry about,' she said quickly. ''Tis just that your husband . . . well, he shared a cell with another man. And this other man, he was convicted and now he's serving his sentence at Dartmoor Prison. And he needs Mr Pencarrow's help.'

Elizabeth was absently stroking her baby's curling hair. 'Yes. I remember . . . Richard did speak of someone. Someone he said didn't seem at all like a criminal. But he never knew what happened to him. Is he . . . is he your husband?'

She looked up, her eyes deep and pensive, bringing a frown to Rose's face. Seth her husband? The question somehow unnerved her.

'I . . . er . . . no. I'm married to . . . to someone else,' she faltered. 'But Seth . . .' She saw Elizabeth raise a surprised eyebrow at the use of a Christian name. 'He escaped. He's innocent, you see, and in a moment of folly, he just . . . ran off into the mist. But he broke his ankle and took refuge in our stables. We live nearly two miles the other side of Princetown. Out on the moor, you see. I helped him, and we became friends. He told me everything that happened. He was convicted on, well, what I think they call circumstantial evidence. But I believe he was innocent,' she stated with firm conviction. 'But he were caught and taken back to prison. Which is where he'll stay if someone doesn't help him. But I really don't know what to do, and Seth mentioned your husband . . .'

She gazed beseechingly into the woman's eyes, her forehead folded with consternation. Elizabeth slowly set the restless child on its feet and watched as the infant tottered across the floor. It seemed to Rose to take an eternity before she spoke again.

'And what about your own husband?'

Rose drew in her bottom lip and swallowed. 'My own husband believes that if you're convicted, then you must be guilty. He doesn't know I'm here. But I *beg* you, Mrs Pencarrow—'

'Beth, please,' the other woman corrected. 'And of course you must speak to Richard, though I'm not sure when he'll be back. He went out at the crack of dawn to check on the sheep up on the moor. There's been so much rain of late, and 'tis said there's liver-rot about. But you're more than welcome to wait if you have time. How did you get here? 'Tis a fair step.'

'Oh, I rode,' Rose replied, filled with relief that Elizabeth was willing to listen to her, and then feeling remorse that, in her anxiety, she had forgotten about Tansy tethered outside.

'Then put your horse in the stables and come back and have a cup of tea.'

'Thank you so much. 'Tis most kind of you.'

Elizabeth turned her tranquil smile on her, and Rose hurried outside, already feeling happier. Elizabeth Pencarrow, stranger though she was, had instilled some confidence in her. She found the stables easily enough, putting Tansy in a stall beside an enormous, dozing cart horse, and finding a bucket of water for her. When she returned inside, Elizabeth was pouring out a freshly brewed cup of tea for each of them. The girl, Chantal, smiled openly at her. She was tall and dark as a gipsy, not remotely like Elizabeth, and Rose wondered how on earth Elizabeth could be her mother. Surely she wasn't old enough!

That serene smile Rose was already beginning to know lifted the corners of Elizabeth's mouth. 'Chantal's my stepdaughter,' she explained easily as she saw Rose looking at the girl. 'Richard was widowed in France. He's a fair bit older than me, you see.'

'Ah.' Rose was becoming interested, her curiosity drawing her mind from the void that Alice's death had gouged out of her soul. 'And 'twas French you were speaking, then, just now?'

'Yes. When we first met, Chantal didn't speak any English, and I didn't speak a word of French. But we've learnt from each other. Oh, do sit down, Mrs . . . I'm sorry, I don't even know your name.'

'Chadwick. Rose Chadwick.'

She sat down, relieved beyond measure that Elizabeth Pencarrow was such a homely, understanding woman despite her youth. But at that moment, the infant struggled to its feet and wobbled across the room in that uncertain way little ones have when learning to walk, chubby arms raised to shoulder level. Its sturdy legs stumbled to the nearest available landing point at the right height for its tiny hands, which happened to be Rose's thigh. The child gazed up at the stranger, mouth stretched wide with a proud grin revealing a set of little front teeth.

The knife twisted in Rose's side. 'How old?' she managed to gulp.

'Thirteen months. Her name's Hannah.'

The child gurgled contentedly, and as she studied her wide, chestnut eyes, Rose could see in them amber flecks the same colour as her mother's. The minuscule face was framed with a cap of coppery curls, and all at once Rose's chin quivered and she felt two fat tears stroll down her cheeks.

'Mrs Chadwick?'

Elizabeth's brow was pleated as she put out a hand, her head tipped in questioning as she sensed the stranger's despair, and Rose felt herself tumbling into the chasm of her pain again.

'I . . . buried my own daughter yesterday,' she croaked. 'She was . . . just eight weeks old . . .'

It was too much, this profound sensitivity and compassion of Elizabeth Pencarrow's, and Rose sank willingly into it, setting free the terrible, savage agony that was her grief. She shook with the tears that engulfed her, choking her, blinding her, as she was comforted not only by the arms of Peter Tavy's wise-woman, but also by her French stepdaughter. It was a moment of release, of cruel torment that was necessary to start the healing process, and when it began to subside, Rose felt freer, at ease, perhaps more so than at any time since her father's death. Elizabeth made her drink something that tasted quite disgusting before she was allowed to sip at her tea, but in this quiet and lonely farmhouse, amongst these total strangers, Rose began to feel some peace. She found herself relating the entire story of how she had come to marry Charles and how her own life had deteriorated since then.

Elizabeth was a good listener and brought her hands together in front of her lips as if in prayer. 'Our first child was still-born,' she murmured in a torn whisper. 'So I know how you feel. But now we have Hannah. So there is always hope.'

Rose lifted her head, wiping her tears on the back of her hand. Elizabeth seemed so calm, so complete, and Rose could scarcely absorb what she had just said. 'But . . . Oh, I'm so sorry. But I don't think I want any more children. Not with Charles, anyway.'

Elizabeth met her gaze, and then breathed out slowly. 'That, I'm afraid I cannot help you with. I love Richard so much it hurts sometimes, so I cannot imagine being in your situation. But we will try and help if we can. With your convict. Though to be honest with you, I'm not sure there's anything we can do.'

Rose felt her heart drop like a stone as she nodded in reply. 'Yes, I know,' she mumbled. 'But I can't bear to think of . . .'

She got no further as they heard footsteps in the hallway, and as the door opened, the man who entered the kitchen was so tall he had to duck to avoid hitting his head on the lintel. He was broad-shouldered but slim of waist and hip, betraying a lean strength, and for a few seconds he was taken up with greeting his wife and children in a fond embrace, while a pair of black and white sheep dogs trotted at his heels. When he at last looked across at the unknown visitor, he lifted his head and his handsome face broke into a friendly smile. As Elizabeth had said, her husband was somewhat older than herself, in his mid to late thirties, Rose judged, but she instinctively knew he was someone she could trust.

'Who have we here?' he said amiably. 'Do you own that chestnut mare in the stable? What a lovely animal! I've given her a hay net, by the way.'

Rose's thanks were lost in the confusion of introductions and explanations, and the large kitchen suddenly seemed to overflow with the four adults, the unsteady baby and the two dogs, one of which was quite young and skittered playfully around everyone's feet. But as the chaos settled, Richard Pencarrow gratefully took from his wife the mug of tea she offered him, and lounged back against the wall next to the range, one foot raised on the fender, to drink it. His dark eyes narrowed as he observed Rose over the rim of the mug, and her stomach turned a somersault, for everything depended on his decision.

'I've often wondered what happened to him,' Richard said at length, his voice low and thoughtful. 'But it was hard enough picking up the pieces of my own life, let alone someone else's I'd only known for a few days, and that not exactly under the best of circumstances. But I feel guilty about it now. Serving twelve years at Princetown, you say? Poor devil.' He spoke the words with passion, and stared silently at the stone-flagged floor for some seconds before lifting his head again. 'So, how do you come to know him?'

'He escaped,' Rose answered at once, eager to grasp Richard's support while he seemed so sympathetic. 'He hid in our stables because his ankle was broken. I helped him. But he was caught again.'

Richard's eyes flashed at her and his generous mouth closed into an angry line as his back stiffened and, pushing himself away from the wall, he crossed the room and pulled out a chair to sit down opposite her at the table. 'You do . . .' he began hesitantly. 'You do realize what will have happened to him?'

His eyes bore steadily into hers, eyes of such a deep brown they appeared almost black, and Rose had to turn away. Her throat had closed, and despite the comforting way she felt him take her hands, she couldn't speak and instead gave a small nod of her head.

'Rose, tell us everything you know about this fellow's case,' she heard Elizabeth encourage her from the other end of the table.

It wasn't easy, for her heart was hammering nervously. She *had* to convince this man of Seth's plight. He listened intently, balancing with one arm his baby daughter who had clambered on to his knee, and eating with his free hand the simple meal his wife put in front of him. He nodded occasionally, interrupting her only to clarify a detail here and there. When she had finished, she held her breath, not daring to hope . . .

Richard's face was totally still for what seemed to Rose an age before little Hannah started wriggling about on his lap, drawing her father's attention from his deepest thoughts. 'Chantal?' he said suddenly, and Rose knew from his tone that he expected his elder daughter to take her part in the situation. The girl obediently stepped forward and took her little sister from her father's arms. Rose gained the impression that Richard Pencarrow was a man who took life face on, practical, his slight abrasiveness merely shielding a deep and hidden sensitivity. She watched his eyes stare fixedly at the table for some minutes, and then he finally sat back in his chair, his lips softly pursed, and ran a hand through his mop of dark wavy hair. He was silent for some seconds before he sighed weightily and slowly rubbed his jaw.

'I don't know that I can help you,' he pronounced with a fierce swoop of his eyebrows. 'I'm a farmer, with only such legal knowledge as that entails. But I do know that once you're convicted, that's it. There's no appeal.'

Ice trickled through Rose's veins, and her whole body shivered. Oh, no. Not after all this. Rescuing Seth would not only be helping him, it would be *her* only salvation, too. It was her only reason for staying alive just now, and she could not have her hopes dashed. 'That's what Seth said,' she mumbled, wringing her hands in her lap. 'But he mentioned something called a royal pardon—'

'A royal pardon!' Richard's voice was so startled it made Rose jump. 'Have you any idea what that means? Not to say how rare and virtually impossible it would be?'

'No. No, I don't.' Rose lifted her chin, her innate stubbornness suddenly glinting so challengingly in her eyes that Richard blinked at her in astonishment. 'But I don't believe Queen Victoria would approve of a totally innocent man suffering twelve years' penal servitude for some crime he didn't commit. Oh, *please*, Mr Pencarrow.' And then a flash of inspiration darted into her desperate mind. 'If 'tis money you need . . .'

Richard's dark eyes were stretched wide with surprise, and

then Rose felt her heart had been ripped from her chest as he solemnly shook his head. 'It's not that. At least, not as far as I'm concerned. It's just that I wouldn't have a clue . . . I'm simply not the right person. But we do know someone who might have a better idea. I can't promise anything, of course, but there's no harm in asking, wouldn't you agree, Beth?'

He glanced across at his wife, and some invisible cord of love and understanding passed between them. Two steadfast faces turned to Rose and announced in unison, 'Adam.'

Rose blinked in confusion, her emotions tossed about as if on a heavy sea. 'Adam?' she repeated with a deep frown.

'Captain Adam Bradley,' Richard explained. 'A good friend of ours. And a man of strong principles who decries injustice of any sort. He's wealthy and far more influential than I could ever be. He's from London. He owns a wine merchant's there, importing wine and other liquor, and he also owns a small international shipping company. I think he'd have a much better understanding of the situation than I do. He deals with lawyers all the time. Only to do with the legalities of his business, of course. Nothing to do with criminal law, but he might have connections. He's actually a sea captain, a jolly good one by all accounts, though he rarely sails nowadays. He had a serious accident at sea some years ago which left him . . . well, you'll see. He's a very busy man, but I'm sure—'

'So where can I find him?' Rose demanded almost accusingly.

Richard gave a serious smile. 'Mrs Chadwick, I'm afraid you'll have to be patient. I know it must be difficult, especially thinking of how Seth must be suffering. Adam inherited a large estate in Herefordshire. His family split their time between there and Morwellham. That's where his wife comes from. Her father's the harbour master there. Has been for years, from back in the days when the place was a busy port. And they also have a small apartment in London. Much of Adam's business is still there, you see. But they're coming to Morwellham at the end of the month to stay for a while. And they always come here for a few days. I can't leave the farm, you see, running it on my own with just a lad from the village to help. But we can send word to you when we know exactly when they're coming here.'

'Not to me,' Rose answered sharply, her expectant mind

racing ahead. 'To my friend Molly Tyler. At the gunpowder mills. My . . . my husband mustn't know.'

Richard's forehead dipped as he shot a glance at his wife, but Elizabeth nodded. 'I'll explain later.'

Rose considered for a moment. She felt sure she could trust these people, believed in their integrity, and she was so desperate, her heart so torn, that she couldn't stop herself. 'Just one last thing,' she faltered. 'I had a horse. A beautiful black thoroughbred cross. We rescued him nearly seven years ago. He was only partly broken in, but he was really spirited and frightened, and they were using such a harsh bit and beating him. All he needed was a little understanding. He and I were . . . well, like one. Only, in retaliation for my helping Seth, my husband sold him. To a dealer. And he won't tell me who. I need to find him. To get him back. Or at least to know if he's being treated all right. I just thought, with you being a farmer, could you keep a lookout for him, please? At livestock markets, that sort of thing.'

She saw Richard suck in his lean cheeks and exchange glances with his wife. 'Of course,' he said, nodding his head. 'What was his name?'

'Gospel. Though that could have been changed, of course.' She smiled thankfully, and then stood up, feeling she had asked enough of them. 'And I'd best be off. I can't tell you how grateful I am. And if Seth were here, I know he'd be thanking you, too.'

Richard caught her arm. 'I know Adam will do whatever he can. But, please, don't get your hopes up.'

Rose bowed her head. 'Yes. Yes, I understand. But at least I feel I'm doing something positive. And thank you again. So much.'

'It's the least we can do.'

'You're welcome to stay—'

'No, no thank you, Beth,' Rose answered resolutely and, squaring her shoulders, made for the door. She would have loved to remain a little longer in that calm, happy household, but it would only be putting off her return.

Twelve

'Where the blazes have you been?' Charles bawled at her from his desk.

But Rose didn't falter as she marched boldly into the study, still in her riding outfit, and calmly shut the door behind her. The long ride home from Peter Tavy had given her time to reflect on the whole situation, and though her muscles ached from such a lengthy period in the saddle when she hadn't ridden for so many months, it had only served to strengthen her resolve. She felt refreshed, even though visions of baby Alice kept torturing her brain, as the comfort she had received from total strangers that day had been more than anything Charles had offered her since her daughter had died. Her grief, for the moment, was locked inside, and all her pent-up emotions were channelled into what she knew would be a detestable confrontation with Charles.

She stood squarely in the centre of the plush rug, her shoulders braced and her chin set with determination. 'Out,' she said simply.

'I know that!' he barked back. 'But where? For God's sake, Rose, it's three o'clock in the afternoon, and you've been missing since dawn. I've been worried sick.'

Rose tilted her head. 'Yes, I'm sorry. But I've told you before not to worry if I'm out on the moor. I know it so well that I'm perfectly safe. And for your information, I've been all over.' She stepped forward and, placing her palms firmly on the edge of the desk, leant on her straightened arms. 'You must understand that I had to do something. Because of Alice. You know I feel at peace out on the moor. It has . . . helped me. I know the moor like the back of my hand. I respect its dangers, and I'm not fool enough to put myself at risk, no matter what you may think.'

'Huh!' Charles grunted. 'Since when did anything *I* think ever come into it? You're my wife, damn you, and you should give that some consideration.'

'Oh, I do, Charles, believe me I do!' she answered, her voice laced with an irony that shook him rigid. 'And you and I must have a frank discussion on that subject.'

'*What!* What do you mean?' He leapt to his feet and came round to her side of the desk, his cheeks puce. His wrath robbed him of his good looks, and Rose wondered how on earth she had once thought him handsome. It was her instinct to shrink away, but she forced herself to turn and face him.

'I do believe you love me,' she began with such coldness that Charles halted in his tracks. 'And once, I truly believed I loved you, too. But once we were married, I found you were not the man I thought you to be.'

Charles's eyes bulged from their sockets and he gripped her wrist, his teeth bared viciously. But Rose merely cast her eyes towards his hand with caustic disdain.

'There you are, you see. The man I thought I was marrying would never have done *that!*' She glared at him, her eyes indigo with rancour, and he slowly released his grip. 'Thank you,' she bristled sarcastically. 'As you say, I am your wife. And I shall remain so. A good housekeeper, and loyal to you. I shall even warm your bed at night and bear your children, though I should appreciate a little more gentleness in that department, especially while I am still sore from Alice's birth. But in return, you will allow me to come and go as I please, visit Molly or anyone else I choose, ride out over the moor, whatever I fancy.'

She stopped then, her mouth firmed to a defiant, mettlesome line and her chin lifted stubbornly. Charles's face was suffused with fury, his fists working at his sides. Rose might have recoiled, but there was no room for fear in her breast. Just emptiness, bottomless grief, and the tiny grain of strength the visit to Richard and Elizabeth Pencarrow had planted in her.

'You little vixen!' Charles spat at her, his eyes slits of venom. 'After all I've done for you! I tell you, I won't have you cavorting all over the place—'

'Rest assured, I'll do nothing to disgrace you, Charles,' she answered without flinching. 'I'll tell you where I'm going and how long I'll be so that you needn't worry. And I apologize

for today. I realize 'twere wrong of me, but I just felt I had
to get away, or I'd go mad. But, if you ever try to stop me,
I'll disappear from your life for good, and you'll never see
me again, and that wouldn't do your precious reputation or
your ego any good, would it?'

Charles's face turned the colour of unfired clay as the
shock of her scathing threat hit him below the belt. He knew
her well enough to realize that it would be foolish to underestimate her. She possessed both the determination and the
intelligence to outwit him in this wild region that she
knew intimately and to which he was an outsider. And yes,
she was right. He *did* love her. To distraction. And he
couldn't bear the idea of being without her. It would destroy
him, just as he supposed he had injured her by selling that
wretched horse. And he could understand her grief over the
child, even if it had meant little to him.

'All right,' he said tersely. 'As long as you keep me informed.
Because I *do* worry about you, you know. But I promised you
another horse, and I will keep that promise.'

'What? Like you kept your promise to help Seth?'

'That was an entirely different matter, as you very well know.
And I should like to accompany you on Tansy on occasion,
so we need two horses anyway. I believe there is the Princetown
Fair at the beginning of September and it has a livestock market.
I would suggest we look for something there.'

She met his gaze, her mouth puckered. She recognized that
he was offering her an olive branch. One she was loath to
accept, but open defiance might not be to her advantage. She
nodded. 'Thank you,' she answered without expression, and
walked quietly out of the room.

He didn't force his attentions on her that night, or the following
morning, and everyone else in the household put the silence
between the master and the mistress down to their bereavement, which in Rose's case, at least, was correct. Her legs were
so stiff after her long ride that she could scarcely walk and so,
dressed in mourning, she ordered Ned to drive herself and
Florrie to the church in the wagonette to visit Alice's tiny grave.
She and Florrie cried unashamedly in each other's arms, and
since she spent the following two days quietly indoors avoiding
the rain, Charles approved, and almost began to think he had

imagined the ugly scene in his study and that his offer of a new horse had smoothed over the cracks in their relationship.

He was mistaken. The hollow pit of misery in Rose's stomach was slowly being filled with bitter plans of vengeance. Or, if not of vengeance, then at least of deceit, since she was noble enough to recognize that, with the exception of his selling Gospel, the situation was not entirely Charles's fault. He, too, had thought he had found the perfect marriage partner – lively, entertaining, the ideal hostess and well-versed in the art of etiquette. But it was that very vivacity that had come between them, infuriating his possessiveness and his desire to dominate. They simply were not right for each other, and when her spirits were low and her grief over Alice was too much to bear, she wept also for the happiness she and Charles had failed to find together.

It was three days before he demanded his marital rights, and he did show her a little consideration, which made it more tolerable, so their bitter exchange had achieved some good. She still felt soiled, used, but at least Charles was satisfied and his attitude towards her was generally more understanding. And if she was to carry out her schemes, she needed to regain his trust.

For the first time in his life, Seth Collingwood – or Warrington, to use his real name – truly wanted to die. Years ago he had returned home on his first army leave to find that the young girl he had wanted to marry in the village had been spirited away in his absence by his father's money. He had exploded with a young man's fury, his hatred for his family and in particular his father driving an irrevocable rift into his heart. But his anger had led him not to suicidal misery, but to seek vengeance. His move into the cavalry and his promotion to captain had both cost his father a deal of money, which he had never recouped when the Purchase System was abolished, and that had given Seth some satisfaction. When he had been arrested and then convicted of a crime of which he was totally innocent, he had been filled with a black depression, and when, in that moment of desperate madness, he had run off into the blanket of mist, the desire to end his life had never entered his head. But now, after two weeks of working in the infamous bone shed, he had had enough, and every night and morning, he prayed God to let him die.

At five o'clock in the morning, the prisoners were woken with a bucket of cold water first to wash themselves in and then to wash out the cell. But no matter how hard Seth scrubbed himself, he couldn't get rid of the stench of human excrement that seeped into his skin, up his nostrils and into his very heart. The previous evening he had been marched with some fellow inmates to the bathhouse for their weekly dip, but it had made little difference. They had then been issued with their so-called clean underwear for the week, and Seth had despaired. As usual, the drawers were stained from the diarrhoea from which so many of the convicts suffered, and he had shuddered with indignity as he had put them on.

On the verge of tears, he cringed as he donned them again that morning, waiting for the moment when the cell door would be unlocked for each convict to slop out, carrying his own daily foul bucket to the tub at the end of the corridor which itself was emptied every other day into the cesspits next to the bone shed. The vile odour started it all up again, reaching into his stomach and tearing at his insides. There were those working in the bone shed who seemed to have got used to the smell, throwing him disparaging glances as he spent all day retching despite his best efforts not to – not for their sake but because once his stomach was empty, it was agony.

Just before six o'clock, the usual pint of 'skilly' or watery gruel and a chunk of bread were pushed through the hatch. Seth eyed it suspiciously. What was the point in forcing it down when he knew he would only bring it back up the moment he entered the shed? So when they were all crammed into the chapel for the brief morning service, the words on his mute lips were not the communal prayers but *Dear God, please let me die today*.

He couldn't help but slow his pace as they were marched past the piggery. The stink was already inside his head, there was no escape. Perhaps he could bolt towards the wall and they would shoot him dead. But they wouldn't, would they? They knew he couldn't get out, so they would merely pin him down manually and set him back to work. He had already lost all his points towards his ticket of leave because of his few weeks of freedom and had been lucky not to have more years added to his sentence, so any futile attempt now would simply put his marks in deficit.

Down the steps to the sunken shed, thus built so that the workers would be on a level with the cesspits next to it. Once drained, the remaining solid matter would have added to it manure from the piggery and the farm, and crushed bones from the shed. Hell wasn't in it, as far as Seth was concerned.

As they were forced inside, he bent his elbow across his mouth and nose in the vague hope that his senses might adjust slowly to the suffocating reek of sewage and rotting bones. They didn't. He was sick almost at once, his eyes watering in the acrid air, and for sympathy received a blow in the back from the warder.

'Clear it up, you milksop!' the warder bellowed in his ear.

Sweet Jesus, he couldn't help it. He was used to malodorous army latrines, but this was something entirely different. In the confined space of the shed, the stink was unbearable. He tried, dear Lord, he *tried* to think of something else, to imagine the scent of lavender, of rosemary and other herbs. The sweet fragrance of *her*. But it was no good.

A fellow inmate tipped a pile of bones in front of him and he took up the hammer, his shoulders slumped wearily. Many of the bones still had rancid meat adhering to them and had been in the heap outside for a week or more, putrefying in the summer warmth and smelling almost as badly as the human manure to which they would be added. The hammering began, and Seth closed his eyes in a moment of despair. Within half an hour, the airless atmosphere was so thick with the tainted dust of the crushed bones that he could scarcely see his neighbour. It settled on his chest, inflaming his already weakened lungs so that he struggled for breath, coughed and spluttered with each blow of the hammer. Crush to dust. With the threat of punishment if the pile wasn't pulverized by the end of the day. Sweat pouring from his face, running down inside his uniform. Retching and coughing until he thought his insides would break. Strangled.

Four torturing hours. Filed out into the open, gulping at the fresh air. Searched for hammers and other tools, then marched back to the cells for dinner. A pint of lukewarm beef soup, flavoured with onion and a slice or two of carrot. The most appetizing meal of the week. It would make good vomit for him, he mused in distraction.

He was right. He crawled on his hands and knees back to

his work place. Couldn't breathe, his lungs fit to burst. Perhaps he would get pneumonia again. He prayed God it would kill him this time.

'Please, I want to see the medical officer,' he choked.

'Get back to work, you blackguard,' was the response.

'I'm going to the powder mills this morning,' Charles announced over breakfast. 'The new manager is facing prosecution over various regulations the government inspector found weren't being properly adhered to. And, as one of the major shareholders, I find that quite worrying.'

Rose looked up sharply from the creamy porridge, sweetened with honey, that her rebellious stomach was just about allowing her to swallow. 'My father would never have allowed that to happen. He was always praised by the inspectors.'

'Yes, I know. My confidence in him was one of the reasons I bought even more shares when trade was lessening. But I was wondering if you'd care to accompany me? You could visit Molly while I carry out a tour of inspection of my own.'

Rose lifted an eyebrow, and the corners of her mouth curved upwards. 'Yes, I should like that.'

Charles returned her smile with some satisfaction. It was a gesture of reconciliation on his part, and she had accepted. Perhaps there was hope yet. Little did he realize he was playing right into her hands!

It was a pleasant August day and they took Merlin and the wagonette, Rose driving as it was something Charles had never learnt to do. While he went off to speak to the new manager, Rose hurried off to Joe and Molly's cottage.

'Rosie! How lovely to see you!'

The younger girl stopped stirring the stew she was cooking for dinner and they embraced tightly. Rose bit her lip, her chin quivering. Dear Molly. How good and kind, like all her family.

'How are you, Rosie?' she asked tentatively, her face taut with compassion. 'How you'm getting on?'

Rose knew that she was referring to the loss of little Alice, and she nodded as they drew apart. 'Well, as best I can, I suppose,' she answered, knowing she could open her heart and talk freely to her friend. 'I feel raw, empty, angry, all in turns. And Florrie's a tower of strength, as you might imagine.'

'Yes, I be certain she is.'

Rose smiled ruefully, and then her mouth widened with delight. 'And look at you! You're really showing now!'

Molly's pretty face darkened. 'Are you . . . are you sure you doesn't mind?'

'Mind? Why should I mind that you're expecting?'

'Oh, I just thought . . . with Alice—'

''Twas not your fault and, well, I can enjoy your little one, can't I? I mean, Joe's like my brother, so I'll be its auntie, won't I? I really am so pleased for you both!'

She grinned, her heart genuinely lifting, and Molly smiled with more confidence. 'Let's have a cup of tea,' she said, turning back to the range. 'Did your husband let you out, then?'

'He's here, too. Because of his investments and the trouble there's been. I don't know how long he'll be, so I'd better come to the point quickly.'

She sat down on a rustic settle, perching on the edge and leaning forward urgently. Molly turned to gaze at her, head tipped to one side.

'You wants me to do something?' She frowned.

'Yes. Yes, I do.' Her voice was low and trembling, and she fixed Molly with her arresting eyes. 'I need you to act as a go-between for me. I'm going to write to some of the local hunts. Ask them to keep an eye out for Gospel. But if there's any news, I need it to come to you. If there's any chance of getting him back – well, if Charles found out, he'd put a stop to it.'

Molly nodded emphatically. 'Yes, of course. Joe's already spreading the word where he can, too.'

'Is he, bless him? Oh, I'm so grateful. But . . .' She paused, her mouth set in familiar determination. 'There's something even more important. To do with Seth.'

Molly lowered her eyes. 'Your convict, you mean?'

'Yes. Do you know how he is?'

Molly's mouth twisted. It was a question she had hoped not to be asked. 'Father'd been working nights, so he hadn't seen him for a while. And a few days after he went back on day shifts, he . . .' She hesitated, bowing her head as if in shame. 'Father found him working in the bone shed.'

Rose stared at her for several numbing seconds while the anger frothed up inside her. 'The bone shed!' she moaned in an agony of despair since the horrors of the bone shed were well known. 'Oh, dear God! With his chest, 'twill kill him!'

'As I say, Father didn't know he'd been moved. Shouldn't have been, of course. Been there two weeks or so when Father found him. Father said he could hardly breathe for the dust, almost collapsed. He had him removed at once and taken back to the infirmary.'

'But . . . was he all right?' Rose hardly dared to ask.

Molly nodded reassuringly. 'Yes. Arter a few days, he were so much better that Dr Power sent him back to the workshops. He said when he passes him as fit, he can work on the buildings as he's actually very strong. 'Tis just his lungs have been weakened, so he's not to work breaking stones or ort dusty.'

Rose had been holding her breath and now she let it out in a deep sigh. 'Oh, thank God he has your father to keep an eye on him. But, oh, Molly, how ever will he last another ten years in that place? And that's another reason why I need your help.' And she proceeded to tell Molly all about her visit to Rosebank Hall and how she had asked Richard Pencarrow to let Molly know when Captain Adam Bradley was to visit.

'Of course. I'll do anything to help, you knows that. But will your husband not be suspicious?'

Rose pulled a long face. 'I don't think so. He's graciously said I can go out on my own. Provided I tell him where I'm going,' she added sarcastically.

''Tis fair enough,' Molly considered. 'If I were to go out, I'd tell Joe where I were off to.'

'Yes, I suppose you're right,' Rose conceded with a shrug. 'But you must start coming to Fencott Place regularly as well, so that when you do have a message for me, 'twill look perfectly natural. As long as you're up to it, of course. 'Tis a long walk in your condition.'

'Oh, I be as strong as an ox!' Molly grinned. 'And I could always send Joe with some sort of excuse, anyways. But, Rose . . .' Her expression became sombre again. 'You take care. 'Tis fire you'm playing with.'

Rose sucked in her cheeks. 'The way I see it, I don't have much choice, do I? And when you come to see me, you can choose which of the puppies you'd like, can't you?' Her face brightened merrily, but inside, her heart was clenched with anxiety. For she knew Molly was right.

Thirteen

'So, did you have a good time with your friend?' Charles asked stiffly as they drove home across the moor.

Rose flashed him a relaxed smile. 'Yes, thank you. And your inspection?'

'Well, I have to admit that I wasn't exactly sure what I was looking for. I nearly came to fetch you as you know far more about it than I do. But I reckon the prosecution will have shaken things up somewhat and everyone will be more vigilant in the future.'

'Good. I'd hate anyone to be hurt again like my father was. By the way, Molly and I have decided upon Wednesdays for me to visit. And sometimes she might come over to me, if that's all right with you?'

She cocked her head to one side, smiling angelically as if it were all perfectly natural, which, she considered, it should be. Charles conceded with a grimace. He didn't exactly approve, but at least one day a week, he would know where she was.

And so, on the following Wednesday, she drove Merlin and the wagonette over to the powder mills as Charles had said he needed Tansy to ride into Tavistock to do some business at the bank. But he didn't go straight there. Instead, half an hour after Rose left Fencott Place, he made a long detour up the Postbridge Road. On nearing the cottages where the track led off towards the gunpowder factory, he spied Merlin unharnessed from the wagonette and tethered in the shade. Charles was satisfied. For now.

Rose, for her part, was playing the game. Each time she went out, sometimes on Tansy or sometimes taking the wagonette, she gave Charles her route or destination, returning at the estimated time. Once or twice, with his permission, she rode into Tavistock, spent some while shopping, and returned with her purchases to show him. It meant she was out most of the day, all in preparation for when she would receive news through Molly of Captain and Mrs Bradley's stay at Rosebank Hall.

The message from Richard and Elizabeth Pencarrow came at last. Rose tore open the envelope as she took it from Molly's outstretched hand, her pulse vibrating at her temples. Was it from them, or had someone replied to her enquiries regarding Gospel? Would she drown in bitter disappointment, or rise on a wave of hope? She gasped with relief. The Bradleys were coming the following week and Rose was welcome to come on any day.

Announcing to Charles that she was going into town, Rose set out in the direction of Tavistock. She was reasonably confident that Charles would not follow, but she nevertheless felt a nervous sweat flush her skin. She must make her outing as legitimate as possible and so she stopped at Tor Quarry at Merrivale to enquire how the new business was faring – their use of powder from Cherrybrook providing a valid excuse – so that she could provide proof that she had at least ridden that far. She also had about her person a couple of trinkets she had previously bought at Tavistock market and had secreted from Charles, but would reveal to him at once upon her return as evidence of her claimed visit to the town.

She heard laughter as she rode up the track to Rosebank Hall, and discovered the happy party on the lawn at the front of the farmhouse. It was the very end of August, and the almost continuous rain throughout the summer had not allowed the general air temperature to rise. So even though the sun was shining brilliantly from a duck-egg blue sky, it was not warm enough to necessitate any protection from the heat when sitting outside. Not that there was much sitting being done! Chantal Pencarrow was racing about the grass with a lean young boy who appeared a couple of years her junior. They were engaged in a game of tag, evidently indulging a pretty little girl of about four years old and also a toddler who were both attempting to join in, to the pure joy of the younger dog Rose had seen on her previous visit. Chasing with them was a man, almost as tall as Richard Pencarrow, Rose judged, though Richard himself was nowhere to be seen, and as he ran and dodged about, Rose realized the man was carrying in his arms a delighted baby Hannah Pencarrow. Two kitchen chairs stood empty by a small table set with drinks, but two others were occupied by Elizabeth and another woman of about thirty years old, petite, beautiful, sophisticated in a dress of ruched pale blue silk, yet laughing uproariously at the antics of the man and the children in front of her.

Rose's heart contracted painfully, for wasn't this the scene of domestic bliss she had once imagined for herself and Charles? Alas, it could never be . . . And the children – ah, *girl* children – who were not only loved and appreciated by their own fathers, but by others as well, since she realized that the man playing with Hannah must be none other than Captain Adam Bradley.

Tansy shied at the shrieks of hilarity from the lively group before them, and Rose slid from her back and patted her neck reassuringly as the mare shook her head with a snort. When Rose turned round, Elizabeth was coming up to her, arms open to welcome her like a long-lost friend, with Captain Bradley close on her heels.

'Rose, this is Adam,' Elizabeth introduced him as she released Rose from her embrace.

The captain's face was still flushed with merriment and he had to catch his breath as he approached. His otherwise full head of mid-brown hair showed only the slightest sign of receding, and that, together with the lines about his eyes, put him at about forty. A handsome man still, though in a totally different way from Richard Pencarrow's dark and brooding good looks, he instantly inspired an awesome respect which anyone but Rose might have found daunting. His expression became more serious, though his warm, honest chestnut eyes still smiled at her, and his mouth was a strong curve of even white teeth.

'Mrs Chadwick – Rose, if I may be so bold,' he said with a quiet confidence, passing the child in his arms to her mother, Rose noticed, in a somewhat awkward fashion. As he shook Rose's right hand in his with a firm grip, he grasped her forearm with his left hand in a gesture of sincerity. Except that the gloved hand was rigid and didn't actually grasp her at all. 'Would you mind if I remove my coat?' he asked politely. 'Running about with the children . . .'

'But of course.' She smiled sweetly, for though she was

perplexed by his character and in particular by his stiff left hand, she had taken an instinctive liking to him.

'Thank you.'

He was slipping with just a little difficulty out of his coat, when the woman Rose assumed was his wife came up behind him and greeted her with such affection that she might have known Rose all her life. Then she turned easily to help her husband, and as the left coat sleeve slid from his hand, the cuff of the glove was rolled back, and Rose saw with amazement that the hand was made not of flesh and blood, but of metal.

Captain Bradley caught her eye with the hint of a wry smile. 'Ah, you've discovered my little secret. An accident at sea that nearly cost me my life *and* my sanity. And would have done so, had it not been for my wife here.'

His arm went about the exquisite woman's waist and she leant against him, the love that they shared seeming to flutter in the air about them, such an intuition between them that Rose felt a lump swell in her throat. Of envy, perhaps, but also of relief, since it was this well-balanced, mature man, who had clearly known his own share of tragedy, who would hopefully be taking up Seth's cause.

'Do come and have some lemonade,' Elizabeth invited her, jiggling Hannah in her arms. 'You must be thirsty after that long ride.'

'Could I put Tansy in the stable first, please?'

'Of course. You know where it is.'

Rose settled Tansy in the now empty stable, as the farm horses, of which she knew there were two, were both out working. Richard had fields in the valley where he grew the fodder for his increasing flock of sheep and the few cattle that were currently grazing on the moor, as well as for the two house cows that were kept at the farm for the family's domestic use. Rose knew relatively little of farming, but it was obvious Richard worked like a slave to make ends meet, supplemented by what Elizabeth made from her herbal remedies and her services as the local midwife. It was a hard life, made even worse by the bad weather that summer and the threat of cheaper wool and tinned meat imports from America and Australia, and there was even talk now of developing refrigeration units that in a few years' time would bring frozen meat from these continents in record time on steamships. Nonetheless, Richard and Elizabeth appeared supremely happy together, and once again Rose cursed Fate for denying her such contentment.

'Beth has told us all about you,' Rebecca Bradley announced quite openly as Rose joined them on the lawn. 'And we're so sorry about your situation, my dear.' She leant forward, squeezing Rose's arm, her sapphire eyes soft with understanding. 'But you're amongst friends now.'

The woman spoke with such compassion that Rose indeed took heart, her fears that Charles might find her out melting to dust. They sat, sipping the cool, bittersweet lemonade for some time before retiring to the farmhouse kitchen for a simple lunch. With so many young children, it was hardly a quiet affair, but none of the adults seemed to mind a jot. Indeed, they encouraged the two older children to join in their conversation, and even the younger members of the Bradley family, four-year-old Charlotte, and James, who was not quite two, were not expected to sit in silence. Rose wondered ruefully if Charles would ever have allowed Alice to dine with them before she reached the sensible age of sixteen. But she would never know . . .

It was when the table was cleared, the washing-up completed, that Adam took Rose's elbow. 'I think we should sit down and talk now, Rose,' he said quietly. 'Richard wouldn't mind us using his office, would he, Beth? And I'd like to make some notes as we talk.'

'Yes, of course. Help yourself to pen and paper. There should be some on the desk. We'll take the children for a walk, shall we, Becky?'

'This way, Rose,' Adam invited her. They crossed through a large hallway with a massive, heavy front door and a solidly turned wooden banister to the staircase – nothing as grand as Fencott Place, but impressive, nevertheless. But the house had an air of having seen better days, carpets with threadbare patches and the whole place spartanly furnished. Richard's office was no different, and a pile of papers was neatly arranged on the desk.

'Better not disturb those,' Adam observed as he indicated that Rose should be seated. Then he put on his spectacles and took up one of two fountain pens that lay on the desk. 'Hmm, when will they invent one of these things that doesn't leak all over the place?' he grumbled, looking at the instant ink stains on his fingers. 'Prefer a quill myself. Now then.' He drew Richard's writing pad towards him, and tested the pen on a sheet of paper. When he was satisfied, he looked up, staring deep into Rose's eyes. 'Begin at the beginning. Take your time. Tell me everything you know.'

Rose did as she was asked. She explained how Seth had just arrived in Tavistock one evening, a stranger in an unknown town since he was originally from the south-east. He had gone to the Exeter Inn for a drink, but although he had a considerable sum in his pocket – what was left of his army pay and wages from various places where he had obtained casual labour on his travels – he didn't want to squander it and so had asked where he might find cheap lodgings in the town. A drunken gambler in the inn had caused a scene, and when he wanted another drink and Seth had suggested he had already had too much, he punched him in the face. Whereupon the publican had thrown the devil outside.

Later, Seth had gone in search of the backstreet lodgings and came across a man being attacked and robbed. He had chased off the assailant, but the victim had been stabbed. An elderly couple had witnessed the event, but had disappeared, not wanting to get involved, and so Seth had torn at the fellow's clothes to get to his wounds and stem the bleeding. Another man had appeared then, but in the dark, had thought Seth was robbing the chap and had gone to fetch the police, who promptly arrested him.

What Seth hadn't realized was that the rogue whose life he had saved was the drunk, and he swore blind that it was Seth who had robbed him in retaliation for being punched. He claimed that the money in Seth's pocket were the gambling winnings he had been boasting about in the inn and had indeed counted for everyone to see. Seth had tried to explain how the money was his, but by asking for cheap lodgings he had given the impression that only half an hour earlier, he was strapped for cash. And on the blackguard's word, he had been convicted.

Adam seemed so calm and unhurried as Rose related the story that she found herself remembering all sorts of details. Adam made notes as she talked, stopping her occasionally to

clarify a fact here and there. It must have been an hour before
he sat back in his chair and removed his spectacles.

'Damned things,' he mumbled with a sheepish smile. 'Had
to give in to them in the end. Couldn't see the navigation
charts properly. Or the plans for the steamship I'm having
built. Had to give in to that, too. Not that I'd sail the wretched
thing myself. Give me sails and the wind any day. But . . .'
He pinched his bottom lip between his teeth, a little gesture
of hesitation his wife Rebecca had come to know so well.
'I'm sure you're not interested in that. You want to know what
I think.'

Rose was sure her heart had suddenly stopped beating. Adam
Bradley was a good man, but he also seemed a realist. She
felt the sweat oozing from her palms as he drew in a breath
to speak.

'I understand from Richard you've mentioned a royal
pardon?'

Rose's throat had dried like parchment, her voice refusing
to work, so she nodded silently in reply.

'Well, it seems to me the only possible way,' Adam began
hesitantly. 'There are some new laws regarding appeals in the
civil courts, but it's quite right that there's no such thing in
the criminal justice system. A conviction's a conviction. And
unless you can produce absolutely irrefutable new evidence
of Mr Collingwood's innocence, you haven't a chance. And
even then, it would be one hell of a business.'

Rose felt sick. Was that it, then? She had wanted so much
to have faith in the captain, and now it seemed he was turning
her down. But then he smiled at her crestfallen expression
and, cupping his chin in his right hand, pushed his thumb
across his thoughtfully pursed lips.

'However,' he went on slowly, 'this is an appalling story,
so I'll tell you what I'm going to do. We'll be returning to
Morwellham in a couple of days. We have someone, Amy
Blatchford – been with us for years – who keeps the house
for us there, so Rebecca will be perfectly content there without
me and, of course, her parents are only a few minutes' walk
away. So I shall go up to London by train and discuss this
with my lawyer up there. Find out all I can about what a
pardon would entail. I'll do all I can, but I have to say that I
don't hold much hope. But just tell me one thing, Rose,' he

said levelly, slowly blinking his steady eyes. 'Do you believe this Seth Collingwood is telling the truth?'

He was staring at her unflinching, his gaze unnerving her. He was testing her, and she met the challenge. 'Without a doubt,' she replied with conviction. 'I've been over everything he said a thousand times, and it all makes sense. But apart from that, yes, I do believe him. And you would, too, if you met him. But . . .' She faltered, lowering her eyes. 'There's just one other thing. He asked me not to tell anyone, but I really think you should know. His real name is Warrington.'

She cringed as she saw Adam stiffen and his forehead creased into a frown. 'Go on,' he urged her enquiringly, and she knew she must explain fully.

'Well, as I said,' she began more confidently, 'Seth didn't get on with his family, and when he resigned his commission, he never told them and he didn't want them to try and find him, so he assumed the name of Collingwood. That was why he couldn't explain fully the considerable sum of money he had on him, as most of it was his final army pay. But if you want to verify it, he was a captain with the Fifteenth King's Hussars. They arrived in Bombay at the end of 1869, I'm sure he said, and from there they were stationed at Mhow for nearly three years. That stands for something, Military Headquarters of War, I think. And then, as I remember,' she went on, biting her lip as she searched her memory, 'they were moved to Meerut, is it? They never saw any action, just the odd skirmish and training. A hundred degrees in the shade, he said. They did go off on exercise for three months at the end of 1873, but it wasn't long after that he resigned. Now, I don't know about you, but how would he have known all that if 'tweren't true? And he told me all sorts of other things about the army and his stay in India.'

She watched as Adam nodded slowly. 'Well, it certainly seems to ring true, and I can try to check out that side of his story. It isn't particularly helpful that he's using an assumed name, but we'll look into that if it's strictly necessary. I should have thought that finding the couple who witnessed the attack by the real culprit would be our best bet. But if we can gather sufficient evidence in his favour – which won't be easy, I shouldn't think – and I can find my way through what I'm sure will be a legal nightmare, then I expect I and whatever legal representative will be required will need to visit him in prison. So I should meet him then. But I really must warn you that as far as I know, a royal pardon is a rare thing indeed. It will take time and influence, not to say money—'

'Oh, I can get you money!' she told him, relieved that there was at least something she could do.

Adam spread his right hand. 'There was a time when I would have had to take you up on that out of necessity. But now I can safely say that my pockets are deep. And nothing would give me greater pleasure than to see such a grave injustice rectified. Besides, I understand that you wish this to be kept secret from your husband, and if, as I imagine, you are referring to a personal allowance, he may wish to know at some point what you have spent it on.'

'Well, I can only thank you from the bottom of my heart.'

'Don't thank me yet. Nothing at all may come of it. But I can promise you, I will try my damnedest. You must be patient. But in the meantime, I would suggest you examine your own involvement in this.'

He watched as she lowered her eyes. To him, she was little more than a child, young enough, almost, to be his daughter. Yes, he would do everything in his power to right this wrong, but even if by some miracle he was successful, what would happen then? This tragic, spirited young girl – and he could see something of his own darling Rebecca in her – was at odds with her husband, justifiably or not. But what did she feel for the wronged man?

Adam shook his head as he followed her out of the room. For he had once known the crippling depths of despair himself, and would he merely be assisting her to topple into the same agonizing abyss? Only time would tell.

Fourteen

'A re you ready, my dear?' Charles asked with a hint of resignation echoing in his voice.

'Oh, yes!'

Charles gave a mildly sardonic grunt. He hadn't seen his wife so animated since before their child had been born. Or possibly since the day of their wedding, he grudgingly admitted to himself. She had talked of nothing else for the last two weeks as the Princetown Fair approached – and the promise of a new horse on which she could charge about the countryside. She had come alive again, more like the Rose who had originally enslaved his heart, yet strangely more compliant. He almost wished in some inexplicable way that by some miracle the black nag she had loved would turn up at the fair, and he would willingly buy it back for her. Not that his pride would allow him to say so unless the occasion arose.

The same thought had inevitably crossed Rose's mind too. She had about her all the generous personal allowance Charles had granted her since their marriage and of which she had spent very little. If she found Gospel, she would buy him back before Charles had the chance to stop her. She knew it was highly unlikely, but she couldn't help but feel euphoric with excitement. Whatever happened, she would have a horse of her own again, and one that would be swifter than good, dependable Tansy. She had got away with her two visits to Rosebank Hall, but she would feel happier if the travelling time could be reduced. She would always tell Charles that she was going to Tavistock, of course, but there was a limit to how much time she could pretend to have spent shopping!

'Let's walk there,' she grinned, hopping around him.

'It isn't very pleasant—'

'Oh, don't be so staid! 'Tis fine – for Dartmoor!'

Charles sighed as he reluctantly gave in. It was blustery with drizzle in the air, and he could scarcely keep up with Rose's athletic gait. She danced ahead, stopping occasionally to tease as she waited for him to catch up, and he watched her with refreshed eyes. She was so beautiful, so spirited, making his heart trip over itself. And she was *his*!

The long road that ended at the Whiteworks Mine out on the moor was deserted, but as they came into Princetown, the place was bustling. The livestock market was held outside the Duchy Hotel, but entertainment booths and stalls selling anything from saveloys and buns to pots and pans or ribbons were set up along the three main converging streets, while pedlars plied their wares as they walked among the crowds. A barrel organ with a tiny monkey in a military uniform sitting aloft had its tinny melody ground out by a man in a medal adorned coat, while further along a fiddler played a merry tune to jolly along the festive atmosphere. Her spirits lifted, Rose knelt to place a silver sixpence in his hat on the ground, and he gave a toothless grin of thanks.

'Rose!'

She glanced up at the familiar voice and sprang to her feet. 'Molly! How are you?'

'I's fine, thank you. Mr Chadwick.' The girl nodded at Charles before turning back to her friend. 'You having a good time?'

'We've only just arrived. We've come to buy a new horse, haven't we?' She linked her arm through Charles's elbow and gave him a cajoling smile.

'Well, we'd better start looking, hadn't we?' he answered stiffly as he drew her away. Rose had been behaving herself of late, but he really didn't approve of her association with Molly Tyler – at least not in public.

But Rose was not to be dominated. 'You go along, Charles, and I'll join you in a minute. I must find out from Molly how the puppy's doing.'

Charles rolled his eyes. 'Well, don't be long. The best will be sold first.'

Rose watched him saunter towards the horse sale, and the moment he was lost in the crowd, she turned anxiously to Molly, her feigned joy sliding from her face. 'Is there any news?' she whispered urgently.

Molly fumbled in her battered basket. 'These came for you during the week. I thought I might see you here. And I'd have come on to the house if I didn't.'

''Twould be a long walk for you, and back again. But I'd take you home in the wagonette, of course, so long as Charles wasn't using it.' But her mind wasn't on what she was saying as she almost snatched the letters away.

'You read them quickly while I keep guard,' Molly instructed, glancing furtively around them. 'I'll tell you if he's coming back.'

Rose opened the letters with trembling fingers and her eyes quickly scanned the writing as her heart swelled on a crest of nervous anticipation, only to drop into a trough of disappointment a second later. She screwed the paper into tight balls and pushed them to the bottom of Molly's basket again.

'Take them home and burn them for me, would you?' she said in answer to her friend's enquiring expression. 'From the Lamerton and the Mid Devon Foxhounds. They've neither of them seen a horse of Gospel's description, but they've both promised to let me know if they do.'

She sighed, her mouth twisting despondently, and Molly squeezed her arm. 'Never mind. Summat'll turn up; I feels it in my bones. Now you'd best go and find your husband.'

'Yes, I had,' Rose agreed, swallowing down her dejection. 'Is Joe here, by any chance?'

'I's afeared not. He were needed to take the new manager into Tavistock.'

'Pity. He could have helped me. He knows more about horses now than I do.' She shook her head wistfully. 'I had hoped Gospel might turn up here, but he was so big, I'm sure I'd have noticed him by now.'

Nevertheless, she cast an expectant eye around the horses' enclosure when she forced her way through the crowds to reach it. There were animals of every description, from unbroken moorland yearlings to cart horses and cobs. Gospel wasn't among them, and Rose experienced that cruel feeling of emptiness that she was growing so used to. But the collection of endearing creatures encouraged her flagging spirits. She could have loved every one of them. A striking piebald pony caught her eye and she spent some time fondling its black and white ears, but tempted as she was by its obviously gentle nature, she must find a larger, stronger mount to convey her at speed across the moor to Peter Tavy.

'This little fellow's charming,' Charles encouraged her. Oh, Rose would look glorious trotting about on its pretty back, an absolute picture, refined and perfect.

'Yes. He'd have been perfect for Alice,' she answered almost scathingly. 'But I need something . . .' She turned, her eyes swivelling avidly about the equine display. 'Oh! Oh, look, Charles! Just being led in. Oh, we must look at that one. The palomino over there.'

'But . . . it's enormous.'

'Like Gospel was, you mean?' she snapped acidly.

'Oh, Rose, I—'

But whatever it was he said, Rose didn't hear. She was already away and introducing herself to the horse before the vendor had tethered it.

'Are you a dealer?' she asked imperiously.

'Er, no, miss,' the surprised fellow stammered. 'I'm selling her for my master. Decided he don't need two horses, like.'

'Right. And you haven't recently come across a black gelding of similar size, by any chance? A thoroughbred cross type, but, well, a bit of a handful? About eight or nine years old?'

'No, I'm sorry, miss.'

'Oh, well, tell me about this beauty, then.' She smiled sweetly as Charles caught her up.

'Fine animal, miss – er, ma'am,' he corrected himself as he looked at the man who must be her husband. 'A good hunter, fast, excellent jumper. But she won't run away with you or ort like that. Lovely temperament. I has to say that I'll miss her. Wish the master were selling the other one.'

'So why is he selling this one?' Charles demanded.

'Well, not to put too fine a point on it, the master's a heavy man and, well, just look at this girl. Fine legs, strong. Master's reluctant to sell her, but he wouldn't want to spoil her with his weight. You'd be all right on her, sir.'

'It's for my wife, here, not me.'

'Well, might I say she'd be a perfect mount for the young lady. Fastest in the field with such a featherweight on her back, and never been known to throw anyone in her life.'

Rose was already studying the animal in detail. Good clear

eyes and ears, a soft mouth, which she didn't mind Rose opening to inspect her teeth and judge her age. Rose ran her hand over the strong withers, along the backbone, and down each leg, which the mare was happy to lift in turn for Rose to check her feet. Her shining coat was at the pale-wheat end of the palomino's golden colour spectrum, her mane and tail ivory rather than a pure white. She turned her head and nuzzled Rose's shoulder, and Rose's heart was lost.

'What is she, sixteen hands?'

'Sixteen one or two, I reckon.'

Rose nodded. Very nearly the same as Gospel and of a similar age, healthy and clearly well cared for. 'What do you think, Charles?'

Charles dropped his head to one side. He had hoped to find something of a more sedate nature, but this was certainly a beautiful, elegant creature, quite suitable for the Chadwick's elevated position in society. Though the animal's size and fine lines reminded him of Gospel, it appeared to be of a far steadier disposition. And Rose seemed to have fallen in love with it. If he allowed her to have it, she might think better of him.

'Could I try her, please?' she asked the groom before Charles had time to answer.

'Oh, I doesn't have a saddle . . .'

'I don't need one. Would you give me a leg-up, please?'

The poor fellow's face lengthened in astonishment and he glanced at the woman's husband for assurance. Charles blinked and then dipped his head in agreement. It would be a good test, and if Rose came off, he would put his foot down and make her go back to the piebald. So the man cupped his hands to take Rose's foot, amazed to catch a glimpse of breeches beneath the riding skirt as the girl swung herself on to the horse's back. In all his life, he'd never seen a member of the fairer sex ride astride, let alone bareback!

'I'll be ten minutes, quarter of an hour, if that's all right. Oh, take this.' To Charles's horror, she pulled off her engagement ring and flicked it at the man who was becoming more flabbergasted with every second. 'Surety that I'll bring her back!'

And with a delighted chuckle, she was directing the steed through the crowded streets. The mare didn't turn a hair at the unfamiliar sounds, the calls and shouts, and responded immediately to the lightest touch on the reins. Rose would take her out to Rundlestone and give the animal her head up the long, steep climb past the humble farmsteads towards Great Mis Tor. The ground would stretch her speed and stamina, and if she came through unwinded, she would be the one.

The road to Rundlestone led out past the gaol. There was no festive day for the prisoners, no welcome rest from the gruelling toil. She brought the horse to a stop and it stood, perfectly still. Another test. And then Rose directed her to take a few paces backwards. She obeyed perfectly. Rose urged her on again, but not before she had spent some moments looking up at the building works within the prison walls. Convicts swarmed over the second of the cell blocks that was being raised to the forbidding five storeys. Seth, she knew, would be somewhere among them. *Oh, for God's sake, take care*, she whispered fervently in her head. *I'm doing what I can.*

And she brushed the tear from her cheek before they trotted on.

'I'm taking Honey into Tavistock,' Rose announced, not cringing at the outright lie since she had received word via Molly that Adam Bradley was at Rosebank Hall with some news for her.

'Do you think that's wise? You've only had her two weeks.'

'Oh, Charles, you and I have been out over the moor together on some long treks, and she's been absolutely perfect.'

'That's true,' Charles conceded with a grimace. He had enjoyed their rides out together so that Rose could get used to Honey. Not that the animal had needed getting used to. The two mares had looked superb together; Tansy's bright chestnut coat contrasting wonderfully with Honey's creamy beauty, and Rose had been overjoyed. Was her heart, broken by the loss of her daughter – and, Charles reflected with a hint of guilt, of Gospel – beginning to mend? She seemed to have regained a purpose in life – though had Charles known what for, he wouldn't have been so pleased!

'All right, then. But be careful. And keep to the roads in case you get into trouble. And *mind* her. She's a valuable animal.'

And Gospel wasn't? she thought bitterly. But the acrimony didn't taint her spirit for long. It was a month since she had met the captain at Richard and Elizabeth's house. It had seemed an eternity, but in the scheme of things, it was little time at all. What was the news? Would the good, upright man have to let her down gently, break the news to her with ultimate compassion that there was nothing he could do after all? She tried not to think about it, not to get her hopes up, but it was impossible, and she felt herself trembling as Honey cantered steadily along the track to the farm.

They slowed to a walk to enter the yard. It was a pleasant morning for late September and the two younger Bradley children and baby Hannah were outside playing with some farm kittens. Just at that moment, Chantal Pencarrow and Toby Bradley, manfully carrying a bucket of milk, emerged from a barn and greeted Rose cheerily.

'What a beautiful 'orse!' the attractive girl gasped in her lilting accent. 'Is it yours, madame?'

'Yes! Her name's Honey. I'm delighted with her. And do call me Rose.'

'All right. Can I put 'er in the stable for you?'

'Oh, yes, please. I can't wait to speak to the captain.'

'Father's in the kitchen,' Toby told her, and then he added a little shyly, 'Chantal and I have just been milking the cows.'

Rose followed the athletic young boy inside. The calm, serene atmosphere of the house once again struck her immediately, the fragrant aroma of dried herbs subtle in the air. Elizabeth was sitting at the table enjoying a cup of tea with Adam and Rebecca, and all three politely got to their feet to greet her.

'I nearly went out on the moor with Richard today,' the captain told her. 'I'm glad I didn't now.'

'You came just at the right time!' Elizabeth beamed, getting another cup.

Rose perched on the edge of one of the chairs as if it were red hot, aware of the nervous sweat that was trickling down her back, and she saw Adam smile knowingly.

'Let's not beat about the bush. You want to hear my progress report.'

'And I'm sorry to say that Richard hasn't had any luck with his enquiries about your horse. He's asked all over the place, but no luck so far, I'm afraid.'

'And I haven't a great deal to report, but at least I've gathered some support.'

Rose's heart sagged. She had hoped for more than that, but she mustn't let her courage flag. 'Go on,' she urged, nodding her thanks as Elizabeth passed her a cup of hot, steaming tea and pushed a plate of freshly baked, mouth-watering biscuits towards her.

Adam Bradley gave her his warm, kind smile. 'Well, I've spoken to my lawyer in London. He has no experience of such things himself, but he does have connections, friends in high places as they say. Including a barrister who's an expert in criminal proceedings and a circuit judge who was really shocked when he learnt all the facts. He reckoned that in his summing up, the judge at your Seth's trial should have tried to sway the jury away from a conviction. It's a difficult situation, one judge criticizing another, but the important thing is that this other judge is willing to take up Seth's cause if we can produce sufficient evidence.' Adam paused, tapping his fingertips together. 'The other thing is that I have also managed to enlist the support of our local Member of Parliament. And I've hired a private investigator to track down the witnesses in the case.'

Rose breathed in deeply, puffing out her cheeks. Every nerve in her body had been on edge, expecting the worse. At least there was still some hope, but she felt deflated, her emotions tangled in a devastating web. 'Thank you so much, Captain Bradley.'

'Adam, please. I'm sorry I have no more to tell you at present, but I did warn you that such things take time.'

A dejected silence settled around the table, but only seconds later, the remaining children all tumbled through the door in happy array.

'You will stay for lunch, won't you?' Elizabeth invited her with a broad smile.

'Yes, thank you, I'd love to.'

'And Rose is very lucky. She 'as a beautiful new 'orse. She's lovely, and Papa will be very jealous because 'e likes 'orses very much!'

Yes, Rose thought, and her mouth curved wistfully. Honey was a dear, a salve to her aching heart. But she wasn't Gospel . . .

Fifteen

'I'm taking these to Alice,' Rose told Charles, glancing down at the last dahlias she had picked from the well-manured flower beds in the garden. They were a strong pink, each petal tipped with white, and she was sure Alice would have loved them when she grew older. When winter came, Rose was sure she could find some variegated evergreen to take to the grave, or a tiny sprig of heather hiding somewhere on the moor. She had already taken some interestingly marked stones, the sort of thing she would have taught Alice to appreciate. Had she been alive . . .

'Do you want to come with me?' she asked, pushing the thought painfully aside.

'Er, no. I'm rather busy at the moment. Actually, Rose, I think I shall need to go to London for a couple of weeks, and I was wondering . . . it might do you some good to come with me. Have a change of scene.' And stop her from going to the churchyard so regularly. He was sure it was only keeping her bereavement alive.

He was both pleased and amazed when she answered at once. 'Yes, that would be nice.'

Little did he know that she merely considered a trip to London might help pass the time before Captain Bradley had some more news for her. It was only the faith she had placed in Adam that enabled her to survive the numbing grief over Alice that bound her in its evil clutches. Although she attended the little grave at least twice a week, Charles never accompanied her. Sometimes Florrie would go with her in the new single Brougham that Charles had finally acquired, with its cosy, plush interior to shield them from the Dartmoor weather, Ned sitting aloft in the driving seat, clad in some fancy attire that Rose thought quite pretentious.

But on most occasions, as today, she went alone, riding Honey whatever the weather.

She left the beautiful mare tethered to the iron gates where she could still see her while she tended both her father's and her tiny daughter's adjacent graves. She arranged the flowers and then knelt in the grass, her head bowed over her tightly clasped hands. Oh, if only they were both still alive, the burden of her marriage to Charles would have been so much more bearable. How could God be so unkind as to take them both from her? She felt the savage pain in her heart, allowing the sorrow to wash over her in the quiet of the churchyard, nothing but the wind moaning in her ears. No one to witness her stultifying sadness. And the tears trickled down her cheeks.

But she couldn't cry for ever, and the tears had eased her misery, at least for a while. She may have lost Gospel, but now she had Honey, who was so sweet and gentle-natured. She had Amber and Scraggles and the one puppy they had kept, Lucky, the runt that Seth had revived after its birth. *Oh, Seth, I haven't forgotten you.* She looked across at the prison, so daunting, so *inhuman*. She gritted her teeth, swung herself into the saddle, and set Honey for home.

The journey to London seemed to take an eternity, Charles studying business papers most of the way. They travelled first class, of course, and ate in the restaurant car. Back in their compartment, Rose returned to the book she was reading, but she couldn't concentrate and spent most of the time gazing out of the window as the countryside flew past. At last they arrived in the capital, the silhouettes of the buildings standing like solid giants against the darkening skyline. Paddington was bustling with passengers, luggage piled high on trolleys, engines hissing out steam, the slamming of carriage doors. Charles engaged the services of a porter and hurried Rose into a cab, and soon they were bowling through the dark, wet streets of London to his immaculate terraced house in a smart, fashionable square.

It was quite pleasant to be back, and the servants greeted her respectfully but with some affection. Would she like a bath run for her after the long journey? Oh, yes, that would be wonderful, not only because she felt tired and dirty, but because she secretly loved to see hot water gushing out of the taps, which was a novelty for her.

Her delight, though, was the private park in the middle of the square to which only residents were entitled to hold a key. Rose would spend hours there, a heavenly oasis in the buzzing metropolis. And she didn't always find herself alone. She met other residents, mainly bored wives and daughters who found this polite young woman with her country accent quite refreshing, even though she chose to ignore certain proce-dures of etiquette such as exchanging visiting cards, but invited them in for tea then and there! Charles certainly approved of these associations, which kept her occupied while he was visiting his bank or his broker, or attending board meetings at one of the many companies in which he had substantial investments. He might have had a fit, however, if he had known that Rose would converse with anyone who happened to be in the square, male or female, and that as word spread, more gentlemen residents than ever before were finding an excuse to visit the garden in the hope of meeting his beautiful and charming wife!

But when she was alone there, Rose would sigh as she sat back on the bench, remembering the period when she had stayed in London before, exactly a year ago. She had known then that her marriage to Charles had been a mistake, but it had provided a comfortable home for her crippled father, which was more important to her than anything. And then she had received the telegram from Florrie and she had rushed home to Dartmoor. Her dearest, beloved father had died a few days later.

Oh, how cruel fate could be! Soon after, she had dis-covered she was pregnant and had then given birth to the child she had hoped would reunite herself and Charles. But then she had lost Alice, Charles had sold Gospel, and the only man who had brought her solace was festering in Dartmoor's cold and brutal prison for a crime he had not committed. Rose would close her eyes, trying to blank it all from her mind. She would listen to the pretty birdsong of the thrush and the blackbird, but would hear in her head the bark of the raven or the wild cry of the buzzard from high on the moor.

Sometimes she would take bread with her and crumble it into tiny morsels to attract a flock of cheeky sparrows to her feet, and one particular fellow would eat out of her hand. She surprised the elderly gardener by chatting to him as he burned the fallen autumn leaves on a smouldering fire. And sometimes a bittersweet spear of regret would stab somewhere about her heart when a neighbour's nanny would push a perambulator into the little park and sit down to converse with her.

Another child. A son. It was what Charles wanted. She hadn't fallen again yet – not that it was for want of trying, she thought grimly to herself. If Charles needed to be out of the house on an early business errand of some sort, she was spared the morning ritual, but it seemed that almost every night he could not sleep until he had satisfied himself. Even when they returned dog-tired from a dinner party or an evening at the theatre, which Rose had to admit she really enjoyed, Charles ruined her elation with his carnal demands. She felt used, like a discarded sack. She felt no other emotion but disgust and resentment as she lay in the darkness while Charles grunted and groaned on top of her. Even if he had shown her some affection, it would be too late now. He had betrayed her, and there was no going back. She could never love him. And she did not know how she could face the rest of her life with him.

One afternoon, however, they were due to attend the opening of a small art gallery for a young painter Charles had met some time ago in a West End coffee house, and whose talent Charles considered deserved a chance. Charles had agreed to pay him a grant for two years to see if he could become established, in addition to which Charles was now to finance the premises and its grand opening. It looked well for Charles, of course, and Rose at least felt pleased that her husband was patronizing the arts and offering the young man a unique opportunity. The artist depicted a whole range of diverse subjects, she had been told, and she couldn't wait to see them.

She was not disappointed. Ladies and gentlemen from Charles's social circle had crowded into what was, in fact, a tastefully converted high street shop, accepting fine champagne and fancy canapés – all supplied by Harrods, of course. Rose had already become acquainted with most of the guests, either at their wedding or during her previous stay in London, and moved easily among them in her role as hostess, refined and looking demurely beautiful, so Charles had told her

approvingly before they had set out from home. She was
dressed in mourning for Alice, of course, Charles having
insisted that she visit whichever London fashion house could
make her two more outfits within twenty-four hours. Black
seemed to suit her, toning down the peachy hue of her skin,
the result of spending so much time out riding, and setting
off the graceful tilt of her head on her swanlike neck.

Charles glanced at her with a proud smile as he gave a
short speech to polite applause. Afterwards, as she was circu-
lating among the guests again, those who knew of their loss
offered their condolences, which she accepted graciously,
burying her grief with a sad smile. She was there to encourage
people to consider purchasing a painting and to spread the
word about the gallery, not to wallow in her own misery,
which might result in the embarrassment of her breaking down
in tears. It was quite a relief when most of the visitors eventually departed and Rose was able to turn her attention fully
to the canvases on the walls.

'Do you like that one, Mrs Chadwick?'

''Tis beautiful,' she said ruefully, and dragged her eyes to
the thin, gaunt man with the nervously drooping shoulders
who had come up beside her. 'Where is it, Mr Tilling?'

'Oh, nowhere in particular,' he answered bashfully. 'Just a
combination of ideas in my imagination.'

Rose turned her smile on him, dazzling despite its under-
lying sadness, and unwittingly robbing him of his breath.
'Then, 'tis no wonder I don't recognize it, though it does
remind me of Dartmoor.'

'Then it's your to keep. As a thank you to your husband
for his patronage,' he added with a shy dip of his head.

'Oh, no, I couldn't possibly!' Her lavender eyes were so
soft that the poor chap wilted at the knees. 'You must agree
a fair price with my husband. Have you sold many this
afternoon?'

'Half a dozen,' he replied with enthusiasm.

'Congratulations!' she exclaimed, his face, flushed with
success, lifting her own heart. 'I'm so pleased for you! Show
me which ones. Though I must say I should find it hard to
choose, they're all so lovely and yet all so different. And yet
. . . You paint *atmosphere*, Mr Tilling. This one is so dark and
stormy, and yet that one over there, with the young woman

and the two children in the garden, is so bright and happy, I can *feel* the sun and the lovely summer's afternoon. And this one . . .'

'I . . . I should like to paint *you*, Mrs Chadwick.' His voice was low, apprehensive, as he stood behind her, his bowed head just above her shoulder almost as if he was whispering in her ear. 'Not a straightforward portrait, but an atmospheric painting, as you put it. You are so . . . if you will allow me to say so . . . so beautiful, and . . . I have been observing you all afternoon, and I should love to capture your sadness, if you would permit me.'

Rose's heart seemed to flutter in her breast and a faint colour tinted her cheeks. 'If you are to paint me, Mr Tilling, I should prefer a happier portrait, if you please, not one that would always remind me of my bereavement.'

She had said it not unkindly, and the young artist dipped his head. 'Oh, but of course, Mrs Chadwick. I do understand.'

'And also, I'm afraid that we are returning to Dartmoor in a few days' time, but perhaps we could arrange something for another time, if my husband agrees.'

'I should be honoured.' And covertly seeking her finely gloved hand, he brought it to his lips.

Across the room, Charles's attention was distracted as he spoke with an elderly gentleman of his acquaintance, and for just a few seconds, he lost the thread of the conversation before recovering himself with a jerk of his head, but the gentleman made no attempt to hide his smile.

'She's a lovely woman, your young wife, Charles. I'm allowed to say such things at my age. But if you insist on showing her off, you must accept that she will gather admirers. You're a lucky devil, you know!'

'Yes, I know.'

But the words were grated between his teeth, and he strode briskly over to where Rose and Mr Tilling were discussing another of his creations. Seeing him approach, Rose twisted her head to look at him with an open smile.

'Charles, Mr Tilling would like to paint me,' she announced innocently. 'What do you think of that?'

Charles's face appeared to close up like a clam. 'And have every Tom, Dick and Harry gawping at you?' he hissed, taking her arm none too gently.

'No! 'Twould be for ourselves, no one else,' she protested. 'I thought as you'd be pleased.'

'Well, I'm not! And is this how you repay my generosity, by making advances towards my wife?'

'I do apologize, Mr Chadwick,' the startled artist stuttered. 'I meant no offence.'

'Oh, no, I'm sure you didn't,' Charles sneered. 'And keep your grubby little paws to yourself, or you'll be looking for another patron. Now, madam.' This turning to Rose with a snarl. 'You will keep to my side from now on.'

Mr Tilling's jaw swung agape and speechless as Charles drew Rose's hand on to his arm and held it there in a grip of iron, despite her efforts to release it. A white, angry line formed around her compressed lips, her eyes snapping violet with outrage as he all but dragged her into the middle of the floor.

'Ladies and gentlemen, I must thank you all once again for coming, but my wife is feeling unwell and so I'm sure you will understand if we leave you to enjoy the remainder of the afternoon without us. Do feel free to discuss any purchases with Mr Tilling.'

A murmur of disquiet passed amongst the remaining guests, and in an instant, Charles had thrown Rose's cloak about her shoulders and was whisking her out into the street where a cab seemed to be waiting for them. Rose was bundled inside before she had a chance to open her mouth, and Charles sat down so close to her, she was squashed into the corner as if he were trying to imprison her.

'How dare you behave like a trollop in front of my friends and colleagues!' he raged at her, his face a fearsome puce.

Rose was flabbergasted, but in her anguish she had no room for fear and she pursed her lips into a knot of disgust. 'You were the one making a spectacle of yourself! I were simply being nice to everyone, just like you said. And if you choose to read anything into it, then you've only got your own jealous little mind to blame!'

Her head rocked on her neck with the force of his hand across her cheek. Her spine stiffened, her brain scarcely registering the stinging pain as she turned boldly back to him and allowed her eyes to travel over him with caustic disdain. 'Very gentlemanly, I'm sure,' she said acidly but with utter calm.

Charles's face sagged beneath her haughty gaze. 'I'm sorry, Rose, but it's just that I love you so much!'

'And hitting me is your way of showing it?'

She shifted in the seat, turning her back on him and gazing out of the window in severe silence for the entire journey home through the London streets. Tears stung her eyes, but what was the point in crying? As if their relationship wasn't bad enough already, Charles had hit her, and there was no way she was going to allow him to offer her comfort. He had gone too far and she hated him more than ever. Dear Lord, she thought, would there ever be a way out?

Sixteen

'Look out, you numbskull!'

The warder's cry jerked the prisoner in the escapee uniform from his reverie and, high up on the scaffolding, he turned to guide in the next massive granite block suspended from the crane and settle it in the bed of mortar. The warder rolled his eyes. Did the fellow want to be knocked off his perch and fall to his death? He was just another felon, but he was a good, strong worker, never risking punishment for uttering a belligerent word, and it would be hard to replace him. It surprised the warder that he had ever tried to escape, but when a man was ground down by the Silent Rule, the gruelling toil, the poor diet, cold and discomfort, you never could tell.

He didn't notice, though, that as soon as the task was done, the convict glanced back over towards the road, taking advantage of his panoramic viewpoint. He hadn't been daydreaming, but *watching*. He squinted into the distance, but even his keen eyesight couldn't be sure. Was it her? He was convinced it was a woman riding astride, so it had to be. Surely no one else . . .? But perhaps it was just wishful thinking. And the horse was a superb creature – at least it looked it from where he was standing – but it was the colour of ripe corn, not as black as night like Gospel had been.

Seth Warrington shook his head with a despondent sigh; the moment of elation was gone. He must be mistaken. What did it matter, anyway? He was condemned to another decade in this hellhole – not that he expected to survive that long. The desire to shuffle off this mortal coil had subsided but little since the torturing time he had spent in the bone shed. He had recovered slowly through the summer, toiling in the workshops until he had been passed fit enough to work on the building site. He hadn't minded too much at first. He enjoyed physical activity and had regained his muscled strength; he had a good head for heights and the views over Dartmoor were magnificent. But day after day, the long hours were killing. Every muscle ached, his shoulders in particular screaming at the constant strain of hauling in the weighty stones. But there was no respite. Eight hours of unremitting labour six days a week, and then a length of tarry oakum to unpick, cutting into the fingertips, before falling into the hard plank bed with its thin straw mattress. He would wake from a fitful, uncomfortable sleep more exhausted than he had gone to bed, only to have to face the same punishing regime all over again.

And now the winter was coming on fast. November was upon them, icy winds already blasting through the inadequate uniforms that were constantly drenched from the driving rain. Hung up to dry in a cold, damp, unheated cell while the occupant shivered his way through the night, the trousers and jackets were little better by morning. Up on the scaffolding was the most exposed place of all, and Seth had begun to cough. He could feel the wheezing inflammation rumbling in his lungs, the pain in his chest. God knew he couldn't go through that again. That he had survived before had been a miracle. He wasn't fool enough to believe he would pull through for a third time. Not that he cared, except that it would be an agonizing way to go. He just cursed himself for not having the courage to throw himself over the edge to the ground below.

He thought of her constantly. The vision of her beautiful, sensitive, caring face filled his head at every minute, giving him the strength to endure. He had never known anyone like her and yet, even had he not been shackled to his penal servitude, she could never have been his. She had her own cross to bear. He wanted to protect her, to lay down his life for her, and the anger of his helplessness ripped through his heart more deeply than the stiffened ends of the cat had scored his back.

He recalled the morning she had come into the stable with the news that her husband would be returning from London the following day. She was so miserable, and her anguish seared into his own heart. She was so unhappy in her marriage, but he had tried to encourage her until she had broken down in tears and he . . .

Oh, dear God, it had been the cruellest, most crucifying moment of his life. He had held her in his arms, feeling against him the mound of another man's child in her belly, comforting her, stroking her back, breathing in the sweet scent of her hair. Jesus Christ, if she could have seen inside him, seen the instant when he had almost lost control, his eyes screwed in torment as he fought to maintain his air of calm, of reassurance. She mustn't, *mustn't* know. And so he had forced himself to go on, talking to her, soothing her. At last, she had gazed up at him through her drying tears and he had thumbed them away. Smiling, while his own soul splintered.

What had happened to her? He knew from Dr Power that she had not been in trouble with the authorities, but had the husband she resented so much punished her for her involvement with an escaped convict? He prayed God not, and that the lie he had dreamt up as he lay writhing in agony at the sergeant's feet had prevented it. And yet she had still tried to help him. Quite what she had done, he didn't understand, but he had only received eleven of the thirty-six lashes that were supposed to have shredded the flesh on his back. The doctor had whispered something about her in his ear, and was it because of her that Principal Warder Cartwright had rescued him from the torment of the bone shed? He had tried to ask if she was all right, if she had come through the ordeal of childbirth safely, but Cartwright was his jailer, after all, and conversation was forbidden.

He should forget her, drive her out of his mind, but he couldn't. Thinking of her helped ease the cold, the hunger. The pain of an empty stomach gnawed at him constantly. He was tall, put to relentless labour and so needed sustenance, yet when the meagre portions of food arrived, it was so unpalatable that he could scarcely force it down. With dry bread and watery gruel for breakfast, five days a week dinner consisted of a pint of greasy soup with a few ounces of grizzly meat floating on the surface. Today, because it was Tuesday, a slab of suet pudding was all that would grace his plate. It always made him feel sick.

He yearned more than anything for vegetables. He knew from his army days how important they were for good health.

A shudder ran through him every time his gums bled. Scurvy. He had a horror of losing his teeth, had nightmares about it. And the slightest knock caused a painful bruise. It was half the cause of the nausea, the exhaustion. And yet he wasn't alone. All eight hundred or so inmates simply had to soldier on. Only if the symptoms became pronounced would a visit to the MO be allowed. If they were lucky, it would lead to a few days in the hospital on the superior invalid diet, and then back to square one.

How would he drag himself through another day, another week, another year? Ten years. All he had to look forward to was the highlight of the day, a pint of cocoa and another chunk of dry bread for supper. Good God. He really might as well be dead.

'You, there! Your real name Collingwood?'

Seth blinked his eyes. Collingwood. He almost laughed with derision. No, his real name wasn't Collingwood at all! Perhaps he should have kept to Warrington. You had a number in the prison, not a name, so to hear it was startling. Unnerving.

He glanced distrustfully at the warder who had just been joined by another evidently bearing a message. He nodded slowly, not wanting to open his mouth and be punished for talking. Christ, he'd had enough of being punished. What the hell did they want with him now?

'Come wi' me. Governor wants to see you.'

Oh, no. For a moment, his head swam with fear and he nearly lost his balance. It was only the felon he was working with grasping his arm that stopped him. A tide of sweat flushed through his body, and he jabbed his head in thanks. Although thanks for preventing him from falling off the scaffold was hardly deep.

His head cleared as he followed the messenger down the series of ladders to the ground, his heart crashing against his ribs. Whatever it was, he simply couldn't face it. Perhaps, after all, they had decided to send him to the Assizes to be tried for his escape and have another five years added to his sentence. If that was the case, there would be no question in his mind. Razor blades were counted in and out, but one quick, deep slash on the wrist, lengthways to open the artery, and Dr Power's skills would be hard put to save him.

The governor's office. He was almost on his knees from

terror. The governor, another ex-army captain, new the previous year and not known for his compassion. Same rank as himself. God, if only they'd known. Two other strangers, one tall, broad-shouldered, distinguished. About forty. Steady, level eyes. The other small, wizened. Hooked nose in an acerbic, beady-eyed face. Seth gulped hard. This was it.

'Collingwood, this is Captain Bradley and this is Barrister-at-law Salford. They want to re-examine your case, although heaven only knows why.'

Adam Bradley sprang forward as the convict dissolved on the floor in a dead faint.

Rose and Charles returned from London, the atmosphere between them in the private compartment so tense it could have been cut with a knife. The bruise on Rose's cheek was coming out, and she knew Florrie would question her about it. She had tripped over and knocked her face on the table, was what she would say. After all, precisely that had happened once before. Charles had raised his hand and she had slipped as she ducked away to avoid it. But this time he really had hit her, and in private, she would tell Florrie the truth.

As Rose resumed her campaign, it became easier to deceive Charles, the remorse she had felt at first fading to nothing. She did her duty as a wife, bearing it with acid resentment, and pleased each time she discovered she wasn't pregnant. She didn't want to replace Alice. Not yet, at least. And not ever really with Charles.

In the meantime, she complied sweetly with all his requests while her contempt fermented deep inside. At his request, she held a dinner party at Fencott Place for Mr and Mrs Frean and the Duchy's agent from Prince Hall. It was an opportunity to enquire about any sightings of Gospel. She spun the same story as before in case Charles overheard, but no one had seen the black beast that was part of her soul.

She accompanied Charles in the new Brougham when he checked on the powder mills, taking the opportunity to fit in an extra visit to Molly, who was growing larger and larger with her pregnancy. Rose also went with Charles when he decided to pay a visit to Foggintor and the other quarries on Walkhampton Common to satisfy himself they were not about to change over to the use of dynamite. Overall, Charles felt pleased that Rose was at last settling down to being a proper wife, and in return, he tolerated her lone rides across the moor. She always returned on time, and made no objection if he decided to accompany her.

But it was all a ruse so that she could spend time in the healing ambience at Rosebank Hall. Elizabeth always welcomed her with open arms, and Chantal – and even baby Hannah – came to look upon her as a beloved aunt. She observed with growing interest as Elizabeth taught Chantal the art of healing with herbs, and chatted with Dr William Greenwood, who was also the mine surgeon for Wheal Friendship, and was a good friend and frequent visitor to the Pencarrows.

'Oh, look who's here!' Elizabeth greeted her one cold and frosty early-November day. 'I'm so glad you've come!'

'And it'll save me writing you a long letter!' Adam Bradley said with his usual strong, dependable smile.

'How good to see you!' Rebecca chimed in, looking as radiant as ever.

'And you, too!' Rose returned her broad smile. 'I didn't realize you were here.'

'Well,' Adam explained, 'the criminal barrister I've engaged unexpectedly had a few days free and he wanted to come down and interview his client in person.'

'Oh.' Rose could feel the blood suddenly circling nervously about her heart. 'How . . . how was he?'

'Not too bad, considering. Perhaps you'd better sit down.' He waited while she did so and Elizabeth poured her a cup of cocoa from the pot on the table. Adam considered for a second or two, deciding it was best not to tell her that, not being in the rudest of health, Collingwood had passed out from sheer shock, and that he was developing a worrying cough again. 'We went over every detail of the case with him,' he went on instead, 'and he stuck to exactly the same story. The governor was present, though, so we didn't mention anything about the army or his real name. Best not bring that in unless we have to.' He saw Rose glance anxiously across at Elizabeth and nodded his head. 'I'm afraid I felt I must be totally honest with Mr Salford, and also with Richard and Beth.'

'Don't worry. The secret's safe with us,' Elizabeth assured her.

'I have, though – and with not a little persuasion and without revealing the reason why – managed to verify the army record of Captain Seth Warrington, and all is exactly as he said, which has confirmed my belief in his claims of innocence.'

'There, I knew it! I knew he was telling the truth!'

'Well, we've also made some progress on the main front. I managed to find the witness who had seen Seth with the victim and assumed he was robbing him. He's agreed to repeat what he said before, that he didn't witness the actual attack, and that he may have jumped to the wrong conclusion. Tracking down the elderly couple who *did* see the real assailant commit the crime and then make his escape, now that's taken a great deal longer. You can imagine why they didn't want to be involved in the first place. They were alone in the street and frightened for their own safety. But they were appalled when they learnt what had happened and are willing to testify in court.'

'Oh, that's tremendous news, isn't it?' Rose cried.

'Well, it is, but unfortunately Mr Salford isn't entirely convinced it's sufficient, but it's a good start. But we're not giving up yet, I assure you. Now, are you able to stay a little while and have some lunch with us?'

'If 'tis all right with Beth, I'd love to. But I'm afraid I must leave shortly afterwards. It gets dark so early and 'tis a fair way to go. And, well, I think this had better be the last time I come, with the days getting so short.'

'Oh, what a pity!' Elizabeth said glumly. 'I'll really miss your visits.'

'Not as much as I will.'

Rose sighed deeply. The farm really had acted as a salve for her bleeding heart, and she always basked in the glow of its peace and serenity. Not that it had always been so. She had learnt once before of the appalling situation Richard and Elizabeth had once faced, though she instinctively felt there existed some secret that neither of them would reveal. But she considered them her close friends and they had always shown her such kindness. Elizabeth had also revealed to her Adam and Rebecca's own tragic tale and of how Adam had lost his hand. Perhaps it was why these good people understood Rose's own anguish now and were doing their utmost to help.

It was as if her visits to Rosebank Hall had maintained her sanity, and she didn't know how she was going to survive without them. She wept openly as she allowed Honey to trot home at a leisurely pace. By the time they reached the prison, her tears had dried. The light was going from the sky and the convicts had already finished their labours for the day. Rose willed the encouraging information Adam had given her through the walls to wherever Seth was sitting in his solitary cell. But her own heart was dragging. She was dreading the long, dark winter, incarcerated with Charles at Fencott Place. She would suffocate, imagining her resentment growing to breaking point. How on earth would she survive through to the spring?

But when she thought of Seth and how he must be suffering, she felt shot through with guilt.

Seventeen

'Happy Christmas, Molly!'
Molly looked up and a surprised grin spread across her face as Rose's head appeared around the door to the little cottage.

'You, too, Rose! 'Tis good to see you!'

'No, don't get up!' Rose cried as her friend went to heave herself from the sagging armchair. 'You stay there with your feet up. Not long to go now, eh?'

'A week or so I reckons.' Molly shifted awkwardly. 'I'll be that glad. I feels like a mountain, and my back aches that much! Oh, Rose, you'm soaking wet. You shouldn't have come in this.'

'Well, I had to come and wish you a Happy Christmas. And I've got some things for the baby that Florrie knitted, and a matinee jacket that I embroidered for you. At least that were something Charles approved of my doing.' She paused, pulling a long face. 'I know 'tis pouring, but I had to get out of the house and away from him for a while. But I mustn't stay too long. I can't leave Honey standing out in the rain.'

'Oh, Rose, she *is* a horse!' Molly laughed aloud. 'They'm supposed to live outside, aren't they?'

'Maybe, but she's been bred for her colour and that could make her delicate, and she hasn't got a blanket on, of course. I couldn't bear it if she got ill. 'Twas the same . . .' She faltered for a fleeting moment and her voice cracked. ''Twas the same with Gospel. Oh, Molly, I wonder if I'll ever see him again.'

'Nobody's passed on any news about him to me, I's afeared,' Molly answered quietly. 'But a letter came for you this morning. 'Tis from Captain Bradley. I recognizes the writing. Joe were going to bring it over to you on Christmas Day as he won't get the chance afore. 'Tis over there on the table.'

Rose picked up the envelope with trembling fingers. 'Oh, God,' she mumbled under her breath as her heart began to race. Her hand went over her mouth and her vision blurred so that Adam's neat handwriting suddenly seemed more like the ghostly efforts of someone trying to knit with fog. There had been no word from him since they had met at Rosebank Hall six weeks earlier, and a deep depression had wrapped her in its strangling fold so that she was convinced the letter must contain bad news.

'Go on, then, read it,' Molly encouraged her gently.

Rose hesitantly opened the envelope and extracted the sheet of paper. For a few moments, the fear of what it might contain made the letters dance on the page, but slowly its meaning took root in her brain.

'Oh, Molly,' she managed to force from her tight throat. ''Tis Jonas Chant.'

'Who?' Molly's freckled brow frowned.

'Jonas Chant. The man Seth is supposed to have robbed. Who swore 'twas Seth who attacked him.' Her voice was low and expressionless, numb with shock, and Molly put out a hand. Rose felt its pressure, and looked up to meet her friend's enquiring gaze. 'Adam's been searching all over for him, and now suddenly he's turned up in the workhouse. 'Twas William Greenwood as found him, Richard and Beth's doctor friend. They've no medical officer at present, so William was standing in and he had to examine this new inmate. He recognized the name at once. And . . . Oh, Molly, he's dying. His liver. Drunk himself to death, William says. Won't last longer than a week, two at most. And would you believe, he's a Catholic and he's asked for the priest? And William's spoken to the priest, and he's agreed that if Chant confesses to lying about Seth, he'll try to persuade him to sign a written confession for the constable.'

She was staring at Molly, her eyes huge and blank in her white face, the pupils so wide, the blue rim of the irises had almost disappeared.

'So . . . it could be what you've been waiting for?' Molly almost whispered.

'Well, yes.' Rose's bloodless lips quivered. 'But what if . . . what if he won't confess? What if he dies, and it all goes wrong? Oh, Molly, I couldn't bear it!'

'But this doctor,' Molly quickly put in, 'you've met him, and you trust him to do what Captain Bradley says in the letter?'

'Oh, yes. And he's been Beth's friend since she was a child.'

'There you are, then. Take some encouragement. I'm sure 'twill be all right. So what else does the letter say?'

Rose took a deep breath as she turned her attention back to the paper in her hand. She scanned the lines of writing quickly, turning over to read the back of the page. 'Adam says,' she told Molly, 'that they've had another stroke of luck. A man who was drinking at the inn that night and remembers the way Chant was behaving, and the scene he caused with Seth. And he also remembers someone else who appeared to follow Chant out into the street. Someone he actually *knows* and can identify. And this chap always wore the same clothes and never had much money, but after that evening, he was never seen in those clothes again and was never short of cash—'

'So, you means, he could be the real culprit?' Molly asked excitedly. 'And he destroyed his clothes cuz they was stained with blood? And if he was caught—'

'And if the elderly couple could also identify him . . . Oh, dear Lord, I daren't even think about it! But Adam says if all this evidence can be established in the new year, he'll go up to London and he'll push and push . . . Oh, he's a good man, Adam! But he says not to get my hopes up. That a royal pardon would still be incredibly difficult, and 'tis such a complicated process . . . Oh, I just don't know what to think!'

'Well, you just keep hoping, Rosie,' Molly said forcefully, 'and we'll all keep praying an' all. And I must thank you for coming all this way with the things for the babby. Proper kind, you are, Rosie, and you deserves some luck yoursel'.'

'And is there anything else you need? You and Joe, you know you're like brother and sister to me, so you mustn't be afeared to ask. And you make sure you send for Dr Power when the baby starts and I'll foot the bill.'

'Oh, Rosie, you cas'n—'

'Oh, yes, I can! It gives me particular satisfaction to spend Charles's money where I know he wouldn't like it! But I really ought to be going. I told you 'twas just a flying visit.' She bent to kiss her dear friend on the cheek. 'Now you look after yourself, and don't forget – if there's *anything* you need! And let me know the minute there's any news!'

But despite her cheerfulness, as she rode home from the powder mills, her stomach was clenched so tightly, she felt sick, and she was scarcely aware of the deluge of rain that lashed into her face. If Seth were working outside in this, it would hardly be doing his weakened chest any good. Molly's father, Jacob Cartwright, was keeping an eye on him, it was true, but it seemed that even though the legitimacy of his imprisonment was being questioned, he was treated no differently. In fact, because of his attempted escape, he was considered to be among the scum of the convicts.

The rain, though, had softened the ground, and Rose was able to let Honey have her head. The mare responded and broke into a gallop, and although with not quite the same zest as Gospel would have shown, she was clearly enjoying herself. When they reached home, unusually Rose left Ned to see to Honey while she herself stumbled indoors on unsteady legs. Florrie. She must tell Florrie, as she could not face the crucifying suspense alone.

It seemed that Charles took her more forcefully than usual that night. He had commented that she seemed quiet and that hardly a morsel had passed her lips at dinner; that it was about time she became pregnant again, and he was damned well going to make sure of it. Christmas was but a few days away, and he was determined there would be another Chadwick – a boy this time – in the nursery by the time the Yuletide celebrations came round again. And so Rose suffered his attentions that night, and all the following nights, in silence. She tried to refuse him once, but he slapped her face so hard, her ears rang.

Christmas was the most miserable affair she could imagine. Florrie, bless her, put on a jolly face to try and cheer her up. They exchanged presents, Charles showering Rose in expensive gifts that meant nothing to her, and they had a little fir tree in the drawing room with minute candles in special holders that were lit in the evening when they could keep a close eye on the tiny naked flames. Patsy and Daisy had spent some time making paper chains to hang around the house, and Rose had attempted to get in the festive mood by decorating the fireplace with glossy, red-berried holly. Cook excelled herself with the dinner and Rose drank more wine than she should have done, which only served to deepen her depression.

She sat by the fireside in the evening, trying to read a book as Charles was doing, but her head was swimming and she couldn't concentrate. Her mind lingered instead on memories of Christmases past when her father, Florrie, Joe and herself would go to the powder mills chapel in the morning, joyously greeting all the workers, and return to open presents and help Florrie prepare the meal and the table. Later they would play games, laughing uproariously, and only towards bedtime would a contented quiet begin to fall upon them. Now she sat in tense silence opposite her husband. This time last year, her grief over the recent loss of her dear father was still so raw, but she had realized on Christmas Day that she was pregnant and that had given her hope. Now, that little child was dead, Charles had sold her beloved Gospel, her marriage was disintegrating around her, and the man she had met who, God forgive her, meant more to her than her husband ever had, was suffering a cruel and unjustified imprisonment.

Charles suddenly glanced up and snapped shut his book. 'Well, my dear, I believe that is the Yuletide over for another year.' He picked up the candle-snuffer and began to extinguish the lights on the tree. 'And I believe we could end the day as we started it.'

He held out his hand, his eyes gleaming, and Rose's heart plummeted.

'Telegram for you, ma'am.'

Rose jerked with shock, her thoughts spinning. But it wouldn't be anything to do with Seth, would it? Adam wouldn't send a telegram direct to her at Fencott Place. But who else would want to contact her so urgently?

She ripped it open. Oh! She snatched in a breath of jubilation. A little girl. The day before – Boxing Day – Molly had been delivered safely of a little girl and mother and baby were doing well.

Rose was swept up on a tide of elation. Oh, what joy! A huge grin split her face, her heart so brimming over with happiness that she almost went in to see Charles in his study to break the news. But no. He wouldn't care, and if he felt peeved when he finally heard that he hadn't been told, then so much the better. It would serve him right.

Florrie had gone down with a nasty cold and had taken to her bed. Rose ran up the stairs to her room in the attic to deliver the glad tidings. Then she pulled on her riding habit, hurried out to the stables to order Ned to tack up Honey and, while he was doing so, she raided the pantry, bundling up two meat pies, some oranges and some dried figs and almost all of a batch of biscuits Cook had just baked for the master's morning coffee. All of which she managed to cram into the saddlebag.

A ferocious wind was hurtling across the moor, but the heavy rain of a few days earlier had at last ceased. Ha, ha! She had gone out without telling Charles where! It was a challenge, a triumph, and only Molly's good news could have given her the strength to do it.

Her euphoria seemed to have washed away all her morose thoughts, and hope blossomed in her heart. A safe delivery was never guaranteed, despite the skills of such dedicated physicians as Dr Power, and the birth of this new life had refreshed her spirit. Honey sensed her excitement and was frisky and straining on the bit, eager to stretch her muscles, and Rose let her go, streaking along the softer earth at the side of the track. Even so, Gospel would have outrun her, but Rose refused to let her pent-up resentment mar the day.

She arrived breathless from the exhilaration of the ride, but knocked gently on the front door in case Molly or the baby were asleep. She needn't have worried. Mrs Cartwright let her in, her face beaming with pride at the birth of her first grandchild.

'Molly's just feeding 'er!' she announced brightly. 'You go on up.'

'And they're well?'

'In fine fettle, my dear, thank you. I 'opes you didn't mind us sending a telegraph from Princetown. Saved us time, you sees.'

'Of course not! Oh, would you like to unpack these while I go up? Just a few things I thought would help.'

'Oh, 'tis very kind on you, Miss Rose.'

But Rose didn't hear as she shinned up the steep stairs. 'Molly! Molly, 'tis only me!' she called.

'Oh, Rose! Come on in!'

Rose stole reverently into the spartan room. Molly was sat up in the bed, her face serene and angelic, almost translucent in her enchantment as she gazed down at the tiny fragment of life sucking steadily at her breast. Rose caught her breath. She looked like a Madonna, she was so calm and fulfilled, her own pale ginger hair falling forward over the fair down on the baby's head. What else could it be, with Joe's thatch of straw-coloured curls? And eyes? They had to be cornflower blue or Molly's soft emerald, or an interesting mix of the two.

'Oh, she's beautiful!' Rose whispered.

'Isn't she?' Molly's face was intense with emotion. 'You can hold her when she's finished feeding. She can get to know her favourite aunt.'

Rose laughed softly but then she asked anxiously, 'And you're all right?'

''Tweren't exactly like shelling a pea, but I's fine. Dr Power were wonderful.'

'Yes. He's a good man. And a good doctor. Oh, isn't she gorgeous?'

They stared down together at the infant, so tiny and innocent, their heads together in rapt wonder as the rosebud mouth worked instinctively, the soft gullet swallowing the life-giving sustenance from its mother. Rose felt the constriction in her throat and had to turn away.

'Here,' she said, reaching into her purse. 'Put this away for her.'

'Rose, I cas'n—'

'Of course you can.' She placed two silver half crowns on the table. 'And now, look, she's finished, so it's my turn to hold her.'

Molly handed her over with a soft smile and Rose held the baby in practised arms, gently rubbing her back. So vulnerable, so helpless, and yet worth the moon and the stars. The milky fragrance of a newborn child. *Oh, Alice . . .*

'We'd like,' Molly began hesitantly, 'with your permission, we'd like to call her Henrietta. After your father. He were so good to Joe, and I were very fond of 'en, too.'

Rose's body became stilled as pride, peace and sorrow settled in her heart. 'Yes. He'd have liked that. And 'tis a lovely name.'

'Thank you, Rose. Rose . . .' Molly's words were low, sacred. 'Does . . . does she . . .?'

Rose nodded, choked as two fat tears rolled down her cheeks. 'We've always been the best of friends, Molly.' She scraped the sounds from her throat. 'You . . . you be happy enough for both of us.'

And her heart broke at the compassion on Molly's face.

Eighteen

January passed, the moor hidden beneath a blanket of snow. Rose tried not to hope, and as the weeks dragged by, she began to despair that, despite all of Adam's efforts, the pardon was going to prove impossible, even with the testimonies of the new witnesses and particularly Chant's confession, by which they had all set so much store. The man it was now believed was the real villain must have somehow learnt of his impending arrest and had evaded capture, a sure sign of his guilt. And yet still Seth was subjected to the horrors of imprisonment.

Rose visited Molly and little Henrietta twice a week. Charles had protested when she had announced her intention to do so, but she had put her foot down and he had conceded. He might disapprove but he supposed it could do no harm. And it was *charitable*, after all.

'A letter for you, Rose,' Molly told her as soon as she arrived one morning towards the end of February. 'And from the writing, 'tis not from Captain Bradley.'

'Oh?' Rose peeled off her gloves and, placing them on the table, unwound the scarf from her neck. Her heart gave a little bound, but her expectancy had been dampened so often that she had taught herself not to get excited. 'And how are you today, Moll?'

The younger girl's shoulders lifted and then fell in an amused sigh. 'Worn out!' she grinned. 'Henrietta woke up again in the middle of the night, just when she'd started sleeping through. However my mother brought so many of us into the world, I doesn't know! Joe's very good, but he cas'n feed her, and he has to be up early for work, of course.'

Rose gave a sympathetic smile. 'Yes, I was lucky with Alice,' she said, ignoring the spasm of pain at the thought of her own child. 'I had Florrie *and* a wet nurse to see to her at night. I see Henrietta's asleep now, though,' she whispered, bending over the little crib.

'Yes, the little tyke. So I'll make some tea while you read your letter.'

'That'd be nice. Thank you.'

She picked up the envelope from the table and opened it leisurely. It was written in a big hand, as if by someone who wasn't used to a great deal of correspondence. Rose raised her eyebrows. ''Tis from the South Devon Foxhounds at Widecombe,' she told Molly. 'They never replied to my original letter so I suppose . . . Oh! Oh, Molly!' She snatched in her breath, a thrill of joy rippling through her body. 'Listen to this! "You are enquiring after a black thoroughbred cross of a difficult temperament. One of our hunt members bought such a horse in Bovey soon after Christmas from someone who was finding him too difficult to handle. He is still being difficult and the owner has asked if you would like to see if it is the horse you are looking for. He is strong and very fast. If it is him, the owner is willing to sell him back. The address is in Ponsworthy." Oh, Molly, you don't think it could be Gospel, do you?'

Her heart was bouncing about in her chest like a rubber ball as she stared, open-mouthed, at Molly. The young mother's face flushed, her eyes wide and shining.

'There be only one way to find out!' she gasped, and danced Rose around in a circle.

I was awake early and it looked such a lovely morning that I've decided to go on a long ride over Dartmeet way. I'll be away some time so don't worry about me. Love, Rose.

She placed the note she had secretly written the night before on the bedside table next to Charles's softly snoring figure and crept into the dressing room, closing the door silently behind her. It was still dark and she had to light the lamp to see to put on her riding habit. Then she extinguished it to steal back into the bedroom and out on to the landing. She held her breath, turning to stone as Charles stirred, but he merely turned over and settled down again.

Rose padded her way down the stairs in her stockinged

feet, knowing her riding boots, polished by Ned, would be waiting in the boot room by the back door. Patsy and Daisy were already up, setting the day in motion in the kitchen. Rose put a finger to her lips at their surprised faces.

'I'm going for a ride,' she whispered. 'I don't want to wake the master.'

'There's tea in the pot, so you have a cup to warm you before you goes out in this snipey weather, ma'am,' Daisy suggested.

'Yes, I will. And I'd like to take a couple of rolls with me.'

'Today's bread won't be ready, ma'am, but yesterday's rolls are still quite fresh.'

'That'll do nicely, thank you.'

Within five minutes, she was outside in a pinching, frosty morning. Dawn was just breaking and it was just light enough to see her way into the tack room to collect Honey's saddle and bridle and then into the docile animal's loose box. There was no sign of Ned, thank goodness, as she wouldn't put it past him to go and wake Charles, master or not, and tell him of her escapade. After all, he had sneaked off to the prison to inform them that the escaped convict was hiding in the stable yard, hadn't he?

Honey seemed pleased to see her and with a small feed, she was ready to be saddled. After all, the ground was rock hard with the heavy frost and they would only be going at walking pace. Besides, it was so early and promised to be such a beautiful sunrise that Rose wanted to enjoy the utter peace and tranquillity to the full. Honey's hooves on the yard cobbles didn't appear to disturb Ned and they were soon off and away over the moor.

They followed the road out past the little settlement at the Whiteworks tin mine and set out along the ancient track above the River Swincombe. They were travelling eastwards and the sun was just rising in front of them, a pale disc in a clear, colourless sky. The white, frost-encrusted grass crunched beneath Honey's hooves, and the mare breathed clouds of wreathing vapour into the glacial air with each gentle nod of her head as she walked steadily forward. They appeared to be the only moving creatures in the entire frozen landscape. Even the occasional group of hardy sheep or ponies stood huddled together and motionless. Rose's face stung with cold and she could smell it in her nostrils, but it was invigorating, filling her with buoyant optimism. Could the horse possibly be Gospel? Would she have enough money to buy him back? If need be, she would swap him for Honey, although she would be reluctant to lose the lovely animal that had brought her so much consolation. But God willing, she would be riding Gospel home and leading the gorgeous palomino alongside.

The sun was beginning its journey heavenwards, taking on a peach glow that it painted across the sky in streaks of coral. The amber light reflected on the pearly wastes of the moor, twinkling on the silvery hoar frost and the dancing waters of the river below. The air was bitingly cold but so still, and Rose could have believed that she and Honey were the only living things in the world.

They came to the lonely crossroads on the moorland track and turned right to cross the river by the ford and follow to the delightful hamlet of Hexworthy and the first signs of human life there. Over the bridge across the West Dart where they stopped for a few minutes for Honey to take a short drink from the river at the natural beach, then along past the tiny wayside mission chapel of St Raphael's before turning up across the fields and down to Dartmeet. They kept to the main road after that, Honey taking the steep hill slowly and steadily and eventually turning left to the little village of Ponsworthy. Rose reckoned it must be eight miles in all, not quite as far as Peter Tavy in the opposite direction but still quite a way, and she would have to allow Honey a good rest before they set off home.

It was mid morning when she found the address she had been given and, after tethering Honey to a tree, she rang the front door bell, her heart jangling with delirious anticipation. She could hardly contain herself, her mind flying to the stars at the thought that Gospel might be just yards away from her. Oh, come on, come *on*!

At last the door was opened and when she explained who she was, the maid went to fetch her master, who was glad to see Rose, and led her at once around the back of the house to some stables. Rose's head was ready to explode with joy. Oh, please, *please* let it be Gospel! Her heart vaulted into her throat as a great black head appeared over a loose box door. She knew at once.

The hope shrivelled and died inside her, dashed to smithereens. But perhaps she was mistaken. Refusing to believe what she knew to be true, she opened the door and went inside. Just in case. Willing it to be him. But she knew it wasn't. Yes, he was so similar, but it simply wasn't him.

Tears raked her throat as she came back out, shaking her head.

'Oh, I'm so sorry, my dear,' the gentleman said with sympathy. 'The one you're looking for obviously means a lot to you.'

'Yes, he does,' she croaked. 'And I really thought . . .'

Her voice drifted away in a thin trail and the man nodded. 'You must be frozen. Put your own horse in the next box and then come inside for some refreshment.'

She spent an hour inside by a roaring fire consuming hot chocolate and oatmeal biscuits and talking to the man and his wife. They were both so kind that she found it hard not to cry, and they promised to let her know if they ever came across any other horse that could be Gospel.

'I'm sorry for my own sake, too. Even I find that fellow hard to handle. I'll have to sell him on at the next sale, but I'll keep my eyes open for you as well.'

Rose thanked them sincerely for their hospitality and rode home, struggling to hold her shattered soul together. Tears froze on her cheeks as grief seeped into every nook and cranny of her being. Oh, what a fool she had been ever to have thought that she could find Gospel again. It seemed that Fate wanted to destroy her life in every way, taking from her everyone and everything she held so dear. At least she still had Florrie and Molly, Honey and the dogs, she tried to tell herself. But it was no good, and as she neared home and the ugly scene she knew would take place between herself and Charles, resentment brewed up inside her.

She was so lost in her misery that at first she didn't noticed the figure on the bright chestnut horse as Honey carefully took the steep incline back down to Dartmeet. It was only as they approached the bridge that she realized it was Charles waiting for her on Tansy, and her aching heart began to patter nervously in her breast.

'Charles, what are you doing here?' she asked tonelessly as she drew level with him.

'Thank God I've found you, Rose!'

'Why? Is something amiss?'

'Only that I was so worried when you weren't home by lunch time that I came to look for you.'

His voice was dry, his lips tight as if he was controlling his temper. Rose had expected a violent tirade, so she decided she should try to avoid a bitter confrontation if at all possible.

'Oh, I'm sorry, Charles. But 'twas so beautiful out on the moor that I hadn't realized how long I'd been and I forgot to take the little pocket watch you gave me. Did you come along the road?'

Charles seemed a little taken aback by her deferential attitude and nodded in reply. 'Yes, of course.'

'Well, let me take you the back way.' She smiled blithely. ''Tis so much nicer and much shorter. Come on. Let's enjoy the ride together.'

She led the way, and Charles appeared to gain a better humour as he was able to bring Tansy alongside her. Rose felt she was treading on eggshells, but the intermittent conversation that passed between them was quite civil and by the time they reached Fencott Place, she felt the danger was over. Charles said no more about her escapade, but she decided she must be more cautious in future. But *what* future? Though it was tearing her heart into tatters, she was beginning to accept that, despite all her enquiries, she would never see Gospel again. Could she possibly put it behind her, her grief over the animal and her resentment towards Charles for selling him? It was a question she couldn't answer. But she was going to have to take a hold on her emotions if her life was going to be worth living.

Charles followed her up to the bedroom that night and sat on the edge of the bed, unlacing his shoes. Rose was removing her necklace at the dressing table and glanced across at Charles through narrowed eyes. She would have to make the best of her life with him. That was what Seth had said to her, wasn't it? And with his words echoing in her head, she would make an effort.

'Charles?' she said quietly.

He looked up casually. 'Yes, my dear?'

'I was just wondering – how is Mr Tilling and the gallery? Is he doing well?'

Charles shrugged his shoulders as he swapped over his feet. 'I've no idea.'

'Really? Oh, then I shall write to him and enquire.'

'You will do no such thing!'

The voice was a sudden, angry snarl and Rose whipped her head round, her eyes startled. 'Why?' she stammered. 'I don't understand.'

The muscles around Charles's mouth were taut. 'I have nothing more to do with Mr Tilling now, since I withdrew my patronage.'

'What?' Rose's heart thumped in her chest as all her good intentions dried to dust. 'What do you mean?'

'Well, what could he expect after his insult upon you?'

'Insult? He simply wanted—'

'Rose! I cannot have my wife posing for some lecherous young artist! I could see the look in his eye—'

'And you read something into it that wasn't there!' Rose fumed, her eyes snapping at him. 'He was polite and respectful and—'

'Oh, yes, my innocent, trusting girl!' he sneered. 'Just as I supposed that damned convict—'

'How *dare* you!' she screeched back, rising to the bait. 'There were nothing like that between us, any more than there was between Mr Tilling and me! What sort of person do you think I am, Charles? I'm totally faithful to you, so why do you doubt me? Why do you want to *possess* me like . . . like . . .?'

A slow smirk spread across Charles's face. 'Oh, I do love you when you're angry. And if you're so faithful, why don't you prove it to me?'

She frowned as she went to step into the dressing room. 'What do you mean?'

He grasped her arm, pulling her back into the room. 'Don't get changed in there. Take your clothes off here. Slowly. In front of the fire. I'll stoke it up so you won't be cold.'

Rose swallowed hard, almost choking. Charles usually took her quickly in bed, getting at her in whatever way he could. It was bad enough, but he obviously wanted more than that tonight. Her punishment for her lone ride. Her mouth thinned to a fine line as fury and revulsion swamped her mind in a savage wave but then ebbed away on a tortured breath. What was the point in resisting? Charles believed he *owned* her. And it would never be any different.

She undressed, reluctantly, bitterly, her fingers shaking on the buttons and ribbons, shivering, her stomach sickened. She stood before him, naked and trembling, while he looked her up and down, licking his lips as he pulled off his trousers without taking his eyes from her slender body.

'Lie down,' he ordered.

Her soul died inside her. She knew from experience it would be worse if she resisted. He sprang down on top of her, pinning her arms out to the sides so that she couldn't move, and proceeded to bite and suck at her breasts until they were marked and bruised. Then he jammed himself into her, cursing as she cried out in pain, drooling and with sweat dripping from his face as he brutally thrust again and again.

'There,' he groaned as he withdrew and let her fall back on the carpet. 'And if I ever have reason to believe you've been unfaithful, you'll have that and more every night of your life!'

Rose glared back at him, her eyes glinting with malevolence. What worse could he do to her? She must fight back, or die.

Nineteen

Rose was as good as gold. Or at least Charles believed her to be. With the coming of spring and the lengthening days, she yearned for the peace and serenity she had found at Rosebank Hall. It would have lightened her heart and she knew she would have been welcomed with open arms by Elizabeth Pencarrow and the family, but she dared not take the risk unless strictly necessary. Instead, knowing she could now get there and back in daylight had only made a black depression settle over her, not helped by the fact that there was no word from Adam. She knew only from Elizabeth's letters via Molly that he remained in London, and had abandoned his own family and his business as he pursued justice for one man. But Rose's hope had tired.

Jacob had told her that Seth had survived the winter one way or another, not exactly in the best of health, but he had never had to be readmitted to the prison infirmary either. He continued to work on the building in between spells of breaking stones to be used on local roads. Above all, he had been spared the bone shed, but Rose was beginning to be convinced that his fate was as sealed as hers.

Her only consolation was visiting Molly and watching Henrietta grow bigger and stronger, pretty as a picture and such a happy little being. But the joyful time spent with her friend and the child had a sting in its tail. Henrietta was already older than Alice was when she died, and the pain stabbed into Rose's side. And as she rode home, the prison dominated the horizon and she could only think of Seth, half starved, exhausted, and forced to work like a slave.

'Found 'en like this in his cell,' explained one of the two warders who between them were dragging the barely conscious felon into the hospital. 'Complainin' of a headache the last few days, he were, but we thought nort of it till we found 'en this morning like.'

'Get him on the bed and I'll take a look.'

'Water,' the sick man moaned, and Dr Power raised an eyebrow. That would all be pretty easy to fake, as many an inmate would to have a few days away from his gruelling labour. Eat soap, candle-wax, even pins they would! Raymond Power took the fellow's wrist. His pulse was racing. Now that was harder to fake, unless it was from fear of discovery. But his skin was hot and dry, and a dusky flush was spreading over his cheeks. The medical officer frowned as he undid the filthy jacket and shirt, turning his head slightly at the stench. The past May week had been unseasonably warm and this chap who had been employed in physical toil on the building works had evidently not washed himself every day. The physician's frown deepened. Lice. Crawling in the folds of the uniform. He quickly pulled up one sleeve. There it was, on the back of the wrist. The mulberry, mottling rash. And there, on the borders of the armpits. Jesus Christ.

He spun round to the two warders who were leaving the long ward. 'You idiots, it's gaol fever! Typhus. This chap must be three or four days into it. Any more like him?'

The two men exchanged glances. 'Not that us knows of.'

'Well, watch out for it. Or anyone else with lice. Spreads like wild fire. Saunders!' he called to one of his medical assistants. 'Give him some water and then get him stripped and washed and have his uniform sent to the laundry. I need to see the governor.'

A few minutes later, he was in urgent consultation with the prison governor. 'I want all uniforms and all bedding washed in chloride of lime,' he was saying in an unusually dictatorial tone, 'and all cells lime-washed. The warders are to ensure personally that every inmate washes himself thoroughly each morning, and I want the bathhouse constantly in use. And anyone with the slightest symptoms is to be brought to me immediately for checking. And the warders had better look out for themselves, too, or they'll be taking it home to their families.'

The governor leaned back in his chair, lips pursed pensively and his fingers joined over his stomach. 'Hmm,' he grunted under his breath. 'Dr Power, I have nearly nine hundred men in this gaol. With the best will in the world, the laundry could take several weeks to wash all the linen and uniforms, and what are we supposed to use in the meantime? We only have a certain amount for rotation purposes, you know that. And I don't want panic setting in, or for it to become common knowledge among the inmates. Half of them would claim they had it just to get a few days off work. Before we knew it, we'd have a riot on our hands.'

Raymond Power ground his teeth in bitter frustration. 'Rather have half of them dead, would you?'

'It's a risk I'll have to take. We can have the devils whitelime their own cells, I suppose. It's done periodically anyway, of course, but I don't want it looking like something urgent. And you must remember these are convicted criminals, not children in a nursery.'

'But they were all human beings. Once,' he concluded sardonically and, slamming his fist on the table, he strode out of the room.

Seth Warrington lowered himself wearily on to the edge of the plank bed and, with his elbows on his knees, sat for ten minutes with his head in his hands. He was bone-weary, every muscle screaming at him, and his head was throbbing. He had noticed that several of the men he had been working closely with had disappeared, but he hardly cared about it. It wasn't unusual. You were moved around, associations being forbidden, as if you could form them anyway with the Silent Rule. Not that he liked the look of most of his fellow inmates. Most of them seemed uncouth devils, swearing under their breath or making obscene gestures at the warders' backs whenever they could get away with it. And all their uniforms were thick with grime and sweat, his own included. Even when you were given a so-called clean one, it was still rank with other men's odours.

It had been a long, hard, back-breaking day, the sun beating down and the forage cap hot and itchy on his shorn head. Now all he wanted was to lie down and sleep, though there was the daily length of oakum waiting to be teased into shreds. Perhaps he could allow himself the luxury of a few minutes on the thin mattress, though if he were caught, he'd be punished for it. Lying down was only allowed from 'lights out' at eight o'clock until five the next morning. Even when the literate were supposed to read for an hour in their cells, they had to sit, since they had to endure the same as those who couldn't read and write and so had to attend lessons. Usually Seth considered the hour engrossed in a book from the prison library the highlight of his day, but this evening he hadn't the energy even for that. And first there was the oakum.

He forced himself, his back aching mercilessly and his fingers bleeding as he pulled apart the tar-hardened fibres. It wasn't often that he cried, but silent tears strolled down his gaunt cheeks, blurring his vision as he worked. He simply couldn't stop them. He felt wretched and a coward, but his misery was so overwhelming that evening that he was helpless against it.

He paused in his work to scratch at his neck. He could feel a small, sore, itchy lump. He had noticed it the previous evening, but you hardly worried about such little things. How to drag yourself through the day or night, the next hour, was more important. For some inexplicable reason, he hadn't slept much the last couple of nights, despite his exhaustion. He had been too restless, and this persistent headache had been unbearable. During the day, he had been so hot and thirsty, drinking water whenever possible, even though it came from the open leat and would probably end in a griping bout of diarrhoea. He was gasping again now, his mouth like sandpaper, but he wouldn't get a drink until the lukewarm cocoa and dry bread of supper came round later on. And he suddenly yearned for a piping hot cup of tea as, amazingly, he began to shiver.

He stopped again, biting so hard on his lip that he drew blood in his attempt to stem his tears. He wiped the back of his hand across his running nose since there was no such thing as a handkerchief in Her Majesty's hotel. And as he did so, something tiny and moving caught his eye. Something crawling in the stale, malodorous blanket on his bed. He looked again, bending down close. And stared in horrified fascination at the scattered platoon of wriggling, creeping lice.

He sprang up, tearing at his uniform like someone deranged. He stripped off, throwing each putrid, infested garment on the floor. Sweet Jesus Christ, he hadn't noticed! Every morning he had always washed himself thoroughly in the bucket of cold water, even all through the winter when he'd had to break the ice on the top. To stop just this. Exactly what they had fought against in the army. Tyhpus!

Half naked, he sat down again on the bed, his hands over his mouth. Then he leapt up again. The bed was contaminated as well. He had done his best to keep clean, but he had lost the battle. He had been working in close quarters with other uncaring devils, and the lice had simply walked across from one uniform to the next.

His hand went to scratch at his neck again, and he stopped. Dear God. He'd been bitten and it was infected. No wonder he felt so rough. He threw back his head and laughed hysterically. After all he'd been through, the way he had tried to keep his spirits up since Captain Bradley's visit – not that he'd heard anything in the six or seven months since – was he to die from gaol fever now? It invariably went to the chest, and with his weakened lungs . . . Ironic, wasn't it? Oh, well, he thought, at least it would put an end to his misery.

He waited for the supper to come.

'I want to see Dr Power,' he begged. 'I feel really unwell. It's gaol fever.'

'Oh, yes? Pull the other one, you shyster!'

Raymond Power put his hands up to his head and literally pulled at his hair. They were going down like flies. Prostrate bodies lay all over the floor, writhing in delirium or deathly still. You could hardly step between them. Nearly thirty had died already. The doctor hadn't slept for nights on end himself. And now they were hauling in another one, tall, already thin as a rake. What chance did they stand, poor sods?

God Almighty, it was Collingwood. The one prisoner he had ever felt a true affinity with. And the one Rose Chadwick had some feelings for. He simply mustn't let the bugger die. For her sake.

He was already delirious, his skin searingly hot to touch, and when the physician pulled off his shirt, the rash was already covering his torso. A large, painful-looking lump had erupted on his neck – site of the original bite, no doubt – and there were sores on his mouth.

Dr Power at once tried to get some water down him, but the poor devil was confused and tried to push him away. But he must drink. And he must get mustard poultices on the inmate's chest before his lungs were attacked.

'Rose. Rose,' the prisoner muttered incoherently, and the doctor's hands balled into fists of frustration.

'Molly, what are you doing here?' Rose cried in surprise. 'And you've walked all this way carrying Henrietta! Well, I'm delighted to see you, but you must be exhausted. Here, let me take her.'

'Oh, thanks, Rose. My arms are killing me.'

Rose took the child from Molly's arms and Henrietta gave a gummy smile to the young woman she now recognized. But as she did so, Rose caught the anguished look on Molly's face and the blood left her head, sending the room spinning before her dimmed eyes. Her heart missed a beat, jerking in excruciating pain. She watched as Molly pulled a crumpled envelope from her pocket, a telegraph message, and Rose's eyes remained fixed on it, though she shook her head in denial.

'The maid said as your husband's out,' Molly whispered urgently.

Rose gulped and nodded, her throat knotted into silence and her gaze still riveted on the envelope. Molly held it out to her, but her muscles were locked in some strange paralysis. Oh, God. Dear God . . .

'I can't,' her lips mouthed, and her eyes glittered with fear.

'But, if 'twere bad news, Captain Bradley wouldn't have sent a telegram,' Molly reasoned. 'Surely he'd have waited. To see you in person. Or at least to have written to you.'

Rose took it then, and it rustled in her shaking fingers. Was Molly right? Would Adam have foreseen her dread? There was only one way to find out, and her heart thudded for several cruel, agonizing seconds.

The first few words gave her the answer. Molly watched as she cried out, crunching the paper in her hands, her head bowed as a tearing intake of breath broke into a wailing sob. Oh, no. Oh, poor, poor Rose. Molly sucked in her lips as her friend moaned and wept, and with such compassion, she prised the paper from her hands.

She began to read, and then read it again, distrusting her own skills of literacy.

'Rose!' she gasped, disbelieving.

'I know.' The tiny squeal uttered from Rose's mouth as she lifted her tear-ravaged face. 'Oh, Molly! He's . . . he's free! But he's so dreadfully ill. Oh, Moll, I can't bear it . . .'

Twenty

O h, why was Peter Tavy so far? Rose groaned in her head. She had ached to see Seth the day after Molly had brought her Adam's telegram, but when she had announced to Charles her intention of riding into Tavistock to do some shopping, he had told her curtly not to be so ridiculous as it was pelting with rain, and the sky promised it would do so all day. Reluctantly, Rose had agreed, for her heart had struggled and strained all night, but Charles's suspicions must not be aroused. She had foamed with frustration all day, and Charles had observed aloud that she seemed on edge. She had replied it was merely because the weather had turned after two weeks of warm sunshine and she was longing to be outside again.

Yes, it was well into spring, Charles had agreed. His own sap was rising and, to prove it, he took her twice that night. She wanted to lash out, but what good would it do? She mustn't anger him. And she supposed she should give him another child. But, pray God, not yet. She simply couldn't rest, couldn't think of anything else, until Seth was well again. But in his telegram Adam had warned her that he was desperately ill with gaol fever and she knew how serious that was. Though she knew if anyone could nurse him back to health, it was Elizabeth.

The next day dawned fresh and clear, and she was away early, champing at the bit and leaving an almost drooling Charles announcing that he had enjoyed the previous night so much he couldn't wait for the day to be over so that he could repeat the experience. Rose cringed and shuddered. But the day was long . . .

Her heart was thundering as she entered the farmhouse kitchen at Rosebank Hall. The wondrous aroma of dried herbs mingled with the smell of fresh baking tantalized her nostrils, the healing tranquillity that naturally exuded from Elizabeth's caring compassion wreathing about her troubled spirit. Elizabeth came towards her with that calm, reassuring smile, her velvet eyes soft with understanding.

'How . . . how is he?' Rose asked without waiting to exchange greetings, her voice choking in her constricted throat.

'You'd better sit down, my dear,' Elizabeth answered gently.

Rose's knees were buckling beneath her and she reached automatically to pull out a chair from the table and dropped into it. Oh, dear God, surely after everything, Beth wasn't about to tell her that it had been too late? That all Adam's efforts had been in vain? Oh, no. She couldn't . . .

'As soon as Adam procured the pardon, he came straight down here by train the same day,' Elizabeth explained, speaking in that steady and serene way Rose had come to know and trust. 'He arrived here late at night, too late to go to the prison, but he and Richard went there first thing the next morning. 'Twas then they discovered there'd been an outbreak of fever, and Seth was in the infirmary. But the medical officer there, Dr Power, who I believe you know, said his temperature had dropped and he was just able to travel.'

Rose's heart soared on a crest of hope. 'He's all right, then?' she cried, leaping to her feet.

Elizabeth contemplated her for an anguished moment and then bowed her head. 'Not quite,' she said slowly, and Rose felt her blood run cold as she resumed her seat. 'The doctor said 'twere just as well someone had come for him if he was going to have any chance of surviving. He might appear to be over the fever itself, but complications can so easily set in, especially with someone with a weakened chest. Fortunately, as Adam doesn't ride, they'd taken the trap, but Seth were still prostrate and they had to prop him up on the seat between them. I must warn you, Rose, he's still very, *very* sick.'

Rose sat and stared at her as a cruel pain twisted inside her. 'And . . . and will he recover?' she dared to ask.

'God willing. He seems over the worst, but sometimes the fever can flare up again and that can be fatal. And his lungs are congested and he's so terribly weak.' She paused, meeting Rose's desperate gaze. 'So, are you ready to see him? You might be in for a bit of a shock.'

Rose nodded, rising unsteadily, and followed Elizabeth up the stairs to part of the house she had never visited before.

Rather than the light and spacious landing at Fencott Place, she was met by a long, dark corridor, but she was hardly interested in the architecture of Rosebank Hall just now.

She heard Elizabeth take a deep, steady breath. 'I'm trying to build him up but he can only take very light things like beef tea and milk,' she uttered in a low voice. 'Even if he pulls through, 'tis going to be a long time afore he's on his feet. So . . . don't get your hopes up.'

Rose nodded, her shoulders dragging in dismay. 'I understand, Beth. And I'm so grateful for everything you've all done. You, Richard, Adam, all of you. You don't know what your friendship has meant to me.'

Elizabeth smiled appreciatively, and then quietly opened the door she had stopped by. She put her head round and beckoned Rose to enter, putting a finger against her lips. Rose held her breath as she shambled forward, her heart pounding. The window was slightly open, allowing the warm spring air to waft into the bedroom, and lying in the bed, propped up on a mound of pillows, was a human form.

Rose approached on tiptoe, every fibre of her being on tenterhooks, and then stood and stared at the sleeping figure. She had tried so often to conjure up a vision of him in her mind, and now here he was. Alive, and in the flesh. Except that his face was so gaunt, so skeletal, that she could barely recognize him. He sported the virtually scalped convict crop once again, but he looked so *old*, his skin ashen, his long brown eyelashes fanned out in a crescent on the dark smudges beneath his eyes. Rose could hardly bear it, and tears from the strain of all those months of waiting and praying, of lying and deceit, trickled unheeded down her cheeks.

She brushed them away with the back of her hand. 'Do you . . . do you think he'll get through it?' she whispered to Elizabeth, who had come up behind her.

But before she could answer, Seth coughed in his sleep. Rose saw his Adam's apple rise and fall as he swallowed, and then he coughed again and his eyelids flickered open, his glazed eyes wandering for a second until they focused on Rose's face. His mouth half stretched into a hint of that winsome smile, and somehow all the frustrations, all the agonies of his years of unmerited imprisonment melted away.

'Rose . . .' he croaked.

There was no need for him to say any more. Rose was
vaguely aware of Elizabeth sliding out of the room behind
her, leaving her and Seth to stare at each other in rapt disbelief. Rose battled to think of some words, but none would
come. Instead she took Seth's limp hand and looked into
the depths of his bloodshot hazel eyes, which had suddenly
come alive. And then restraint was thrown to the four winds
as she leant over the bed and gathered him in her arms,
feeling the frailty of him as he tried to hold her in response.
All the unsung pain and suffering of her marriage to Charles,
the loss of her father and baby Alice, her yearning – oh,
yes, she knew it now – to be with this man who might not
survive, brimmed over in a drowning torrent.

She held him for seconds, minutes, before she felt his body
sagging in exhaustion and she lowered him back with the
same care she had lavished on her child. Her gaze was locked
on his face, and she could see his eyes were glistening with
moisture, unaware of her own fresh tears until he managed
to lift his hand and thumb them away.

'Rose,' he repeated, his sore-covered lips moving painfully.
'I can't thank you enough.'

'Me?' she almost squeaked, her throat was so tight. 'No,
'tis Adam you must thank.'

'Believe me I have.' He coughed harshly, dry and wheezing,
and nodded towards the jug of water on the table. 'Would you
mind . . .?' he choked, coughing again.

Rose jumped up in alarm, pouring some water and holding
the feeding cup for him since she could see how weak he was.
He drank slowly as if even that was exhausting for him, but
he swallowed all of it at last and she was thankful for that,
at least. She had just replaced the cup on the table when there
was a knock on the door and Elizabeth entered the room
carrying a tray with a small glass of deep green liquid and a
medicine bottle and spoon.

'Take the decoction and then the syrup straight after,' she
instructed. 'One of my best remedies for chest infections. And
I'll bring you up your steam inhalation. In a little while,' she
added knowingly, and left them alone again.

'How long can you stay?' Seth croaked when she had closed
the door behind her.

'Not too long. I told Charles I was going to Tavistock.'

'Ah, Rose, I . . .'

He broke off, coughing again, and Rose stroked the back of her hand across his cheek. 'Hush now. There's no need to talk.'

'But . . . you've come all this way,' he spluttered.

'It doesn't matter. 'Tis just so good to be with you again.'

She pulled up a chair and just sat, holding his hand in silence, watching as his eyes closed and he drifted off again. She heard little Hannah wake up from her sleep, calling out some baby gibberish that only she understood and Elizabeth came to pick her up and take her downstairs. A little later, Richard and Chantal, who had been helping her father with the sheep, returned for their lunch and came up to see her, and Seth was roused from his sleep again.

'Feeling any better?' Richard asked in his concerned manner.

Seth nodded. 'A little, yes, thank you.' Though no one was sure he really did.

It seemed that the two men had struck up a good friendship in the few days they had known each other. Observing both men, Rose's heart lurched. With his shock of dark, lustrous hair and his face radiating with good health, Richard appeared the younger man, although he was seven years Seth's senior. Rose caught her lip as the pain struck her full in the chest. Seth should regain a more youthful appearance as he recovered – *if* he recovered – and his shorn hair grew back . . . But she must not think like that! She was a married woman, and one day, with God on his side, Seth would be well enough to leave Rosebank Hall, resume his travels and no doubt find a wife of his own.

The thought sobered her already sorely tried spirit. Through Adam, she had rescued Seth from his grim prison sentence and given him a better chance of surviving the dreaded gaol fever. But there could never be any more to it than that, and though it slashed at her heart, she must resign herself to being Charles's wife for life. She lowered her eyes, knowing she went quiet as Richard and Chantal went back downstairs.

'I was so sorry to hear about the baby,' Seth rasped, trying to suppress another cough. 'It must have been dreadful.'

She managed a wan smile. 'Yes. It was. Eight weeks old, poor little soul.' She raised her head and found him looking at her intently, his tired eyes deep pools of concern. 'Charles didn't care much for her,' she told him suddenly. 'She was a girl, and she was sickly. So perhaps 'twas for the best she died before she were old enough to understand and to suffer.'

'You . . . you don't really think that, though, do you?'

She grunted. Seth understood precisely, while Charles . . . 'No, not really. But I think if I keep telling myself that, I'll come to believe it and 'twill help me. I still feel . . . so raw. As if the grief is trapped inside. 'Tis all very well to cry with Florrie, or Molly or Beth here. But I needed to cry with Charles. With her father. But he'll have none of it. And . . . you heard he sold Gospel? In retaliation for helping you.' Her voice had cracked with sorrow, and as she looked at Seth, her eyes misted.

'Yes. And I'm really sorry. I feel it was my fault.'

'No! Never think that! If Charles had been a different man . . .'

She shook her head, her mouth quivering wretchedly as tears raked her throat. Seth spread his arms and Rose had no strength to resist. She half lay on the bed, her face against his chest as she sobbed inconsolably until slowly, very slowly, the torture eased. But in its place was a barb just as cruel.

'Oh, Rose, that husband of yours is a fool,' Seth choked miserably. 'He doesn't know how lucky he is to have you, while I . . . I thought of nothing else but you. The risks you took to help me. And all those months, everything they put me through, I just kept imagining your face. Otherwise, I just couldn't have taken it.'

Rose stiffened and drew back, swamped with guilt, for surely he had suffered far worse than she had. And now she had emptied her weary soul on him when he was so ill. All she wanted was to stay with him, to nurse him through every minute until he was fit and well again. But she couldn't.

'Oh, Seth, I don't want to go—'

'But you know you must.'

She gulped. 'Yes. You will get yourself better, won't you?'

He gave a wry shrug. 'I'll certainly try. I couldn't have better care than I'm getting here. But . . . you will come again?'

'Yes, of course.'

'Well, goodbye then, Rose.'

He held out his hand, deliberately. For what else was there?

Rose shook it, and fled the room without looking back. What if . . . what if he took a turn for the worse and she never saw him alive again?

She ran down the stairs, blindly, and back into the kitchen. The family were sitting around the table having lunch and Elizabeth looked up with a smile.

'You will have something to eat, Rose? And then I'll be making Seth an egg custard in a minute if he can manage it.'

'Oh, 'tis most kind of you, but I think I'd better set off home,' Rose answered, glad of something practical to discuss. 'But I really must thank Adam for all that he's done.'

'He went straight back to Herefordshire,' Richard explained. 'Toby's starting school there next week. Proper boarding school. Adam wanted to be there to see the boy settled. To make sure he wasn't feeling he was being got rid of, especially because, well, I think you know Adam's not actually his father. And Rebecca will miss Toby terribly, so Adam wanted to be with her.'

'Yes, of course. I can understand that. I'll write to him instead, if you can give me their address.'

'I'll jot it down for you,' Richard replied, getting up and making for his study.

'Thank you. And you will look after Seth, won't you?' she asked earnestly as she turned to Elizabeth.

'Of course I will, my dear.' The good woman nodded vigorously. 'But remember what I said. He's far from out of the woods yet. So far, so good, but sometimes there can be a serious – and I'm afraid to say *fatal* – relapse. His lungs need to recover and sometimes the parotid gland becomes hugely infected in the third week. William would drain it for him if that happened, but 'tis a sign of deep infection. So, keep praying for him.'

Rose bit her lip as fear and worry bore down on her again, but just then Richard came back, handing her a piece of paper.

'That's the address.'

'Thank you. And thank you both so much for all you've done.'

'Don't mention it, Rose.'

'I'll come out to the stable with you,' Richard announced, following her to the door and out to the yard. 'I'm still making enquiries about your horse, by the way,' he said as he put

Honey's saddle back on for her and tightened the girth strap. 'But I'm afraid I've drawn a blank so far.'

'That's very kind. But, you know,' she added with a forlorn sigh, 'I don't think I'll ever find him. I'm becoming resigned to it now, and Honey here's such a dear. The most important thing for me now is that Seth gets well.'

'Well, he couldn't be in better hands. You know,' he faltered, his voice fading to a whisper, 'I nearly died once, from an infected wound. Beth saved my life. Nursed me day and night, just like she's doing with Seth now. She's right to warn you, of course, but take heart. And take care.'

'Yes, I will, Richard. And thank you again for everything.'

'Not at all. And you come any time you want. We're always here.'

'Yes, I will.' And she urged Honey into a trot, a tangle of emotions heaving in her breast.

Twenty-One

'Where have you been?' Charles asked coldly on her return to Fencott Place.

'To Tavistock. I told you.'

'What? All this time?'

Rose was standing in the dressing room clad only in her chemise and drawers, having just removed her riding habit and shirt, and turned in a casual manner to put them on hangers, though inside her heart was beating hard and furious. But Charles grabbed her wrist with such force that she dropped the garments with a squeal of pain, and found herself being backed up against the wall.

'And what have you bought then, eh?' he spat into her face. 'That it took you so long?'

'Nothing!' she snarled back. Her heart had been lost in sadness, torn beyond all reasoning, as she had ridden back from Peter Tavy trying to put a curb on her own devastated emotions. She would visit Seth as often as she possibly could until . . . Dear God, he *had* to recover! It would kill her if he didn't. And then, one day, it would be time for him to move on. And then memories would be all she had of him. Her sorrow, her gnawing despair, had turned to anger, and if she had to fight Charles tooth and nail to acquire those precious, bittersweet moments with Seth, then so be it. For after that, there would be nothing left, and she really wouldn't care what became of her.

'Well, you've been a bloody long time buying nothing!' Charles's hot breath was like fire against her cheek.

'Exactly!' she sneered, her eyes snapping dangerously. 'I couldn't find anything I liked, so I went on looking.'

'I don't believe you, you lying little slut! You've been with someone, haven't you? Haven't you!' he bawled deafeningly into her ear. And not content with wrenching her forward so that he could then bang her head backwards on the wall, he flung her across the room so that she tripped on the discarded garments and fell on to the floor. He was on her in seconds, throwing her on her back. 'Well, I'll teach you to be unfaithful to me!'

Rose glared up at him as she regained her senses, chin lifted stubbornly and her eyes flaring with unleashed wrath. 'Oh, yes! You would, wouldn't you?' she hissed through clenched teeth. 'Some gentleman *you* turned out to be! Well, if I *had* been with someone else – which I haven't – 'twould have been with a far better man than you!'

The biting sarcasm in her voice, the challenge that glinted in her fearless eyes, scorched into his pride. His face seemed about to explode, his mouth knotted so that his cheeks were puffed out like footballs. He let the breath out through his nose in a squall of hate and indignation, but after what seemed like hours to Rose, who thought her heart had ceased to beat, he slowly lowered his raised fist.

'Well, I'll damned well make sure you're not cuckolding me, you trollop! I'm going to London tomorrow, and you're bloody well coming with me!'

'If that's what it takes to prove I'm not lying!' she railed at him, her tongue burning with contempt as he got to his feet and stomped out of the room, slamming the door behind him so that the whole house shook.

Rose lay for some minutes, stunned and lifeless. Oh, sweet Jesus! Why had she given in so easily? She hadn't, though, really, had she? She had forced Charles to stand down, not the other way around. But now she must go to London. For how long? Would Seth still be alive when she returned? If he survived, Beth had indicated that it would take four to six weeks for him to recover fully. Surely they wouldn't remain in London for so long? But Rose couldn't blame Seth if he grew fit enough to leave in her absence. Were his feelings for her as strong, as savage, as hers were for him? But what did it matter? It was hopeless. And perhaps it would be better if he left, disappeared from her life, without saying goodbye.

She crawled across the floor, found the clothes in which she had leant against Seth only hours before, and hugged them to her breast.

*   *   *

As it turned out, Charles planned to spend a whole month in London. A month in which she played the dutiful wife, behaved with perfect etiquette in the society circles Charles frequented. But inside, her soul was slowly bleeding to death. She thought of nothing but Seth, his spirit filling her every waking minute with ecstatic joy and tearing grief, and her restless nights with dreams and nightmares. When Charles took his pleasure with her, which was almost every night, he took her passiveness for compliance, not knowing that as she lay there, behind her closed eyes was the vision of a handsome, lithe young man with light hair and hazel eyes and a tender, gentle smile that lit up the sky.

She managed, just twice, to write him a short letter, praying he was alive to read it, and put it in the post before Charles returned from some business meeting. She didn't give an address, it was too dangerous. And she did not write of love. How could she, when she knew – they both knew – that destiny had sealed their fates long ago? On the day she had married Charles. The letters seemed ridiculous, farcical. For she could merely say she hoped he was recovering and feeling stronger. That she thought of him every day, and would visit him immediately upon her return. Whenever that might be.

The moor was enshrouded in a dense, grey mist the day they returned. The road from Tavistock to Princetown, however, was quite discernable in the early summer evening as Ned drove the Brougham up the steep hill. Rose's heart contracted, bringing a slick of sweat to her skin, as they passed the turn-off to Peter Tavy. She forced herself not to turn her head. *Oh, dearest Seth. Are you still alive? How I long . . .*

It was good to be home. To be with Florrie, who hadn't known what to do with herself in Rose's absence. Charles only kept her on, he had told her curtly, because she had proved herself a good nanny to Alice and would be so again to the son he intended Rose should bear him. Not that there was any sign of it yet.

'I need to take Honey for some exercise,' Rose announced boldly at breakfast the following morning, though her heart was hammering not so much at the idea of deceiving Charles but at what she might find at Rosebank Hall.

'And where will you go, madam?'

'Oh, Charles, when will you learn to trust me?' she sighed

wearily. 'Haven't I done everything you've required of me? I am utterly faithful to you, you know.' That at least was true. 'But since you ask, I think I'll ride out to Vixen Tor, and then down along the Walkham to make a circle. 'Tis so pretty down in the valley.' And then a flash of inspiration – said with her fingers crossed behind her back. 'Won't you come with me? 'Tis such a lovely day after yesterday.'

Charles looked up in surprise, and Rose's pulse thudded painfully while he seemed to consider. 'No. I don't really think I can spare the time. I thought, though, I might go to the powder mills to make sure they've pulled their socks up now. You could come with me. See your precious friend, Molly Tyler.'

'Hmm.' Rose tilted her head to one side, pretending to be making a decision. 'I'm tempted. But my head's bursting after so much company in London and I'd just like some quiet on my own. But if you see Molly or Joe, you might tell them I'll be over in a day or two.'

With that, she deliberately came over to him, and though it stung her lips, she kissed him affectionately. He caught her hand for a moment, whispering in her ear something about what he would do with her that night. She smiled. And felt sick.

She was away, her spirit flying between excitement, despair and fear as Honey's strong legs ate up the ground. The road was so familiar to them both, and when they clattered into the yard at the back of Rosebank Hall, Rose felt she might faint. She hurried inside, trembling, and not even stopping to knock.

There was a figure sitting in the battered chair by the side of the range, a small, petite young woman who looked dreadful.

'Rose!' Elizabeth nevertheless greeted her brightly as she stood up.

Rose was numbed. Something must have happened. Oh, not Seth. Please God, no. 'Wh . . . what's the matter?' she stammered as she tottered forward.

Elizabeth smiled. 'Nothing. Just the opposite in fact. 'Tis just that I'm pregnant and I feel awful. Even my own reme-dies aren't helping with the sickness. And late morning, this is the worst time. I'm just having a raw carrot.'

'Oh, yes! I used to find carrots helped. Or an apple. But

. . . what wonderful news! I'm so happy for you! And Richard must be pleased. I . . .' She paused, shying away from her own thoughts. Molly, and now Beth. But she gritted her teeth and went on, 'I expect he's hoping for a boy.'

'Yes, I think so.' Elizabeth's smile was content now. 'He's never said as much. I mean, he's always joking about being surrounded by women. 'Tis why Seth being here is so good for him. But a farmer needs a son. Chantal's a great help. She's out in the vegetable garden now. Hannah's helping her. Or supposed to be,' she chuckled. 'But you need a man's strength. Talking of which, you'll be wanting to see Seth.'

Rose gulped. And nearly melted into the floor with joy. 'He's still here then?'

Elizabeth glanced at her sideways. 'Of course. He's much better, though he still needs to build up his strength. He's been going out with Richard the last few days. They're down in one of the fields near the village. Planting flatpoles. Richard's asked him to stay on when he's fully recovered. We can't afford to pay him, but you know we've an old farm worker's cottage just on up the track. Used to be old George's, but both he and his widow have passed on now. We've said Seth can live there if he wants. He's still thinking about it.'

'Oh.' The sound that issued from Rose's lips was devoid of expression, she was in such a state of shock. She didn't know what she thought, what she felt, at this unexpected news. Not only had Seth survived the fever but there was a possibility he might stay on at Rosebank Hall. That she could continue to steal away from Charles to ride over the moor to see Seth for . . . for how long? Until Charles found out? And his jealous rage led him to the wrong conclusions? For it wouldn't be an affair. Not in the carnal sense of the word. No. In that, she would remain utterly faithful. It would be a deep and intimate friendship, no more than that. She owed Charles that much. And one day, Seth would find a wife. It would tear at her heart. But to know he was happy and safe, and to see him on occasion, would perhaps get her through the bleak and barren years ahead with Charles.

Elizabeth gave her directions to the field that sloped down to the River Tavy. It was not difficult to find, with one of the farm horses pulling a cart loaded with seedlings that the two men were planting in the neat furrows while a young boy was keeping them supplied with seedling trays and working ahead of them, watering the furrows with a can he was refilling from the river. It was laborious work, and both men straightened up, arching their backs, when they saw Rose approach. She slipped from Honey's back, tethering her to the gate, and hurried towards them, almost keeling over with happiness.

'Congratulations, Richard!' she called as she neared them. 'I hear you're to be a father again!'

A proud grin spread over Richard's weather-browned face as he used the back of his shirtsleeve to wipe the sweat from his brow. 'Thank you, Rose! Good to see you!' He was still smiling as his dark eyes swivelled across at Seth. 'But it's not me you've come to see, I'll be bound. Go on, Seth. Take a rest. Beth wouldn't be very pleased with me if I allowed you to work too hard, and I think you've done enough for today!'

He went back to the monotonous, arduous task, and Rose's heart gave a little squeal as Seth came towards her, stepping carefully over the planted rows. He met her gaze then, a wide smile lighting his face, and she couldn't believe how much better he looked and so much more his real age. His gentle, hazel eyes shone, the dark hollows beneath them vanished. His ashen skin was now a healthy amber and his hair, not straw-coloured like Joe's but a deep, golden blond, was an inch-long cap on his head and already showing a tendency to curl around the nape of his neck. There was beginning to be a little flesh on his bones, and the hand he held out to her was strong and firm.

'Oh, I'm sorry,' he said, bowing his head sheepishly. 'I'm covered in earth.' But then he looked up again, his handsome mouth stretched once more in a broad grin. 'Oh, I'm so glad to see you again. How was London?'

Rose couldn't answer for a moment. Seeing him so recovered, so virile, more attractive even than the vision of him she had conjured up in her mind, had quite taken her senses away. And yet it was a spear in her side.

'London was . . . London,' she laughed at last, shaking her head. 'Busy. Tedious. I hated every minute of it. Apart from the two concerts Charles took me to. I loved those. At one of them they played an orchestral piece based on *Romeo and Juliet*, by some Russian composer called Tchaikovsky, I think his name was. 'Twas very moving.' She broke off breathlessly.

It seemed incongruous, telling him this here, nearly three hundred miles from the capital, when her soul was empty of everything but her love for this man. Who could never be hers. 'And you, Seth. How are you?'

They had reached the rear of the cart now, and Seth pushed back some of the empty seedling trays so they had room to sit. He brushed the worst of the dirt from his hands, then took her around the waist to help her as she jumped up backwards to perch on the end. Their eyes engaged, awkward, wishing . . . but he stepped back and glanced down at himself, his palms spread.

'As you see, much improved. I get tired pretty quickly, but it'll come.' He bounded forward, leaping up on the cart and twisting round to sit beside her, legs dangling over the end. 'Did Beth tell you, they've offered me a cottage in exchange for work, if I want to stay on?'

'Yes,' Rose murmured as her stomach turned right over. 'And will you?' she hardly dared to ask.

His voice was serious now, cautious. 'If *you* want me to.'

She gulped, her heart suddenly racing. 'Yes. I do. But you know . . . you know there can never be anything . . .' Her words trailed off in a broken sigh, the pulse vibrating at her temples.

'Yes, I know. I understand. But we can still be friends.'

She turned to him, her mouth twisted in a wistful half smile, so grateful to him. As if some intangible thread linked them together. 'Of course. But my husband must never know. He's . . . well, a very jealous man. Which is why I should be getting back.' She wriggled off the end of the cart and turned to face him as he, too, dropped to the ground. 'I'm so glad you're so much better. And you will take care?'

He answered her with an anxious smile. 'I think you're the one who needs to be careful. Come again soon, Rose. But only when it's safe.'

They stood, facing each other, for just a few seconds. And then, once again, they did the only thing they could. They shook hands.

'Did you have a good ride, my dear? You didn't say.'

'Yes, thank you, Charles. 'Twas good to be out on the moor again. You know how I begin to feel stifled in London after so long, even though I realize you try to make it interesting for me.' She prayed her voice didn't betray the uneasiness that thrummed in her chest as she turned down the sheets that night and began to unfasten the ties of her dressing gown. She had been prepared, though, ready to deceive, and though the falsehood came easily, she hated herself for it.

'You're not a very good liar, you know, Rose.'

His voice was suddenly ice-cold and she threw up her head. 'Pardon?'

'We weren't back twenty-four hours before you were off to see your lover.'

'My lover?' Her eyebrows arched in derision, her mouth open in a mocking, contemptuous laugh. 'Oh, a chance would be a fine thing with the way you keep a check on me!'

'Well, I shouldn't have to, but first it was that convict, and now it's . . . Well, God knows who it is! Joe Tyler, perhaps—'

The fury spiralled up within her, grasping her by the throat. She could scarcely believe she had heard right. 'Joe?' she rounded on him, her eyes flaring. 'How dare you! Joe's like a brother to me, and he's Molly's husband! My God, your mind's even filthier than I thought!'

'Well, you're the one having the affair, not me.'

She watched as his eyes hardened to steel, his mouth in a cruel, compressed line, and in that moment of confrontation, her heart turned to stone. 'An affair! Good God! And suffer what *you* put me through every night at the hands of another man as well? You must be joking!'

Before the bitter words had even left her lips, he had gripped her by the upper arms and with a violence that terrified her, shook her like a rag doll so that her neck cracked in agony and for a sickening instant, she feared for her life.

'So, it's all my fault, is it, you little whore?' his roar bellowed in her ears. 'You're only doing your duty as my wife, may I remind you!'

'I know that!' she yelled back at him with such anger that he at last stopped shaking her and they glared at each other like two rutting stags, Charles panting heavily while she flared her nostrils with vitriolic disdain. 'But at least I'm *trying* to do something to make our marriage work,' she succeeded in spluttering as he seemed to be calming down. 'I want another child as much as you do,' she lied convincingly. 'But I do wish you'd be gentler with me. Show me that you love me as much as you say you do. And I swear on Alice's grave that I'm not sleeping with another man.'

He was glowering at her, his forehead dipped in a wary frown as he turned his head to study her sideways, his cheeks sucked in distrustingly. 'Show me, then,' he rasped, releasing his grip.

Outrage, disgust, the triumph of deceit, pain, grief and an unfathomable despair. None of these and yet all of them were tangled about her soul as she stripped off her nightdress and stood naked before him.

Her spirit died as his hungry hands reached out . . .

Twenty-Two

'Rose?'

She couldn't hold the tender concern in those clear hazel eyes, and slowly averted her gaze. She wanted to lean against him, let him see her pain, soothe and comfort her wounded heart, but she must try to hide it from him, for there was nothing to be done. It was the same every time she managed to escape from Charles's jealous vigilance, meeting Seth at some pre-appointed hour, changing the venue but always nearer to Princetown now, since she could not rely on Charles's absence for long enough for her to ride to Peter Tavy and back. Ned, too, was a problem, as she had found to her cost that he would relay her movements to Charles, and it tested her ingenuity to have him out of the way, even if it meant spiking his tea with laudanum! She communicated with Seth through Molly, but often Seth would wait hours for her and she did not come. It was not always safe, and she must give Charles no grounds for suspicion. Once he had locked her in the bedroom again, but she had climbed out of the window, letting herself down on knotted sheets stripped from the bed, and then marched boldly into his study to smile at him audaciously.

The bruises had lasted for weeks.

And now she knew Seth would not be satisfied with a denial. She had winced when he had held her at arms' length as they found each other in the woods along the Walkham valley. It had been more than a fortnight since last they had managed to meet. The summer was drawing to a close, the stolen moments they snatched together the only flickering candle in the damning obscurity that her life had become. Half an hour at most they would sit and talk, no word or gesture of love passing between them. For it was impossible. A mere shaking of hands, or a natural touch of greeting, as just now, was all they allowed themselves.

But somehow, this time, the fight had gone out of her, her courage, her spirit exhausted. The memory of Charles's attack on her the previous night was too much. She had told him wearily not to bother to make love to her because her period had started, and he had lost his temper, cursing her for not being pregnant. And now she stood, her liquid eyes riveted on Seth's face as he unbuttoned her riding jacket and slid it from her trembling body, and then unfastened the shirt beneath just enough to slip it over her shoulders. Her stomach, already aching, constricted even further and her pulse beat fast but quietly as she watched Seth's eyes move downwards and he sucked the breath in through his teeth.

'The bastard,' he muttered as he took in the livid finger marks on her arms and even around her neck, the scratches visible on the pearly skin above the neckline of her chemise, angry welts which he rightly guessed reached down to her breasts. His eyes met hers again. She thought she would drown in them, and hung her head in shame.

'Not again, Rose.' His voice was thick, choked. 'This can't go on. I can't just sit back and let . . .' He rolled his head with an agonized sense of helplessness, shaking his fists dementedly in the air before he let his arms drop limply to his sides. 'You know, I was so livid that first time that I told Richard. I just had to tell someone! He flew into such a rage—'

'*Richard?* But he always seems so . . .'

'Yes, I know. But I think something else happened a long time ago that they never talk about. But he was so incensed that Beth and I physically had to restrain him. He was all for giving that bloody husband of yours a taste of his own medicine. Well, that's just how I feel, too. And how often has it happened since, tell me that, eh?' He shied away, his jaw clenched in maddened frustration. 'I feel such a coward, doing nothing to protect you.'

He turned his back on her, his head tipped skywards and his eyes wildly searching the trees for an answer that simply wasn't there. Rose stepped up to him, her fingers patting the air in hesitation before she leant her cheek against his shoulder.

'There's nothing to be done,' she whispered. ''Tis not your fault. 'Twill be better once I'm with child again.'

'And what then?' he barely murmured. 'I'll never see you once you have a family to care for. I just couldn't live, thinking of you under the thumb of that . . .' His voice faltered, and he gulped hard before he croaked, 'You must know I love you, Rose.'

'Yes.' The word was hardly breathed. Miserable, wretched. Lodging in her throat like a stone.

He spun round so suddenly that she started, her shoulders jerking backwards. 'Then leave him,' he said gravely.

She blinked at him, and he watched her pupils widen. 'What?' she mumbled.

'Leave him. And come away with me.'

Her fine brow puckered, her eyebrows arched as she shook her head. 'He'd find us,' she moaned piteously.

'No, I mean *really* come away. America, South Africa. Wherever you want.'

His eyes were piercing earnestly into hers, and she felt the shiver reach down to her toes. 'But   .'

'I know I'm a pretty poor catch. I've nothing to offer you but my love, but we could start a new life together. I'd work hard for you. We could travel under my real name. As Mr and Mrs Warrington. No one would know any different. We could sail on one of Adam's ships to France or Spain, so there'd be no passenger list for your husband to find us on, even if he knew what name to look for. Then we could take a ship from there. He'd never find us.'

He was speaking urgently, his expression sharp and alert as she stared at him, her eyes stretched wide. Escape. Travel. Adventure. But most of all, to be free. Her heart began to bang against her ribs, her reeling senses vibrating with each beat of her pulse. But . . . the *enormity* of it . . .

'But . . . leave Dartmoor?' she stammered, the sadness stabbing into her soul. 'I don't think . . .'

'Yes, I know.' His voice was low, deep with understanding. 'You'd have to leave the place you love. And all your friends. Without saying goodbye. It'd be best that way. We couldn't risk anyone knowing that we were leaving. Except Adam, of course, and Richard and Beth. They'd have to know.'

'Oh.' Her white lips trembled and the world seemed to drop away as she felt herself swooning. But she was being supported, and she could hear Seth's heartbeat, strong and steady, as her head drooped against his chest. If she left, she would never have the chance to find Gospel. But was she likely to, after all this time? And she would have to leave Florrie and Joe and Molly, everyone she knew and loved.

'The dogs?' she squealed desperately. But she knew the answer.

She felt the shock drain from her limbs, and acceptance trickled into the void. Seth was right. It was the only way, though it would break her. Shred her heart. And what did she *really* know of Seth? But *love* had touched her. And it was nothing like the uncertainty that had made her hesitate over Charles. This was so strong . . . With Seth beside her, there would be no more fear.

She lifted her head, and his dear, beloved face was there. Ready, waiting. Trusting.

'Yes,' she croaked.

And when his lips brushed against hers with the softness of gossamer, she knew her heart was lost for ever.

Charles sauntered into his study to fetch a cigar to go with the large brandy he held in his other hand. He had to look over some papers his agent had sent him that morning, outlining an opportunity for investment in a new business enterprise in Exeter. The returns from the South African diamond mine were proving a major success, but he was always looking for new avenues to explore. It would certainly be more practical to keep an eye on something in Exeter than some of his other interests. Take the powder mills, which he knew so well now. And when he had studied the proposals, he would sit and drool over what he had in mind to do with Rose when he went up to join her in bed a little later. She was back 'in working order' now, and he would make up for what he had missed. By God, he'd have a son out of her, and he'd bloody well enjoy the making of it!

Oh, drat it! The fire was nearly out. He went to ring the bell, but the thought of Rose's enticing, lithesome body exposed to his greedy eyes had put him in a good mood, and he supposed he was quite capable of rekindling the moribund embers. A pile of old newspapers was stored in the corner, and he languidly reached out for one and began to crumple the sheets into balls.

He stopped as if an electric charge had shot through his arm as his eyes focused on a minor headline. *Royal Pardon for Escaped Prisoner at Dartmoor.* The tiny print blurred as he forced his brain to concentrate on the short article below, and his heart jerked in his chest. He could not believe it. Yes. The very same. That damned bloody convict Rose had hidden in his own stable, under his very nose, had proved his innocence and had been released – over four months ago. Where was he? And *who* had helped him? Must have been someone on the outside, since a royal pardon was a bloody difficult thing to achieve.

There could only be one answer.

The strangling anger, the *hate*, grappled in Charles's throat and he had to tear open his necktie and collar as blood suffused into his face. Good God Almighty! That lying, cheating, whoring little harlot! He'd kill her! He could feel his fingers closing around her neck, throttling the life from her.

But that would be too good. He'd make her suffer first. Bloody well make her tell him who had helped her, since there was no way she could have done it alone! He'd deal with whoever it was later, but first of all, he'd deal with *her*! And he'd make her wish she had never been born!

'I'm going into Exeter tomorrow,' he told Rose casually later that evening, when he had taken his fill of her raw, tender flesh. 'A new business my agent has got wind of. I'll ride Tansy there. It's too far to go and come back in one day, so I'll probably stay overnight. I've told Ned he can take the day off if you don't need him. He can spend some time with that tart of his.'

Rose didn't reply. She was stinging and swollen from Charles's onslaught, for the mild consideration he had shown her just that once had long since been forgotten. She was so tired of it, and lay there in submission, as complaining only made things worse. How many more times would she have to suffer his attentions? Not too many, she prayed. Somehow, the notion that one day soon she might escape his clutches for good made it even worse. But she didn't feel the resentment, the fury, any more, just the humiliation and shame. Her head was full only of the plan to escape. Would it work? Was it the right decision? All she knew was that she could not possibly go on living – existing – the way she was.

So Charles and Ned wouldn't be there tomorrow. Her spirit should have soared, but it didn't. Charles had driven out the courage, the valour, that had once been Rose Maddiford. She waited half an hour after they had both departed, and then brought Honey in from the field, saddled her, and set off for Rosebank Hall. She went a different way now. The farm was a mile or so out of Peter Tavy up on the moor, and Richard had pointed out to her a more direct route following an old track now used by those men from Peter Tavy who had taken work at the new quarry at Merrivale.

Honey cantered along at a steady pace, and Rose sat astride her, devoid of all thought, her heart saddened. How many more times would she ride over her beloved Dartmoor again? Was it worth the sacrifice? Her vision misted with tears that spangled on her lashes in the early autumn sunshine, forlorn and despondent. But she would be free from Charles. She *had* to do it, but she would do it in great pain. And as time healed her, as she was sure it would, she would have Seth. Good, kind, gentle Seth, who wanted nothing from her. Who had kissed her just that one time, and fleetingly. But whose love had flowed into her in that precious moment and given her faith.

She hadn't wanted it to be this way. She had wanted, *expected* her marriage to Charles to be whole and fulfilling. If it had been, this appalling situation would not have arisen. If Charles had been the man she had once thought he was, a man like Adam or Richard, he would have *helped* Seth as they had done, and there simply would not have been room in her heart to entertain the idea of loving someone else. But now she knew her salvation lay only in Seth's embrace.

She could see him now, with Richard and the two dogs, driving some sheep down from the moor, ones Richard had selected for market, she supposed. She stopped and waited, not wanting Honey's presence to scatter the animals if she went too close. The two men saw her, exchanged a brief word, and then Seth came towards her, leaving Richard to carry on down to the farm.

She slid to her feet and was in Seth's arms. And the doubt fled as they turned towards the tiny cottage.

It wasn't easy following her over the open, barren moorland, as much of the time you could see for miles and she only had to look back once . . . Charles had to use the contours of the land, the long sweeps of the road, keeping well behind her, sometimes losing sight of her for five or ten minutes, before reaching the crest that would bring her into view in the far distance. She was easy to spot, a horse and rider moving at speed when most of the traffic consisted of lumbering farm wagons or perhaps a cart from the powder mills carrying carefully sealed kegs to the quarries or outlying storage magazines. Oh, yes. Charles knew all about the business now. It was one of these carts turning into Merrivale's Tor Quarry that helped him to spy Rose when she seemed to have vanished into thin air. He had reached the brow of the hill a little past the quarry, and the road ahead was deserted. He drew Tansy to a halt and, turning round in the saddle, his eye followed the cart he had recently overtaken on the road, and there was Rose, skirting the quarry and heading steeply up hill over the moor. His emotions turned from fuming acrimony to fear and disappointment, as there was nowhere for him to hide and if she glanced around and saw him, his ruse would have failed. But she didn't. And as soon as she disappeared, he cautiously urged Tansy up the hill, cutting off a corner, towards an outbreak of rock of whose name he was ignorant. He dismounted, leaving Tansy to crop the short, springing grass and, scaling the boulders, he used them as cover to spy on his unfaithful, adulterous wife.

She was heading almost straight across a long dip in the land between two further tors, greater and on higher ground, he judged, than the one where he was hiding now. A natural pool somewhere between them had attracted a small herd of cattle to drink, but Rose did not deviate. Where was she heading?

It was an area Charles was unfamiliar with, but it appeared an empty, infertile wilderness inhabited only by lonely sheep and cattle and the occasional Dartmoor pony. Could it be that he was mistaken? That she really was doing nothing more than enjoying a long ride out on the savage moor? He climbed back down to where Tansy was patiently waiting, and swung himself into the saddle. Should he ride to wherever it was he would decide to spend the night in order to disguise his own trick, satisfied that Rose was telling the truth? She didn't love him. She had told him so. But she insisted upon her fidelity, and heaven knew he wanted it to be true. He loved her. Worshipped her. Wanted to possess her as he had the right to do. Just grant him the son he wanted, and it would bind her to him.

But . . . the thought of her in another man's arms. Another man's bed! Those long, slender legs, the curve of her tiny waist, the roundness of her breasts and that hair . . . The image brought the saliva to his mouth and he drew the back of his hand across his lips. She was his. *His!* The law said so.

She had suddenly dropped out of sight and he set Tansy at a gallop to catch up with her. He *must* be sure!

He passed enclosures, fields, a brook in a narrow gully. Signs of cultivation. Habitation. He slid from Tansy's back again, using the stone walls and tall boulders for cover. He peered out. And his heart froze into a lump of ice. Two men, two dogs and some bloody sheep. Both men were tall, but the slightly shorter of them came towards Rose. She dismounted and – damn and hell and bloody damn again – she melted into his arms.

The breath left Charles's body. He turned round, leaning back against the wall, half slithering to the ground, choking and spluttering as he battled to make his lungs draw in some life-giving air. His heart catapulted forward in his chest, ramming frenziedly against his ribs as the blood pounded in his skull and he had to tear open his collar. The bloody lying, conniving, deceitful, wanton, whoring bitch!

He had so nearly believed her! She had almost got away with it! And after all he had done for her, buying the house on this God-forsaken moor and abandoning his luxurious life in London! His hands tore at his hair, his eyes wide and brutal as the perspiration oozed from every pore. He was gasping, struggling to stay conscious as the realization seeped through his shocked brain. Surely he was mistaken. He turned back, hoping . . . But there she was, arm in arm with the blackguard, Honey ambling behind them as they headed – dear God above – to a small, isolated cottage and disappeared round the back.

His instinct was to fly down the hill and barge his way inside, drag the hussy out of bed, naked if need be, and trail her, screaming, by the hair all the way home where, by God, he'd flay her until she begged for mercy. But that would be too good for her. And besides, she had the bastard to protect her. They hadn't been so far away that he couldn't recognize him. It was that bloody convict! He'd kill him! He'd take a meat knife as he stormed through the kitchen and ram it into the cur's belly as he lay in bed with Rose, and she could watch her lover die in agony. Charles wouldn't care about the consequences, he wouldn't bloody care! He wouldn't be cuckolded! But . . . there was the other chap. Tall, broad-shouldered and athletic, one of those strong farming types. Might he come to the rescue? And if Charles didn't manage to disable the – oh, he couldn't believe it – the *convict* with his initial blow, he certainly wouldn't want to grapple with *two* strong men!

Charles's face was puce as the doubt wormed its way into his deranged fury. Take a hold. Think. Perhaps . . . He waited. But half an hour later, they were still inside. Satisfying their lust. No doubt she didn't lie like a wet fish in *his* bed. She deserved to die. The trollop deserved to die. But he'd take his fill of her first! Take her by force every night until . . .

The thought set him panting harder, his lips drawn back from his closed teeth in an ugly snarl. And as the idea came to him, the irony struck him clean between the eyes, and he threw back his head in a mindless, diabolic laugh.

Twenty-Three

Charles was going to London. So . . .

This was her chance to get away. To escape. To slip from Charles's bed and the ever more brutal way he was treating her in it, as if he were deliberately trying to hurt her. She should be light-headed with joy, tingling with anticipation. But how could she be when it meant she would be leaving Dartmoor and everything she held dear and sacred, never to return? The savage realms of the infinite, windswept wastes where hardly a stunted tree would grow, the spongy grass topped only by strange and chiselled outcrops of massive, barren rocks; the swathes of purple heathers and the dazzling banks of prickly yellow gorse; the lush green fields enclosed by old stone walls, or the merry chatter of clear, spangling water as it tripped and swirled over ancient boulders in a gravel river bed, carving its way through a mystic, wooded valley. The magnificent, craggy landscape that was at the very core of her being, the moods and impassioned seasons of the moor that pulsed in every beat of her heart. But the days of gilded contentment were vanished, destroyed by her husband's vicious jealousy.

Everything was in place. She and Seth had sat at the rustic table in the tiny cottage for more than an hour that day, sipping tea as they made their plans. Richard and Elizabeth, and Adam and Rebecca shared their secret, of course, but not a word was to be whispered to another soul. A glistening teardrop had slipped from Rose's liquid eyes at what felt like betrayal of her lifelong friends, but there was nothing else for it, and Seth had squeezed her hand with infinite compassion. No more than that. Just a gentle, trusting kiss when they had parted.

She had gone to visit Molly and the baby the previous day. Saying goodbye, that she would see her next week, when she knew it to be a blatant lie, fragmented her strung nerves, and yet she must not give herself away, for Molly, she knew, would find it hard to contain her emotions and might let it slip out, and if it reached Charles's ears . . . Should she tell Joe? Her tormented soul asked when she saw him at a distance and he waved cheerily. Better not. Her vision blurred with moisture as Honey trotted away along the familiar track, and she drew the mare to a halt outside the manager's house that had been her happy home for so long. She turned in the saddle to take one last look at the powder mills, the three sturdy fortresses of the incorporating mills strung out on the far hillside, the various buildings along this side of the river, the tall stone chimneys drawing the smoke and fumes safely away from the danger areas. Grief clawed at her throat like barbed wire, and she felt if she stared at the place an instant longer, she would drown in the rip tide of her misery. And so she dug her heels into Honey's flank and they shot forward, turning their backs on Cherrybrook for ever.

She watched as Ned turned the Brougham out of the driveway, knowing that inside it, Charles was unaware that he was heading out of her life. But there was no relief in her breast. She had gone too far for that. Her mind had been long overtaken by the numb indifference of fatigue and despair, of suffering and abuse. Of regret that instead of bringing her a lifetime of peace, the man she had once thought she loved was now driving her away from the place that gave her life. She would be with Seth, of course, and he would be the cornerstone of her existence from now on. Kind, thoughtful, sensitive Seth, who knew what it was to suffer physical and mental torture, and so understood her pain. He had asked nothing of her but to accept his help. If the physical aspect of their love ever blossomed, she would welcome it without fear, since she knew that he would treat her with gentleness and respect, but as yet a natural, comforting embrace and a fleeting touch of their lips was all that had passed between them.

She must time it perfectly. On Honey's back, she could move so much more swiftly than the Brougham, and cutting across country to avoid Princetown so that no one would see her, she didn't want to catch Charles up as she crossed over the road at Merrivale. But, by the same token, she mustn't meet up with Ned on his return journey from Tavistock station.

She took nothing with her but the personal allowance

Charles gave her weekly – like a child, she always thought grimly – and of which, thankfully, she had spent very little over the past year since Alice's death, so that it amounted to a substantial sum. To take anything else might arouse Florrie's suspicions, and though Florrie had been like a mother to her, she wore her heart on her sleeve and could easily give them away if she knew of their plans. She would be demented with worry when Rose did not return that evening, and would doubtless send Ned out to look for her. But Peter Tavy was not far short of ten miles away, and there would be no reason for him to search there. Besides, they had planned to leave on foot under cover of darkness, arriving at the river port of Morwellham at dawn. From there, they would cadge a lift on the first vessel heading downstream to Plymouth – on Adam's barge if it happened to be in port – and there they would await one of Adam's sailing ships to take them to wherever it was headed, and hence on to a new life on some distant shore.

'I'm just going out for a ride,' she had announced with a forced smile. 'Quite a long one, I expect. I think I'll head out towards Dartmeet for a change. So I won't be back till later this afternoon.'

'Well, you be careful, young miss!'

'Of course, I will!' Rose assured her.

She saw Florrie's face, as familiar as a favourite old slipper, relax into its usual, comforting lines, and the pain seared into her throat. She swept across the room as tears stung at the back of her eyes, and she enveloped the older woman in her long, slender arms. For a split second, she was lost, her resolve all but dissipated. 'I do love you, you know, Florrie,' she mumbled into Florrie's grey hair, and had to grit her teeth to tamp down the torment.

It was Florrie who pushed her away. 'Get away with you, cheel! And take care. 'Tis coming on for a mist, I reckons.'

Rose battled to disguise her deep swallow. 'Possibly. But I'll keep to the road, so I'll not get lost.'

'That's my little maid.'

Rose nodded, her pulse flying, and steeled herself to walk calmly out of the room, pausing for a moment as she closed the door behind her, her head hung low, before heading for the stables. She moved mechanically, as if in a dream, fetching Honey's tack and saddling her up. For the very last time. Her limbs, her fingers, worked as if of their own accord as they slipped the bit into Honey's mouth, fastened the buckles, the girth-strap of the saddle. Honey was a beautiful, faithful animal and Rose would miss her dreadfully. But she wasn't Gospel, and that emptiness would never be filled any more than her grief over her father and her daughter ever would.

She opened the loose box door, and her eyes gave a final sweep of the dark corner where Seth had lain hidden for all those weeks. And now she was going to him. But she felt nothing. There was no excitement in her, nor even relief or fear of discovery. Just a pall of sorrow, her eyes dulled to the colour of slate. Eager to be off, Honey gently nudged her shoulder, but no smile of amusement tugged at Rose's lips as she led her out into the yard and her hooves clacked on the cobbles. The dogs had pattered outside, Amber and Scraggles and the runt – the one puppy Charles had grudgingly allowed her to keep and that was now a playful young adult. Rose tried to catch it, but it pranced away, thinking this a merry game. So with a heart-wrenching sigh, Rose ruffled instead the comical mongrel head of its sire, and then, squatting on her haunches, buried her face in Amber's thick, golden coat. The tears came then, unstoppable, a deluge of misery, and she knew the only path open to her was to swing herself on to Honey's back and set her at a blind gallop across the moor in the opposite direction from the one she had indicated to Florrie.

The barren uplands of Walkhampton Common were cloaked in low, swirling cloud, a desert of springy grass and endless, unidentifiable contours to anyone but the likes of Rose Maddiford. She slowed Honey to a walk, using the customary trick of staring directly ahead, focusing on a blade of grass, a clump of heather, and making straight for it, thus following a line as rigid as a mine-rod through the shroud of disorientating vapour. She crossed the main highway leading down to Yelverton, and sure enough, shortly came across the distinct route of the horse-drawn tramway, just as she knew she would. She glanced to her right. Somewhere out there, a mile or two away, her father and her daughter lay together beneath the cold, damp earth.

The tramway now showed her the direction to follow, and she was able to set Honey at a canter, glad that the heavy curtain of mist was providing a shield of invisibility. They passed without meeting a soul the sidings that wound their way to the massive quarries at Foggintor, and still met no one as they continued to follow the track westwards. At last, the tramway swung round on itself to the left to reach the quarry at King Tor, but Rose must head straight on, crossing the River Walkham at Merrivale, and gaining higher ground once more. The banks of iron-grey mist began to roll away as they finally began to descend towards the Tavy valley, as if they were emerging from the godless depths of some infernal hell to the pale, watery light of a new world beyond . . .

'Now, don't you worry about Honey.' Richard smiled down at her. 'If I ever have to, I'll say I bought her from a pretty young woman who was selling her in Tavistock. It'll be a privilege to own her. Thank you for entrusting her to me.'

''Tis little enough after all you've done. For both of us.'

She turned and glanced up at Seth as the four of them stood in the pool of glimmering light from the open back door of Rosebank Hall. This was it, the moment when she would leave Dartmoor for ever. It was late and Chantal and Hannah were fast asleep upstairs in their beds, unaware that their parents were saying a final farewell to their friends.

'Well, good luck,' Richard said a little gruffly, since he was sorry to be saying goodbye. 'Look after her, Seth.'

'Oh, I will. And thank you for everything. Especially to you, Beth. For saving my life.'

'Oh, I think we all had a part in that.' Elizabeth nodded, sucking in her lips to hold back her tears.

'Goodbye, then, Rose.'

Richard opened his strong arms and hugged her, a lump like an apple swelling in her throat. But it was as she was locked in the embrace of the petite, serene herbalist that the teardrops began to meander down her cheeks. The pair of them stood apart then, laughing softly in an attempt to cover up as, next to them, the two men shook hands and then clapped each other on the back.

'When we're settled,' Seth said in a strange tone, 'wherever that might be, we'll write.'

Rose nodded, strangled by the tears that were welling in her throat again, and she quickly turned away. Seth put his arm around her and her limp body sagged against him as she sobbed helplessly, her heart breaking and grief closing about her in a merciless knot. So blinded by her tears and pain that she scarcely noticed as Seth began to walk her up the track, her feet trailing as he supported her in his arms. He halted after fifty yards and they turned to take one final glance. Richard and Elizabeth had come to the farmyard gate and waved one last time before turning back to the house. And then Rosebank Hall and its outbuildings were merely a solid black outline against the dark night sky.

Seth tenderly smoothed the wild hair back from Rose's face and dropped a kiss on to her forehead. She blinked up at him gratefully, sniffing hard, but the smile she tried to offer him twisted into an agonized grimace as her chin quivered threateningly again, but she was calmer now, trusting herself into his comfort and understanding.

'They're good people, Richard and Beth,' he said, his voice choked.

Rose nodded, unable to speak, and they set off again, her head resting on Seth's shoulder, and thankful for his arm tightly about her. The night was dry, though heavy granite clouds hung low above their heads and they prayed it would not come on to rain for their long walk to Morwellham Quay. Rose's weary heart was empty now of all but the strange mystery of the hushed darkness. They would walk quietly through the silence of the sleeping world, meeting only the nocturnal animals that would scurry from their presence.

But first they must return to Seth's cottage to collect the old and battered carpet bag that Elizabeth had originally brought with her to Rosebank Hall as a servant so many years before. It contained some spare clothes for them both – poor, working garments, far less remarkable than the smart riding habit Rose had been wearing, but had exchanged for an old skirt and blouse of Elizabeth's, and a tattered shawl. Every tie with Rose's former life must be broken. Elizabeth and Richard would remain their only contact, and Rose's shoulders drooped with shame and guilt at the devastating anxiety her disappearance would cause her dear Florrie. She knew that, when after months she still could not be traced, Florrie would leave Fencott Place to return to living with her sister, and perhaps in a year or so, Rose would feel safe to write to her there. The thought eased her dejected spirit and gave her some purpose as they began to progress more swiftly along the track.

Seth suddenly stopped dead, pulling her up short, and she glanced sharply at his tense profile as her heart began to batter against her ribs. A horrible sinking feeling gripped her stomach, twisting it viciously.

'Oh, God, we're not being followed?' she whispered as her skin broke out in a hot nervous sweat.

'No,' Seth murmured back, his keen eyes searching into the darkness ahead. 'But did you see that? I'm sure I saw a light. Small. A candle, perhaps, or a match. Moving about in the cottage. Yes, look! There it is again! There's someone downstairs.'

A tremor of fear shuddered down Rose's spine, and she felt herself shrink with dread, cowering against Seth as she braced herself to turn her gaze towards the cottage. Sure enough, she saw the flicker of light through the window of the one downstairs room, and then it disappeared again. She went cold. An intruder? That was hardly likely. Such a humble dwelling would hardly house anything worth stealing. No. There was only one explanation. It had to be Charles.

A tiny squeal died in her throat as she snatched in her breath and clung on to Seth with digging fingers. Charles must have tricked her, just as she had believed she had duped him; followed her instead of catching the train, watched the cottage and the farm. And now he was lying in wait, ready to drag her back home and do God alone knew what to Seth. And if Ned was with him to help . . .

'Run!' she croaked frantically into Seth's ear, her whole body quivering. 'Get away before he sees us!'

She shook his arm with a violent force, torn with agony as he stood rigid, staring ahead at the cottage. And then, somehow, she sensed it, too, that appalling instant of clairvoyance, of fate or predestination, when the earth stands still for one horrific moment and the human mind is endowed with second sight. Her gaze joined Seth's in time to see the flash, and then that ominous silence, the hiatus of terror when time stops and the heart explodes . . .

'Get down!'

She heard Seth scream at her, though it had no time to register in her shocked brain, and as the crashing blast reverberated in her skull, she found herself thrown to the ground with Seth lying protectively on top of her. The booming peal rolled away and she lifted her head, but Seth pushed her face back into the grass as she heard the clatter of splintered timber and broken glass and slates landing all about them. She lay still, breathless, waiting, until Seth's weight lifted from her, and they crouched together, stunned, staring through the shattered windows at the flickering light as the inside of the building was instantly catching fire.

They staggered to their feet, each lost for some seconds in a private, silent world, rooted to the spot like dumb marionettes as the flames spread rapidly through the half-demolished cottage. Most of the roof had been blown away, the remaining shattered trusses standing like broken bones in the lurid glow as the fire took hold. And as they stood, mesmerized in fascinated horror, there came another jarring crack, perhaps a beam giving way, and another shower of sparks shot into the shroud of smoke that was gathering in the dank air.

It was Seth who recovered from the shock first.

'He could still be alive!' he yelled at her above the din, and Rose was crippled with terror as she realized what he was about.

'*No!*'

She put out her hand, her fingers clawing towards his arm, but he was already out of her reach.

'I'll try the back!'

Her legs, her whole body, were locked in damning paralysis as she watched him run forward, vault the low stone wall that enclosed the little garden, and disappear around the side of the cottage. She tried to cry out, to screech at him to come back, but no sound came from her strangled throat, and she could only stand and offer up a silent prayer to a God who had never listened to her before. She trembled, her limbs shaking convulsively, her teeth chattering as she slithered down to her knees. No. Oh, sweet Jesus Christ, no . . .

She didn't turn her head as Richard stampeded up the track and joined her in silent contemplation of the burning ruin, his awestruck face set like stone, before he, too, raced forward. Rose's heart shrieked in agony, for he not only had a wife, but two children and another on the way. She could never forgive herself if anything . . . Cold shards of ice attacked her breast . . . And then her senses all but slipped away. Was her tormented mind hallucinating, making her see only what she wanted to see . . .?

She knew then. And the tears spilled unheeded from her eyes.

The tall figure of Richard Pencarrow met the stumbling silhouette of another man sagging under the weight of what looked like a sack of coal, and together they carried the lifeless form towards the girl who waited, collapsed on her knees with dread. They laid the body on the grass before her, and she bowed her head in sorrow, too drained, too weak, to look.

'He was just outside the back door,' Seth spluttered as he coughed harshly from the smoke. 'So I don't think he got . . . the full force of the blast. But . . . I don't think . . .'

He didn't finish the sentence. He didn't need to. Horror pulsed down through the very core of Rose's being as she dragged her gaze to the man stretched out on the ground. Scarlet tongues of flame were now flicking out of the windows of the burning building, lighting the night sky with a fluorescent orange glow, fire spitting and crackling and consuming everything inside. In the flaring inferno, Rose could see Charles's clothes were charred, his face blackened, red raw and grotesquely blistered in places, half his hair gone and one ear lost in a distorted, bubbling mass. And when his eyes opened like two glowing pearly orbs in the satanic, burnt mask, the horror seared into Rose's heart.

'I thought you . . . were upstairs . . . in bed . . . with him,' the cracked, ghoulish hiss scraped in his throat, and his scorched mouth twisted. 'But then . . . I asked myself . . . what was I doing? Killing the woman . . . I love? And . . . I couldn't do it, Rose. But then . . . I dropped the match. On to the trail . . . of powder. I tried . . . but I couldn't . . . put it out.'

Rose's chin quivered and she sucked in her lips, drowning in the all-engulfing sadness as she wept with grief and shamed compassion. She took his hand, burnt beyond pain, in hers, and stroked it against her cheek.

'No, Charles,' she breathed in a hushed, dead, tortured murmur. 'I told you. I've never been unfaithful. I *was* leaving you, though. I just couldn't live as we were. 'Twasn't how 'twere meant to be. I *wanted* us to be happy. Truly I did. And . . . I'm so sorry . . .'

Her throat closed, aching, agonizing, as she cradled his mutilated head in her lap.

* * *

Charles died the next morning, the pain of his horrendously burnt and broken body eased by the administrations of Dr William Greenwood. Richard had insisted on fetching the constable from Mary Tavy to take down Charles's confession. In the dark, he had tried to stamp out the phosphorous match but it wouldn't be extinguished and Charles had realized too late that the trail of powder had already ignited. He had tried to escape but the keg of powder – such a huge amount within the tiny cottage – had exploded as he had reached the door. The blast had thrown him outside, otherwise he would surely have been blown to pieces, but his injuries were too severe for him to survive. It was a horrific end, and the constable went off to make enquiries at Cherrybrook, where he learnt that the dying man had quite openly bought a large amount of gunpowder *for his own purposes*, and as a known and respected shareholder, the manager had not questioned it. Poor chap must have been demented, the constable thought wryly. But then if you had such a beautiful, exquisite wife as that, and she was being unfaithful, it would be enough to drive you insane, wouldn't it? Nevertheless, to try to *kill* her . . .

The silent widow sat, motionless as a statue, scarcely breathing, and staring sightlessly out of the bedroom of Rosebank Hall and across towards the moor. Another young woman came and knelt before her, and carefully washed her grimy hands and face. She appeared not to notice, her eyes blank, swallowing obediently the odd-tasting concoction in the glass that was put into her hands. But she would not move when begged to take to the bed. A young man, his own clothes still smudged with ash and smoke-smuts, was summoned, but she merely shrugged off the compassionate hand he lay on her shoulder and clearly did not hear the anxious words he spoke.

They left her alone, then, moving quietly, like ghosts, around the house. But while they sat about the kitchen table, eating a meal none of them wanted, they looked up in unison as they heard the clatter in the farmyard. The young man sprang to his feet and skidded to the back door, just in time to see the elegant horse, its coat as pale as wheat, streak out of the yard, the slight, fragile rider glued to its back.

Twenty-Four

Rose buried him in London.

She was gone three weeks, accompanied by the ever-faithful Florrie. Passengers on the train to the capital, ignorant of the scandal Charles Chadwick's death had caused, turned their heads and sighed at the tragic beauty of the young widow's grief-ravaged face, the dark shadows beneath her striking lavender-blue eyes echoing the rich, black velvet of her mourning weeds. They judged the older woman with her to be her mother as she consolingly touched the slim, black-gloved hand, but it seemed the girl was encased in some impenetrable trance as she watched the miles race past the window, her expression impassive as the engine rumbled its way through the countryside, pulling the rattling coaches behind it. But despite the state of hypnosis in which she appeared suspended, there was an air of purpose, even determination, about her when the train finally drew into Paddington with a great roaring of steam. Undertakers were waiting on the platform to receive the heavy oak coffin with its solid brass handles, male passengers and railway staff respectfully removing their hats, and ladies bowing their heads. The handsome widow spoke but a few words to the funeral director as the pall-bearers shouldered the solid wooden box containing her dead husband, and then she and her mother swiftly made for the row of waiting cabs.

She had instructed Charles's solicitor, his agent and the butler to put their heads together to compose a list of his acquaintances to inform of the funeral arrangements. To everyone's amazement, she did not hold a wake, since she scarcely knew any of them, and her face was a mask of stone as Charles's earthly remains were laid to rest. Did they consider her a gold-digger, an adulterous, wanton hussy, for the story of Charles's demise must surely have filtered through to them?

Only the inhabitants of Rosebank Hall, together with Captain and Mrs Bradley, knew of what she had suffered at Charles's hands. And now Florrie, who, although she knew something of Charles's treatment of his wife, had hidden her face in her apron as Rose had finally revealed to her the detailed truth about her marriage.

She closed up the house, entrusting its sale and that of its contents to the solicitor, and dismissing the servants, though not without providing each one of them with an excellent character reference, a month's wages and some item of value from the house to keep or sell as they chose. She held a meeting with the bank manager, the lawyer and the agent, setting up a system for the control of her financial affairs, and when everything was in order, she returned to Fencott Place – her home.

Florrie watched her keenly from the opposite seat of the first-class compartment. Would the sight of the moors bring some animation to her set face, some ease to her heart? Apparently not. She had not telegraphed ahead to tell Ned to meet them. Dusk was gathering fast, and she decided to spend the October night at the Bedford Hotel, whose opulence over-whelmed Florrie, who had never slept at a common inn, let alone such a renowned establishment. And first thing next morning, Rose hired a carriage to take them home, the driver wilting under her sharp, brusque words.

'Oh, ma'am.' Patsy dipped a curtsy at the unexpected return of her mistress. 'We didn't know you was coming. I must tell Cook.'

'Tell her not to worry about preparing any fancy dishes,' Rose told her, the first hint of a smile twitching her mouth. 'We'll eat whatever's available.'

'Oh, right, ma'am. And, ma'am, there's been a gentleman calling for you. Several times. Leastways, I *think* 'er's a gentleman. 'Er spoke and acted like one, though 'er was dressed like a worker.'

'Mr Collingwood?'

'No, ma'am. I think 'is name were Warrington.'

'Ah.' Rose dropped her chin for a few seconds, then lifted it haughtily. 'If he comes again, tell him I'm still in London.'

'As you wish, ma'am. Shall I serve some tea, ma'am?'

But Rose had no time to reply as, with a scurry of claws

scratching on the highly polished floorboards, Amber came bounding in through the kitchen door with a bark of delight, the long hair flowing from her flank and legs, while Scraggles and young Lucky skittered about in an array of confusion, tails wagging nineteen to the dozen. Rose dropped to her knees, her arms about Amber's thick yellow ruff. The stubborn shield of indifference she had drawn about herself against the horror of Charles's death was momentarily fractured, and the damning guilt speared into her soul. But then Scraggles was pushing his snout into her face, his tongue rough and rasping against her cheek and driving away the welling tears from her eyes.

She stood up, breathing in deeply as her shoulders stiffened with cool resolution once more. 'Just give me five minutes, Patsy, and then tea would be lovely. Or perhaps coffee. Florrie, you decide.'

Florrie's head rocked backwards in astonishment as Rose flicked her skirt and strode purposefully towards the back door, the dogs scampering about her knees as she disappeared out into the dank and dismal autumn air. Out in the yard, a cry of bitter fury strangled in her throat at what she was about to do. But as she passed Gospel's old loose box where she had concealed Seth all those weeks, Honey who occupied it now put her pale gold head over the top of the half-open stable door and whinnied to her. Rose stopped and wrapped her arms about the mare's strong neck. She wept then, her tears soaking on to the creamy coat and making it glisten with long, wet streaks, her emotions taut and twisted into a tight, confused knot.

When she heard Ned whistling, her brittle nerves cracked. Ned, who had betrayed the escaped convict for the sake of five paltry pounds. Within seconds, her tears had dried and she was marching across to him and thrust an envelope and a small purse into his hands.

'There you are,' she said with utter control, though her eyes were black with anger. 'Your thirty pieces of silver. Go on. Count them. They'll see you through until you find another position. I've written you a good character, though you don't deserve it. I want you out of here by dinner-time, and then I never want to see you, *ever* again!'

*   *   *

She thought she saw him as she climbed the stairs to bed, and she shivered. It wasn't possible, of course. His bones and mutilated, decaying flesh were lying deep underground nearly three hundred miles away. But it was as if he stood there, waiting for her, glaring at her, a thing of torment to haunt and unnerve her. She knew it wasn't real, just a figment of her tortured imagination, but she nevertheless gave the apparition a wide berth, and hurried into the bedroom. Was he there, too? No. And her heart sagged with relief. A welcoming fire blazed cheerily in the grate, setting apricot and peach shadows dancing merrily on the walls. The room was warm, the furnishings she herself had chosen before she had known what she would have to suffer there, suddenly fresh and pretty once more, the carpet deep and luxurious beneath her feet. She changed quickly into one of the new nightdresses she had bought ready-made from the pleased seamstress in Princetown in the few days she had spent at Fencott Place between Charles's death and leaving for London. Lovely as they were, she could never again bear against her flesh the nightgowns that had witnessed the abuse of her innocent body in her marriage bed, and she had ordered them to be burnt. And now she stood, staring at that very bed she had shared with the man who had been her husband, but who had wanted to possess her in every way, and to crush the life and the vitality that had once belonged to Rose Maddiford.

She was free. But the brilliance had gone from her lavender-blue eyes, leaving them dull and lacklustre. A bewildering numbness held her as if in some deadened state of limbo where no feeling could enter, suspended in a futile void. She slid between the crisp, snowy sheets, the corners of her mouth flickering upwards at the comforting stone hot-water bottles Florrie had placed there. Dear Florrie, whom Rose had insisted was to move down from her servant's room in the attic and occupy instead one of the bedrooms on the same floor as herself. They were five women now – Rose, Florrie, Cook, Patsy and Daisy – living alone in the isolated house, with not even Ned sleeping outside in the stable yard. The three dogs were no longer banned to the stables at night, but guarded their mistress and her female companions by sleeping inside the great hallway of the house. Rose planned to take on some male servants in due course, one to live in, perhaps with a boy as well, to take care of all those duties in a large house that required the strength of a man, and another to take Ned's place and perhaps assist with the gardening. As Rose closed her eyes, she wondered idly if the lad who helped the gardener who came a couple of days a week knew anything about horses and might be interested. But she was deathly tired, her strength drained, and her exhausted mind slipped easily into unconsciousness.

But Charles crept into her sleep like some fiendish, slithering snake from the depths of hell, his blackened, scorched face leering at her, his burnt disembodied hands reaching out to drag her down into the inferno that raged about him. She sat up, the haunted scream strangling in her throat, her body drenched in sweat and her eyes blank with terror in her white face as the ghoulish spectre faded into the darkness.

Oh, God. Though she knew it had been but a nightmare, it had pierced into her heart, causing her physical pain, and her pulse raced frantically, refusing to be calmed. 'Oh, Charles, I'm so sorry. I really didn't want it to be like that. I wanted us to be happy. But I just couldn't go on as we were. 'Twas my fault. I was the wrong wife for you. And now you can never forgive me.'

She slid out of bed, moving as if in a dream, and floated across to the window. The glass was cold against her cheek, the night so dark that she could hardly distinguish the garden let alone the moor beyond. But that was what her bleeding soul hungered for, the solid eternity of the land that no man could ever tame. Scar, perhaps, with the quarries, the mines, the failed attempts to conquer the wilderness and turn it into farmland, the only success the prison fields that broke the convicts' backs to clear and cultivate. But one day, she was sure, the moor would reclaim it all, proud and unforgiving. Constant, powerful, the very core, the bedrock upon which her life was founded.

The moor flashed beneath Honey's hooves early next morning, the purple heather, the tufty grass, the dying bracken, the golden swaths of autumn-flowering gorse, the pale shafts of sunlight filtering through the scudding clouds as if illuminating her path to some elusive salvation that teased and tantalized, and was gone before she reached it.

Rose stood atop Sharpitor for perhaps an hour, gazing out across the southern moor and the winding River Tamar in the west, while Honey languidly cropped the grass. And then away they raced down to the picturesque Walkham valley, to what she had always fancifully called the fairy wood at Eggworthy, where ancient moss clung to boulders forged in the realms of time in the watery glen, and where she had met with . . .

No! She forced him from her mind. It wasn't right. She didn't deserve it. She had been the cause of her husband's horrific death, and the guilt, the shame of it, sliced into her very existence. She dug her heels into Honey's flank and the willing mare stretched her muscled limbs to bound up the steep incline towards the tiny hamlet of Sampford Spiney. Then out on to the moor again, past the familiar crags of Pew Tor and Heckwood Tor, and the unmistakable piled rocks of Vixen Tor. She paused when she came to the main road. She could quite easily turn left . . . towards . . .

She set Honey's head for home, her heart ripped into incomprehensible shreds. But there was one visit she must make as she walked Honey solemnly through Princetown. The churchyard. There were fresh flowers on the two graves: chrysanthemums, whose glorious colours she recognized from the garden at Fencott Place. So Florrie had been there before her. She bowed her head, and in her fragmented mind, she was holding Alice in her arms, and she felt her father touch her hand.

It was the same, day after day, once she had seen to the needs of the three horses, since she had done nothing as yet about employing any new staff. To Florrie's consternation, she did nothing at all beyond giving her the money to pay the household bills. She ate, almost in a trance, whatever Cook chose to put in front of her, hardly speaking at the table or as she sat with Florrie by the evening firelight, her face pale, the skin taut and transparent, as a miserable autumn deepened and the first snow of winter peppered the heights of the moor. She seemed impervious to the biting, lacerating wind, the penetrating cold and damp as she spent her days traversing the moor on Honey's back. Even the swirling, treacherous mists did not deter her, as she could navigate a straight line even in the densest fog, and knew exactly the clear path or track she would intercept. She visited Molly and the baby once, but she barely heard what her dear friend said, and was soon wandering desolately again in search of her lost self, scouring the high exposed ridges, the sheltered, tumbling river valleys, drowning in a deep, unbearable grief, and never able to find the peace she craved . . .

'You cas'n keep turning that poor lad away,' Florrie berated her. 'Twice a week he comes, regular as clockwork, and all that way! Now that I've met him, I can see why you made such an attachment to him, and now you never even opens the letters he leaves, nor those he brings from those good people he lives with. You should be ashamed on yoursel'! No matter what the weather, he's on the doorstep, and you'm either not here, or you refuses to see him. Handsome fellow like that . . .'

'I just can't see him, Florrie.' Rose's voice was flat and expressionless, as if she had gone beyond despair, locked in a world where nothing seemed to matter any more. And Florrie shook her head. For where had the tempestuous, spirited child gone?

The bundle of papers arrived from London during the second week of December, and Rose opened the package with a ponderous sigh. Both the lawyer and the agent had sent letters, begging her to come to the capital, and since she had ignored them, they had got together and sent the papers to her instead. The London house and its contents had fetched a sum Rose could scarcely believe, but the small fortune must now be invested. The sheaf of papers made various suggestions of stocks and shares, new and existing opportunities with what risk or return each might carry, plus the most recent reports on the investments Charles had held, and which had made him rich but might now need reviewing. Rose's heart sank. It was all very well to be monied, but it meant you had responsibilities, not just to the household you ran and the servants you employed, but investments could make or break a new or struggling company. Or you could suddenly lose a devastating amount if you weren't constantly looking ahead. Charles had been brought up to it, but she had not . . . Domestic economies she understood, and those of the moor. There was talk of Sir Thomas Tyrwhitt's horse-drawn tramway being replaced by a steam railway, coming back into Princetown again, and linking up with the existing steam line from Plymouth up to Tavistock possibly at Horrabridge. The proposed new railway would not only serve the quarries far better, but would be greatly welcomed by the prison and the civilian population of isolated Princetown. Sir Thomas himself would surely have been as delighted as he would have been to know that his prisoner-of-war depot had been reopened as a gaol back in 1850, though whether he would have approved of the barbarity shown to many of the convicts was another matter. But what did Rose know of national companies, or of those Charles held all over the world – of which there were more than a few!

Having fed and groomed the horses, turned them into the field for the day and mucked out the stables, she had changed into her riding habit and had been about to saddle Honey when the package arrived. She cast an eye over the accompanying letter and put it disparagingly to one side. But it was nagging at the back of her mind, and she cut her ride short.

It was during the third day of sitting at the massive desk in the study, trying to make sense of the columns of figures and other documents, that Rose's head was brought up by a commotion in the hallway. The dogs were barking and voices were raised, and Rose wondered what on earth had broken the peace of the female household. Not Ned come back to cause trouble? Good God . . .

'Sir, you really cas'n—' she heard Daisy's offended voice just seconds before the door flew open.

Rose's heart reared in her breast. Seth stood on the threshold, snow dusting his shoulders and with the bitter cold outside having put a red spot on each of his cheeks. Rose had unconsciously risen to her feet, and as her eyes locked with his across the room, her pulse almost faded away.

'I'm so sorry, ma'am, but I couldn't stop 'en. Came bursting in through the kitchen, 'er did, bold as brass . . .'

''Tis all right, Daisy,' Rose said, though her white lips hardly moved. 'Leave us now, if you would.'

'Yes, ma'am.' And Daisy retreated with a confused curtsy, though not without a glance at the good-looking fellow who had been trying to see the mistress for weeks.

They stared at each other, motionless, and Rose was aware of her heart knocking painfully. The clock ticked, the fire crackled in the grate, and still neither of them moved.

It was Seth who broke the silence. 'I just wanted to be sure you were all right,' he said quietly and with utter calm.

Rose was numbed, paralysed. To see him again was just too much to bear, and she knew why her tortured soul had wanted to blank him from her life. She was still trapped in a helpless mire of futility, her brain too tired to unravel the tangled threads of her life.

'I am well, as you see,' she answered, her voice cool and indifferent.

'Yes. I do indeed.' His words were crisp, tainted with bitterness, and she saw the spasm of hurt flinch across his face. 'And you are obviously busy with your new life, so I shall intrude no more.'

His shoulders stiffened and he stood to attention, his years of military training providing a stalwart reassurance for a moment before he turned on his heel. Rose gazed at his retreating back, and her knees buckled as panic flooded into her limbs.

'Seth, please, no! Don't go!' Her heart was tripping furiously as she sprang around the desk and her hand grasped his arm. 'I'm so sorry. I was just . . . so engrossed in all these papers.' She let go of him, waving her hand flippantly at the chaos on the desk, wanting to apologize though without making a fool of herself. 'It seems I am a wealthy widow, but I don't understand the half of it. I really don't know where to begin.'

Seth's troubled eyes moved across to the desk, and then slowly and deliberately back to her anxious, tentatively smiling face. 'Can I help?' he asked gravely.

She shrugged, and her shoulders sagged. 'I don't know. Can you?'

'Well, I can't tell unless I have a chance to study them. My family were a little like your . . . your late husband. Made most of their money out of speculating on the stock exchange. I was quite young, but I was brought up with it, so I have a reasonable idea about such things. Even when I was in the army – before I went to India, of course – there were always business matters to discuss when I was on leave.'

'Oh, would you take a look, please, Seth? I'd be so grateful. 'Twould be such a weight off my mind.' She looked up at him with a searching frown and the relief swept through her as his mouth broke into a wide grin, revealing the strong set of his even teeth.

'I think I'm going to have my work cut out, mind.'

Rose almost danced about him. 'Let me take your coat. Warm yourself by the fire. I'll get you a cup of tea. And we'll be having lunch soon. Nothing special, but you will stay, won't you?'

'By the looks of things, I'll need to.'

'Oh, thank you, Seth!'

She skipped out of the room, the colour flaming into her face. She had been caught in a mesh of despondency for so long that she couldn't grasp the enormity of her sense of relief. And as she sat by Seth's side all afternoon long, she found it hard to concentrate as she fought against the curious draw of his masculinity. He was still too thin, but there was a healthy colour to his cheeks and he had lost that gaunt, haggard look. His thick fair hair curled pleasingly around the nape of his neck, his firm jawline had been recently shaven and, she noted, the dark shadows had gone from beneath his eyes. He explained so much to her, and they made reams of notes and sorted the papers into neat piles, instilling Rose with confidence.

'I really should go now. I don't know the moor as well as you do, so I need to be home by dark.'

Rose felt the arrow dart into her side. 'Oh. Do you have to? I mean, 'twill take days to sort this out.'

'At least.' He nodded in agreement. 'Let me talk with Richard. I can't let him down after all they've done for me, but perhaps I can come and stay for a while to get everything straight. There's less to do on the farm this time of year, and Chantal's a great help to him.'

'Oh, yes! 'Twould be very good of you. And take Tansy. 'Twill be quicker than walking. And how's Beth? Can't be so long till the baby now. Do give her my love.'

'Of course.'

His voice was dry, perfectly polite, but efficient and businesslike. Nonetheless, for the first time since her return from London, Charles's ghost did not come to haunt her that night.

Twenty-Five

Christmas was only days away. Seth had been staying at Fencott Place, occupying one of the guest rooms along the landing. They were gradually organizing Rose's affairs, the decisions Seth had helped her make meeting with the broker's approval, and she was to keep an eye on the situation regarding the new railway. Seth had remained distant as they worked together, but she didn't mind. It was enough that he was there, his health regained. She barely noticed the quiet contentment creeping into her heart, the inner peace that at last invaded her soul. And now she could retire to bed safe in the knowledge that the cruel, charred spectre would no longer come to curse and haunt her.

Seth was mucking out the stables one day, steam rising from the straw and fresh dung as it collided with the stinging, frosty morning air. Rose had been helping with the ironing as the laundry woman was laid up with a nasty influenza. Then she had retired with Florrie to the drawing-room fireside to discuss their plans for Christmas Day, which she wanted to be extra special. For the first time since her father's accident, she was actually looking forward to it. A sense of blithe anticipation pervaded the house, and that afternoon they were to start making paper chains and other decorations.

Florrie took herself off to perform some task, and Rose stayed for several minutes, gazing, relaxed and at ease, into the flames. It was good to feel like this after so much fear and abuse, and she wouldn't let herself slip back. She still had affairs to deal with. She always would, since Charles's legacy had turned her into a woman of enterprise and business. But, hopefully, help would always be at hand.

She smiled softly to herself. But she couldn't sit there all day. She must put out clean towels in all the rooms – Daisy's job really, but they were all busy in the kitchen, and Rose felt there was more purpose in her life carrying out domestic chores. More like the Rose Maddiford of old. She saw to her own first, and Florrie's, then sauntered into Seth's room, her vision half obscured behind the pile of thick fluffy towels in her arms as she hummed happily to herself.

She snatched in her breath. The limpid winter sun was streaming through the tall windows, its brilliance dazzling her so that the contents of the room were thrown into deep, confusing shadow, and at first she had been unaware of the tall figure by the wash stand pouring steaming water into the bowl. She could see by his dark silhouette that he was stripped to the waist and she gulped hard. But surely the best way to avoid any embarrassment was to act casually.

'Oh, I'm sorry. I thought you were seeing to the horses.'

'I've finished.' His voice was strange, grating. 'It's hot work and I . . . well, I needed a wash.'

Rose had bustled forward efficiently, nodding as she placed the towels on the bed and now, as she turned around, the gasp stuck in her throat. Seth had his back to her, and the light from the windows was falling directly on to his bare torso. He clearly knew she had seen, and he held himself rigid, staring blindly at the wall in front of him, his muscles tense beneath the scarred skin. For some seconds, neither of them moved, scarcely breathed, and a wave of horror, of anger and sorrow washed down to the pit of Rose's stomach. The agony he must have suffered, the cruelty and barbarism of his unjust punishment, seared into her heart. She knew he would be marked for life, but . . . to see it for herself, in reality, was a saddening, sickening shock.

But it wasn't something to be brushed under the carpet. It had to be faced. She padded up behind him, each beat of her heart vibrating hard in her chest so that her hands shook. 'Oh, Seth,' she murmured, her appalled voice no more than a whisper as her trembling finger traced one of the ugly lines that latticed his shoulders and lower ribcage, some no more than faint scratches healed to a healthy white, others deep, the flesh seamed, and even after eighteen months, still purple and angry where the skin had hung in shreds that Dr Power had done his best to stitch back into place.

Seth flinched at her touch, lifting his head further, his lean jaw set like hewn granite. 'Not a pretty sight, is it?' he said, almost inaudibly.

Rose said nothing for a moment, allowing the grief of it to sink into her heart. 'Does . . . does it hurt?' she asked lamely, since she was so stunned she couldn't think of anything else to say.

She heard him swallow. 'No. Not now. It doesn't hurt exactly. But sometimes it does feel tight. Beth's been rubbing something on to it. Some lotion made with honey and other things. It does help it feel more comfortable. And she says it'll help it fade over the years. But the scars will never . . . they'll never . . .'

His voice cracked, and his chin drooped on to his chest, his eyes closed, and Rose felt his pain tear into her. It was instinctive and she leant forward, her lips brushing the disfiguring scars.

She felt him shudder. 'Rose, *don't*. Please.' He turned round abruptly, his hazel eyes dark and scowling. 'I must leave. This afternoon. Go back to Rosebank Hall.'

Rose took a staggering step backwards. 'Go back?' Her tiny voice faltered.

'Yes. I must. Richard needs my help. Poor sod's got to keep up with all the debt repayments his father saddled him with. He's got to have the farm running at full capacity, and it's impossible for just one man. He can't afford to employ anyone properly, but I'm happy just to have a roof over my head. I've one of their attic rooms now, but a farm labourer would need a tied cottage and since, well . . .'

Rose stared at his cold, hard face, and her chest clenched with panic, the peace that had been seeping into her soul draining away again to a bottomless chasm of desperation. 'I have money! I'll pay for the cottage to be rebuilt. 'Tis only fair as 'twas my fault it were destroyed. I should do it anyway. But . . . please don't go, Seth! I need you!'

Her voice had risen in a howl of anguish, but Seth threw up his head with a bitter laugh, harsh lines suddenly forming about his mouth. 'No, you don't. You're a woman of substance now. You can pick and choose who you want.'

'But I only want you!'

She was clinging to him, his biting words slashing into her as he pushed her aside.

'Then why did you refuse to see me for so long?' he protested acidly. 'Going to London to bury your husband where he belonged, yes, that I can understand. But turning me away for two whole months! That . . .' He broke off, his eyes glinting savagely and his hands clenched into fists, and Rose recoiled, battling to hold on to her shattered emotions.

'But . . . but we were running away together. I was giving up everything for you—'

'No, Rose.' He took her hands calmly now, his steady gaze boring earnestly into her tear-streaked face. 'Everything's changed. We were equal then. I was a penniless wretch and you needed to escape from a brute of a husband. But *now* . . . You're a rich widow. You have a respected position in local society. And I'm nothing more than an ex-convict with the scars on my back to prove it.'

Rose slowly lowered her eyes, her white lips trembling. Dear God, he was hurting. Hurting more than she had ever realized. Not just the physical pain he had suffered, but a mental torture that had gone deep into his soul. But no one understood that better than she. And since when did Rose Maddiford give up so easily?

She flicked up her head. 'Do you think that matters to me? To someone who knows the shame of being abused by her husband for over two long years? I'm sorry I turned you away. 'Twas just that . . . Charles, he . . . It took some getting over. But I feel free of him now. With you here. What they did to you, in the prison, 'twas dreadful. You were innocent and yet they . . . But 'twill be with you for ever, and you *must* accept that. Just as I must accept that I was once married to a man who . . .' She straightened her shoulders, her chin lifted haughtily. 'I love you, Seth Warrington, and a few scars can never change that!'

He had shied away, biting his lip, but now, as he turned back to her, his haunted eyes were glistening with moisture. He opened his mouth as if to speak, but no sound came from his throat and, reaching up on tiptoe, Rose brought her lips against his, smothering any words in a kiss so deft and fervent, it sent a shiver down his spine. It took but that one second of overwhelming love, of intense harmony of two broken spirits, for his taut nerves to snap, and a moment later, his hand reached into her hair, his entwining fingers loosening the pins so that it fell about her shoulders in a froth of ebony silk. Their bodies clung, reverently, hungrily, and he tucked her head beneath his chin as he absorbed the very closeness, the soft sweetness of her to his tortured breast. Her cheek was warm against his bare chest, and she turned her head, kissing the lightly haired skin, drawing her moist tongue across his flesh in a natural, fluid movement that had never even occurred to her with Charles. This was something she had never known before, a deep passion, a need borne of understanding, respect, devotion, that plunged down to her loins, and when Seth lifted her head to kiss her nose, her closed eyes, her slender throat, and his hand moved tentatively to her breast, she welcomed it with a deep, heaving sigh, lost in a world of desire, of something so powerful it would not be denied, everything falling away from her but her love for this sorely tried man.

He laid her on the bed, slowly undressing her, inspecting every inch of her flesh as it was revealed. Stroking it, kissing it, loving it. She stretched her arms above her head, languidly, lasciviously, for him to peel off her shift, and she arched her back, purring like a cat as his mouth closed over her breast, gentle and caressing. Just for a split second did the vision of Charles – clawing at her, abusing her, with no care but for his own gratification – stab into her memory, and then the pain and the fear were gone, cast aside for ever by this man who truly loved her. She knew he would not hurt her and he entered her gently, carefully, drawing her on to the sublime heights of ecstasy, driving out her demons, until she moaned with pleasure and he let out a joyful cry as their love exploded in unison and their flesh became as one.

She gazed up at him, mesmerized, breathless, drowning in his glorious, smiling eyes that roamed tenderly over her face.

'God, I love you,' he muttered as he kissed her again, and then he rolled away on to his back, drawing her against him so that she lay, wrapped in his arms, her head resting on his shoulder and her naked body, unashamed and unafraid, pressed against his. A supreme and exquisite peace washed through her, and she wanted the moment to last for ever.

But the room was cold and she shivered as her passion subsided. Seth lifted his head, sensitive to her needs, and reached out to gather the counterpane about them, reluctant to let her go. 'There. I can't have my beautiful darling catching cold now, can I?'

She snuggled down beside him, her arm across his chest, breathing in the masculine scent of him, intoxicated by his closeness, the wonder of what had just passed between them silencing her until she felt him push his head back into the pillow. She raised her eyes and watched, fascinated, as his prominent Adam's apple rose and fell as he swallowed.

'That's what kept me going, you know. Thinking of you,' he croaked, staring at the ceiling, and all at once, the hairs bristled down the back of Rose's neck. 'When I was . . . being flogged, I just concentrated on thinking of you. Creating a picture of you in my mind. It was . . . the only way I could take the pain.'

His voice was thick. Ragged. Choked. And the enduring compassion that was Rose Maddiford swamped her in a tidal wave as she drew his head against her breast and he wept wretchedly like a child. She smoothed her hands over his shoulders, feeling the scars, the ridges, beneath her fingers. Oh, yes. She had wept for her own lost soul, but she had found herself again because of this good, worthy man. And now she must be strong for him.

'We can get through this, Seth,' she whispered into his tousled hair. 'We have each other now. Look at poor Adam, what he went through. He says 'twas having Rebecca that saved him. And Richard, too. He could never work the way he does if he didn't have Beth to support him.'

She paused, and waited as Seth drew back, pushing the back of his hand against his mouth. 'I'm sorry,' he sniffed awkwardly. 'You must think me—'

'Don't say another word, Seth Warrington. I love you. And to my mind, a man who can't cry isn't worth his salt. However.' She sat up abruptly, tossing her head so that her hair swung enticingly down her back. 'I *am* getting rather cold. I suggest we get our clothes back on,' she said, picking up his discarded underdrawers and throwing them at him with an endearing grin, 'and go over to Rosebank Hall. I'll tell Richard to work out how much the repairs to the cottage will cost, and I'll also pay Beth for her services in looking after you. But on one condition: that you're living back here with me by Christmas.'

Seth stared at her, his eyebrows raised in astonishment. 'Are you sure? I mean, that'll set tongues wagging.'

'And since when do you think I ever cared about that?' She stopped to pull the shift on over her head, then added cheekily, 'Of course, you'll be sleeping in your own room. Although I won't mind if you sneak along to mine once in a while.'

The corners of Seth's handsome mouth turned upwards with amusement and then he threw up his head with a roar of laughter, his eyes dancing rakishly as they settled on her face again. 'I won't mind if I do. You know, I do love you so much.' And he took her in his arms once more.

Rose felt like a child again, free and happy and rocked in a glorious, warm cradle of harmony and peace. There were regrets, of course, things she could never change, but with Seth beside her, she was awash with a deep sense of euphoria. She hadn't been so content since before it had all happened, since her dear father's accident which had set the horrific chain of events in motion. Now she could look forward to a future without fear.

It was into January when the telegram arrived for Seth. Rose frowned as he read it, for she couldn't think why he should receive such a thing. They were in the morning room having breakfast, and when he had finished reading it, he screwed it into a ball and tossed it into the fire where it uncurled slightly and burned in seconds. His face was set, his lips pursed as he stared into the flames for a moment before turning to look at her.

'Seth?' she asked in a panic, her heart squeezing, for surely nothing could spoil their happiness now? 'Seth, what is it? They . . . they can't revoke your pardon, can they?'

'No, no. It's nothing like that. But . . .' He dropped his head before lifting his eyes to her again. 'Rose, I need to go away.'

Rose's heart turned to a solid block in her chest. 'Go away?' she murmured. 'For . . . for how long?'

'I don't know,' he answered evasively. 'And . . . I'll need money. A great deal of money.'

She felt the agony penetrate somewhere beneath her ribs. Go away. With her money? Dear God. She knew the colour drained from her face and she began to tremble. Seth stepped forward and took her hands, but she turned her head away.

'I'm sorry, Rose, but . . . I can't tell you why. Not yet. But please, I beg you, trust me in this. You've trusted me in everything before, and this . . . I just can't tell you, for your own sake.'

His words were spoken with such gravity, his voice so thick, that her gaze was drawn back to his earnest face, his eyes dark with anguish.

'How much money?' she hardly whispered. 'And . . . you will come back, won't you?'

He looked horrified, his jaw dropping. 'Yes, of course I will. Just trust me, Rose.'

Her face was alive and intense with pain as she stared back at him and then swallowed hard. 'When will you go?' she muttered.

'As soon as possible. Today.'

'Oh . . .'

She twisted her head away in an agony of shock, and brushed him off when he tried to take her in his arms.

'Rose, *please*. You know I wouldn't be doing this unless I absolutely had to.'

'Will you take Tansy?' she asked frostily now.

'No. Thank you. I'll be going by train.'

'Train?' That meant he was going far. To London? ''Tis nothing to do with my investments or . . . or your own family?' she suddenly thought to ask.

'No, thank the Lord. But I would appreciate you taking me into Tavistock. In the wagonette, perhaps, as it's dry.'

It was indeed a beautiful crisp and sunny winter's morning, the sort Rose loved, but as she drove Merlin down into Tavistock, she hardly noticed it. Seth was going away, and he wouldn't say where or why. He tried to talk to her, but she didn't want to know. They went to the bank, the clerk frowning at the substantial amount Mrs Chadwick withdrew and then entrusted to the tall and handsome man by her side. And when Rose saw Seth off at the station, a black tide of suspicion and dismay ripped through her heart. Would she ever see him again?

With a broad, confident smile, she told Florrie, and Molly when she went to visit her, that he had gone away on business and would be back in a few weeks. But inside she was torn to rags. Had she been wrong about Seth all along? He had been proved innocent beyond a shadow of a doubt, but was it possible that in all other ways he had deceived her? Alone in her room, she wrung her hands in frustration and banged her fists on her head. She had been betrayed too often before. She was free from Charles, but was Seth really just as bad?

Dear God, she had *given* herself to Seth on several occasions. Perhaps even now she was carrying his child. He had been so caring, so gentle, awakening her body to some ecstasy she had never known before. But had it all been a trick? Surely not! But she had learnt to distrust, and she felt dragged down by a deep and gnawing depression.

The days passed and she heard nothing. Sometimes she was hard and bitter, a knot frozen solid in her chest. At others, she felt drained with grief and degradation. For what would she say to Florrie if Seth never returned? How could she admit to her shame and her weakness at being taken in by his handsome smile? And yet, at every minute, something inside her still believed in him.

It was more than two weeks before she heard the furious clatter of hooves thundering up the drive and scattering gravel in every direction. Rose was coming down the stairs and by the time she got to the window, the horse had disappeared round the side of the house. Rose's heart tripped and began to gallop as she ran out of the back door and along the terrace towards the stable yard. Could it possibly be . . .?

'Rose! Rose!'

Seth's voice rang in her ears. Yes! He had kept his word. He was back! Joy sizzled through her body like a bolt of lightning as she scudded through the gate in the high wall. And there she stopped dead, every muscle in her body stilled. Locked in all-encompassing paralysis.

The great sable horse in front of her lengthened its neck, gave a trumpeting whinny and then did what he always had when he couldn't contain his excitement. He did a standing leap from all fours and then bucked wildly, almost unseating his rider.

'Whoa!' Seth called, bringing the animal under control, and then sat, grinning down at Rose while his magnificent mount shook his head and snorted, jangling the bit in his mouth and breathing great white wreaths into the cold air.

Rose still stood senseless, staring, unable to believe. Slowly, as the horse whinnied again and came forward, nudging demandingly at her shoulder, the numbness unfurled and she shrieked to the sky.

'Gospel! Oh, my God! Gospel!'

Her arms were around his strong, hairy neck then, trying to draw him into her very being, and when Seth swung his leg over the saddle and jumped down beside her, she didn't know which of them to hug first.

'How . . . how did you find him?' she spluttered at last through the tears of pure joy that strolled down her cheeks.

'It was Richard, not me,' Seth told her, smiling down at her utter jubilation. 'The telegram was from him. He's not a gambling man. Can't afford to be and he's passionately against it because of his father. But he'd heard through the grapevine of a new phenomenon in the racing world based over at Exeter racecourse. A black thoroughbred cross suddenly appeared on the scene and was taking the racing world by storm. Had a reputation for its temper, though, and Richard just wondered if it couldn't possibly be Gospel. That's why I couldn't tell you. I couldn't break your heart by getting your hopes up and then have it turn out to be a wild goose chase. And that's why I needed the money. Successful racehorses don't come cheap, but I did manage to knock the price down a little and I have some change for you.'

Rose gazed up at him, at the light in his smiling, shining eyes. How could she ever have doubted him? The world dropped away as her soul filled with her love, her need, of this good, kind, sensitive man.

'How can I ever thank you, Seth?'

The elation slid from his radiant face and his muscles moved into a sombre expression that dampened her euphoria.

'You can do one thing for me,' he said seriously, and her heart bounced in her chest. 'But it's an awful lot to ask, and I will understand if you won't . . . Marry me, Rose, and make me the happiest man alive.'

'What?'

He lowered his eyes, his face crestfallen. 'Please. Think about it, Rose. Not yet, of course. You've been widowed barely three months. I know I have absolutely nothing to offer you. And when people find out who I am, which they'd be bound to in time, they'd say I was after your money—'

'But we'll know differently.'

It was Seth's turn to be stunned as her words sunk into his brain. He slowly raised his eyes, his brow puckered. 'Is that . . . is that a *yes*?'

'Yes.' She shook her head, gave a grunt of surprise and delight. 'Yes, I suppose it is!'

Her breath fluttered in her throat, and nothing else in the world seemed to matter as the anguish of all that had happened faded away and she stood, wrapped in Seth's arms. Her heart soared. For, at long last, she had found the man with whom she wanted to spend the rest of her life . . .

Dr Raymond Power slowly signed the letter, then leant back in the chair with a wistful sigh. He would hand it to the governor in the morning. The position of prison surgeon had provided him with a decent wage and reasonable accommodation for his dear wife and family, allowing him also to attend the more impecunious inhabitants of the area at nominal fees. But it was time to move on, and now he had secured a partnership with an elderly physician in a fashionable quarter of Bristol, and with luck, he would acquire the entire practice in time.

His wife had hated Princetown. The dismal settlement cut off from the rest of humanity, the lack of acceptable society, the appalling climate – snowdrifts and lacerating winds in winter, damp, driving rain and swirling mists even in summer, and no protection from the sun on the rare occasions that it did shine. But it wasn't because of his wife that he was leaving.

He was a man of medicine. Of healing. And he simply could not reconcile his vocation with the position he held. In the early days, Dartmoor had been used purely as a sanatorium for consumptive and other infirm convicts, sent there for the fresh air and the benefit of their health. Ironic. For soon the gaol had also become the dumping ground for the most notorious criminals in the land, to be punished by sleeping in cold, damp cells, existing on a starvation diet with a decidedly dubious water supply, and expected to work like slaves. And when they caught pneumonia digging drainage ditches on the open moor in impossible conditions, had a limb blown off or were blinded by explosives in the quarry, or fell from the high prison blocks they were building, *he*, Raymond Power, was the one who had to patch them up in whatever way he could so that they could return to some other gruelling task. And then there had been the outbreak of fever when all his efforts had not prevented so many from dying. Not that anyone cared particularly, as the regime was such that there were few warders like Jacob Cartwright who felt able to exercise a little compassion.

But the worst part of being prison surgeon was having to pronounce a man fit for punishment, to be subjected to the inhuman procedure of being birched or flogged. He had reached the stage where he could stand it no longer, but the turning point had been the begging, passionate letter from the young woman he had admired so deeply and who had implored him to help the recaptured escapee. Poor beggar had turned out to be totally innocent and now, it seemed, he was to marry his saviour. Well, good luck to them both. They deserved some happiness after what they'd both been through.

Raymond had never liked that husband of hers. He didn't like him being wed to the vivacious young girl who had captured his own heart so many years previously. He had reared away from his feelings, shot through with guilt, but it was a secret he had thankfully managed to keep safely locked away. He was already married with a family that he loved dearly; was old enough to be her father, and yet . . . he couldn't help dreaming. She wasn't just beautiful. She was captivating. With a generosity of heart, a fervent compassion, a wild, free spirit. He would miss her terribly, a slender, ethereal figure charging over the moor on that enormous, elegant horse of hers that seemed to have reappeared, as reckless and head-strong as she was. But it was better that way, though he would never forget her. Rose Maddiford from the Cherrybrook Gunpowder Mills. Rose from Cherrybrook.

Cherrybrook Rose.

Author's Note

All details regarding conditions at Dartmoor Prison at the time of this novel are believed to be correct, but this is a fictional story and should not be considered a statement of fact. George Frean was the real-life proprietor of the gunpowder mills and he is portrayed as the kindly gentleman he is believed to have been.

The ruins of the gunpowder mills stand on private land and can only be viewed from the public footpath. Anyone who trespasses does so entirely at their own risk.